HIGHER POWERS

HIGHER POWERS

JIM WARREN

HIGHER POWERS

iUniverse books may be ordered through booksellers or by contacting:

iUniverse
1663 Liberty Drive
Bloomington, IN 47403
www.iuniverse.com
1-800-Authors (1-800-288-4677)

ISBN: 978-1-4917-8025-1 (sc)
ISBN: 978-1-4917-8026-8 (e)

Library of Congress Control Number: 2015916974

Print information available on the last page.

iUniverse rev. date: 10/09/2015

PROLOGUE

Power. In its simplest forms, it is one of the few constants in this world. Those who seek it, and those who have it. For those without, power was craved, bled for, died for. It was the greatest treasure, and the greatest hunt. The beings that had harnessed power, bent it to their will, were revered as Gods.

The Asgardians, warriors all, were renowned for their skill in battle. Those with the blood of Asgard in their veins were artists, able to turn the greatest of battles into a delicate dance of death and destruction. The Olympians, rulers of another quadrant of the cosmos, were the builders, the architects. But perhaps the eldest and wisest of the Gods, were the Labrynthians. The Labrynthians, sheltered from the squabbles of petty children that fancied themselves Gods, created the Ancient Ones, the soldiers and protectors of the divine. Given to the Sovereigns as peace offerings, the Ancient Ones garnered respect for the Labrynthians, so much so that no one would approach them for favor so long as the Labrynthians remained neutral.

The Elders populated the cosmos, in all their wonder, once Orion had completed his campaign. Riding with the Hunters against Lucifer and his army of the Dark Ones, Orion ultimately succeeded, bearing Lucifer from his pedestal and casting him down into Exile. The pendulum had few swings left before the Ragnarok, especially after Omega had constructed his system, which failed. The Ancient Ones were able to declare their independence from the Sovereigns, and the Hunters were able to build Dark Purge borders for their campaign against the Destroyer gods. The Forces That Be watched silently as all of the pieces of their grand puzzle fell into place, while the Sovereigns desperately attempted to avoid slowing the universal pendulum any more than they already had.

Eventually, after eons of pointless war and death, the Sovereigns were able to find a pivotal piece in their game. They realized that, in their game of pawns and thrones, if they played this piece correctly, it could very well save everything from the brink of oblivion. Odin, one of the newer elder gods, had discovered a unique power. Something that none of the others could boast; Odin had fallen in love. Considered one of the most chaotic flaws that a god could suffer, love allowed Odin to be the only great power in creation that could break the laws of the Universe. It made him invisible to the consequences of breaking the rules, being a creator god in love with a soul. All the Sovereigns had to do was wait and let the pieces fall where they would.

For the first time in all of eternity, the Sovereigns felt a loss of control. They had no choice left, but to rest the hope and fate of the entire Universe on this one play. Even Kronos, the mighty god of Time, knew that Odin was the key to their ultimate victory. So, through the ages, Odin was watched, studied, to see if he was truly to be their savior.

The only thing that could be done, was to wait.

Book I

THE HERO

CHAPTER 1

Odin and Jade watched the Ropens danced together along the low clouds in the night sky. The crimson glow of the bird-like creatures pulsed and burned. Below, the two Dryads lay holding each other, quietly conversing on Odin's recent victories and Jade's recent struggles. The Ropens began to screech in excitement, as Odin and Jade joined their lips together and touched each others' faces.

"Are you ready?" Odin asked.

Jade nodded and Odin touched his forehead to hers. Their minds melded together and their thoughts were unified. Jade was overwhelmed with thoughts of Odin's love. She knew what he felt. She felt what was in his heart. She loved what he was and what he had become. This connection had never been made possible until now. This kind of intimacy was so brand new. It was perfectly balanced, perfectly matched, perfectly fixed. Jade dug further into his thoughts, wandering through past events he had faced. Battles, conflict, accomplishments, creation, pain and joy. Odin had fought his brother, nearly killing him, and ensnared him in realm of the Labrynthians. All of this for his home. All of this for her.

Odin held tight to Jade as she rested in his arms. Her body rose and fell with every breath. The touch of her skin, the warmth of her chest; everything was so intoxicating.

"All of this is for me?" Jade thought out loud.

Odin answered by kissing her neck.

"But why? Why me?" She felt so unworthy of these efforts. "What makes me so much more important than your life with your family, or the life of your brothers and sisters? More important than your own ascension?"

He turned to her and answered thoughtfully, "This moment that we're sharing right now is what makes my family envious. For an elder to become intimate; become one flesh with a mortal, it's dangerous."

"But you can't ascend, now," Jade replied.

"It doesn't matter. I'd rather have this for one lifetime than spend an eternity without you."

"Won't they hate you for that?"

"Jade, I'm not letting go," Odin whispered.

Her light brown hair fell on his chest as she clung to his tattered pale shirt. "Odin, I don't want to lose you again, but-"

He kissed her again and held her tighter. "I'm not going anywhere," he told her softly. "I'm never leaving you again."

She looked up at him as he placed her hand on his heart. The desperation in his eyes for her to understand the depth of his feelings for her engulfed her attention. "I promise," he whispered.

She felt his heart pound like a steady battle drum under her fingers. Her eyes, which were like diamonds under the light of the stars, slowly closed. She had never felt such a love. She had never felt such an appreciation. She was precious to him. No other person or object would hold more value than she would to him.

They held close to each other. Odin looked up and saw a shooting star trail across the sky above the Ropens. Odin thanked the Father for blessing the two Dryads and for bringing them together again.

With a sudden deafening crack, the ground shifted and broke and up through the crevices, little demons hopped out as flames erupted from the ground behind them. Smoke and reflections of fire burned from the ground. Odin jumped to his feet. He drew his sword, and readied it for battle. They were pygmies, almost as tall as Odin's knee, but they could jump great distances. Their bodies completely composed of flame, they scorched everything that contacted their body. Odin's heart pumped at double time. His focus sharpened. He counted how many came up and calculated their attack. The group jumped as one for him and Odin sliced through them in the air, blocking each one from him and Jade.

Two arch-demons climbed up from the ground. They stood about the same height as Odin and Jade, but their arms were much longer and their hands dragged along the ground next to their feet. They wrapped their arms around Jade and took her captive and waited as Odin continued warding off the pygmies. She put up a fight, even without a weapon. She twisted, bent and dodged, but it was no use. Their arms were too long and their strength outmatched hers. When she saw the insignia on their backs, she knew who commanded this particular company, and she hated that they had found her. She didn't want to go back.

"Release her! I command you! Release her! Now!" He pointed his legendary blade towards them as he shouted.

When they didn't move, he dug his heels to the soil and prepared an attack.

Another figure emerged from the ground. He stood taller than the rest. Odin held his sword ready and true, as the figure opened his cloak into the wind and stood on solid ground.

"Magnus," Odin muttered.

"I have returned." Magnus growled, opening his hands to present himself: his long and wavy black hair fell past his shoulders. His skin was smooth and tight. All other features seemed to match Odin's. Magnus' dark shaded tunic was battened down by his large black belt. He grinned and nodded at the arch-demons. They nodded back and took Jade, screaming and pleading for mercy, back under ground.

"You have a debt to pay, Odin, and I'm calling on you to settle it now."

Odin glared at Magnus. "Leave Jade out of this. Keep our fight between you and me."

"No!" Magnus' voice was stern, but his emotions were kept in check. "You brought her into this. You committed the sin. By the authority of our father, your atonement is either death or her. The redemption from this sin is simple enough. You confront me in my courts, fight me to keep what I'm rightfully stealing back, and I will relinquish your obsession."

Odin sheathed his sword, "You've plagued my planet too many times. What are your plans for the titans?"

Magnus smiled. "Reading my thoughts, are we? They are still in your prisons. But even now, my agents work to release them."

"You can't do that! If they get free, they'll lay this entire world to waste. My work has come so close to completion!" Odin shouted.

Magnus laughed now. "Odin, my brother. This land is no longer yours to save-"

"And it's not yours to destroy!" Odin replied.

"I didn't come here to destroy. I came to serve," Magnus scoffed. "A message needs to be sent to the one that rejected his family and abandoned his responsibility. And for what? To save the lives of the Dryads? You had the powers of the elders themselves in the palm of your hands and you wished it all away, embodied yourself as a Dryad, just so you could keep this planet. You are a fool! And what would you do for this young love of yours? Give your life, no doubt." he finished.

Odin scowled at him. "I would go to the land of Lucrid and back for her. I assure you, I will meet you in your courts. I will fight you, and I will kill you."

Magnus circled Odin laughing to himself.

"You would face the monsters that were born of our father? You would go to the armpit of Galarah and back and even face the Jorns and Skord of my world just to save the life of this girl?"

Odin glared at him. "I would make friends with death itself for her!"

"Again, I say unto you, you're a fool! If you take this journey, you do it alone. The elders will not help you. I assure you of this: you will make friends with death. You will know my pain. You will know my loss. You've crossed the will of the elders for the last time, brother."

As rapidly as he appeared, Magnus dropped through the ground. Odin drew his sword and dove after Magnus. Magnus laughed and was engulfed by a flame. Odin appeared back on the grassy plain that he and Jade were lying on. Odin reached up and sheathed his sword once again, and shouted to the skies. His eyes welled up and he uttered in agony, "I'm not letting go."

The wind howled and rain poured. Trails of water flowed down the crevices of his plant-like skin. The signs of Jade's sadness struck the ground and Odin pained with her. A conversation subtly echoed in his mind.

"A time will come when you and I will be taken away from each other. As long as we're apart, the heart of my creation will match yours. Your sadness will fall on me like rain. Your anger will bite me through the wind. Your joy will be reflected in the light of the star."

"So I can communicate with you?"

"So I'll know whether I've failed you or not."

*****

Trudging back to his home village, all inhabitants were inside their shelters, hiding from the heavy wind and rain. Little huts were staggered along the street and a temple was under construction.

Odin opened the door to his small barn and found his centaur friend, Sashi sleeping there. Odin closed the door and opened his armor case under the mattress he slept on. The smell of battle polish and oil escaped the container. Boots of steel sat to one side, each with a dagger on the side. He fitted them on his feet, reminiscing the last time he wore them. His breastplate was thin and minimal for faster maneuverability. His gloves were weathered, but firm.

Sashi yawned. "Where are we going?" He asked.

"You don't. You stay. I go." Odin replied.

"No. I'm going with you. If this is your average adventure, you'll need me. You always do."

Odin turned to the brown coated steed-man.

"He took her, Sashi," Odin answered. "Magnus took Jade from me. I'm going south, to his miserable excuse of a fortress. I'm going to bring her back. You stay. I go."

Sashi drew his swords. "I'm ready. I'm going with you and you can't stop me. It's best you climb on and we both go, rather than fighting me until I win … physically," he said with a smile.

Odin smiled back, "You arrogant beast," he retorted and mounted up. Sashi kicked the door open and darted out of the village.

*****

Jade sat curled next to a bail of hay, scared that she might never be set free. She closed her eyes, leaned her head back, and wept. Through thought, she called out to Odin, but she heard no reply. He was too far. The distance had planted a sharp pain in her chest. She wanted to get out of this brick chamber. She wanted to be safe in Odin's arms. She wanted all of this to go away. But, before they could be together in peace, Odin would have to fight for his rights to solitary peace. She hugged her knees again, and dreamed of Odin. She prayed to the elders that they would keep him safe and she drifted into a peaceful rest.

CHAPTER 2

Odin woke from his rest on Sashi's back. He'd found it hard to sleep with all of his thoughts screaming for Jades Safety. The rise of the morning star gave a bleak colored, clouded sky. Sashi galloped on, across hills and over puddles. His arms hung down and back to catch the wind, letting it spread across his body.

"So this venture we're on: it's all for a bit of young love?" Sashi asked.

Odin wasn't in much of a talking mood, but he answered. "Not so young anymore. This is for justice to be served. Magnus can keep me from protecting and providing for my planet, but he can't keep me from the soul I purchased with blood."

Sashi raised an eyebrow. "Odin, if this ends like it did the last time, you'll be sacrificing multitudes for the sake of one woman."

Odin tried harder to concentrate on communicating with Jade. "If you would ever find a centaur for yourself, you'd understand how she is worth the cost."

Sashi kept his smile and grunted as he leapt over another puddle. "I don't think there are anymore centaurs left."

The morning star crept above the army of mountains ahead. The trail was not too steep, and Sashi moved quickly and confidently, remembering the harder times; surviving on small rations, making a weeks worth of supplies last a month or more. Things were good now, and he relished in it.

"If I remember right," Sashi said, "there should be a freshwater spring in these mountains. We can rest there for the day and travel by night."

Odin grimaced. "Night? Wouldn't it be wiser to get on the way while we can?"

Sashi glanced back at Odin. "As long as we're traveling through Ogre territory, I'd like to go through with as little trouble from them as possible."

Odin felt shivers go through his body. He felt vulnerable in this mortal form, unable to fight things like ogres., "How do you know that ogres live in this area?"

"The stench," Sashi replied.

Odin didn't smell anything, but took Sashi's word for it.

The climb up and down the mountain would be long enough through the day, but would leave some room for resting. One of the advantages of being a Dryad was having low metabolism. The centaur; however, would need more water after the climb, and some food to withstand the rest of the trip. Sashi, had trained himself to miss out on a day's worth of food without any side effects during the Skord sieges. The battle between Centaurs and Skord lasted for a few days, and he couldn't eat even a scrap of grass until the battle was over. After the army of Skord retreated, Sashi was the last surviving centaur. Any other centaur had either been killed, or wounded beyond the possibility of recovering and died shortly after.

The climb was easier than expected. The trail wound on the mountain face through trees, giving them an easy trip. They would reach the middle by midday. The trail wrapped around, below the peak, and down the other side.

*****

Jade woke up to the creaking of the chamber door. Her monstrous captor stood before her. She got up and met him at the center of the room. His arms crossed over his dark brooding robes and cloak. His dark blue eyes began to burn bright and then calm back to the color of a peaceful sea.

"Welcome to my home. I hope you've enjoyed your stay so far," Magnus muttered.

"As a captive, I believe I'm entitled to one dying request," Jade said plainly.

Magnus smiled and took a breath. "Well pray, tell me your wish, then," he gave off the smallest hint of surprise in his tone.

"Give me the north sky. I want to see the morning star rise and the reflection of the one I love in the stars," she requested.

Magnus raised his palms. "You shall have it, but think on this. Were I in your position with one last wish, I would've requested that Odin be kept safe."

With a wave of his hand, a window appeared in the concrete walls. She gazed out and saw the drop from her window. Just a slip would instantly kill her. Magnus backed out and closed the door. She sat and stared at the mountains. Something out there was drawing her attention. Miles upon miles away, she could see each individual leaf on each tree. But what could be on the mountains?

Then, she saw a tree move, only slightly, but enough to make her notice.

"Treants" she thought.

The ancient race that resembled the trees had made their way up the south side of the mountain toward Odin and Sashi. They stood taller than other trees, with limbs like branches. They moved as a lumbering tower, bringing down anything that had not already gotten out of the way. Sashi could probably fight his way out of that, like anything else. But, Odin would have a much harder time not getting crushed.

Another figure caught her eye, a small ogre was caught in the mess. It had its sword drawn and fought hard to keep the treant away. Branches swatted at it, and roots came up to crush it. Finally, the ogre fell and was overtaken by a griffin. She closed her eyes prayed that the elders would have mercy on Odin and Sashi, and that the treant would do no harm to them.

*****

Odin cut through a thicket of trees and listened closely for the sound of rushing water. The spring was close by. As he slashed and cut the vines, tainted water fell on him from a deposit in the poisonous plants. But he couldn't let any of it in.

"We'll be there soon," Odin grunted, cutting past another large bush. Sashi brayed in frustration and galloped in front of Odin, swords drawn and head down. With one swift move, he darted through the trees and swiped everything away. He stopped once he arrived at the spring. Odin stood surprised.

"Maybe we should start with that next time," he scoffed and joined Sashi at the spring.

Sashi drank for long lasting moments, storing most of the water he consumed.

Odin lay down and watched the evening star dip beyond the grey and green horizon.

Sashi stood and nibbled from the vegetation. It was hardly edible: most of the trees were either covered in fungus or naturally poisonous. But other leaves escaped complete corruption. Sashi felt a soft tremor rumble through the ground. He turned his head and sniffed the wind. All he could smell was the ogres around the mountain. But ogres weren't heavy enough to make the ground tremble like that. Sashi sniffed the air again to make sure that it was in fact nothing. Satisfied, he continued eating. A gust of wind blew birds and leaves through the wood. He looked out again, his ears pointed and his entire body tensed up, alert. He brought his front hoof up and tapped it on the ground twice, adjusting his position as he did. He drew his swords ready for a fight. Something was on the move. The evening star was setting behind him, and he took the opportunity to leave.

"Odin, something is here." Sashi said in a low tone.

Odin saw Sashi's swords drawn. He felt the ground shake. The evening star was down but cast color through the clouds. He stood up and scanned the area.

"What is it?" Odin asked.

"I don't know but we need to go," Sashi warned.

The wind rustled and a tree cracked in the distance, almost like it was breaking down. A low groan stretched faintly in the wind. The darkness quickly closed in on them. They could feel the forest growing thicker. Something was on the move, and it knew they were there. Magnus was using his influence to try to prevent them from making it any further.

Odin climbed onto Sashi's back and they quickly disappeared. Sashi risked the plummet to their deaths and galloped down the slope. They ran down the mountain face, between trees and through the swaying and swinging branches. They could feel the leaves and vines attack at them. Branches swung down to knock Odin off. Sticks grabbed at their ankles to bring them down.

The sky had already turned a dark shade of blue, and light was leaving them fast. Sashi sliced the branches that came down in front of him, and Odin blocked from other falling debris.

Sashi felt his hooves get caught on a root and at that speed down the mountain, lift was more dangerous than gravity. Odin was thrown into the air and Sashi started to lose his footing. Stumbling to maintain his gallop, Sashi pushed back to his feet, and continued down the mountain. He picked up Odin and continued to descend down the mountain face. Still a long way from the bottom, the blue shade in the sky grew ever darker, and the horizon promised nothing to save them.

Gripping the mountain under his hooves, Sashi remembered what it was that made these ground tremors: "Treants!" he shouted to Odin.

"On the mountain?" Odin asked.

"Magnus must be behind this." Sashi guessed.

"How much further?" Odin asked.

Sashi quickened his pace. "It won't be long now. Once we escape the mountain's forest, they won't venture past the border."

They finally reached the bottom of the mountain and the night had begun. The only sound that could be heard was the sound of Sashi's hooves galloping on the ground. Swords still drawn, Sashi kept his eyes peeled for the ogres on the planes. Odin kept watch all around. The stars were bright and reflected on the dust Sashi kicked up. Trees were sparse along the planes. Everything could be spotted easily.

An object launched and blinked out the light of the stars as it passed them. Odin looked up and saw nothing. They both heard a distant crash in the trees off to the left. Odin brought his sword up and saw another flying object shimmer in the night.

"Up high!" Odin roared.

A mace stuck in the ground next to them and dust burst up all around it. A boulder came from the front and a club from their right. Sashi maneuvered around the falling objects, dodging more as they fell. Odin blocked anything that came too close and watched for any ogres that would charge at the intruders. He saw them across the field. A small group of ogres gathered in a defensive line. With their arms raised high, the blubbery skin jiggled as their full bodies pivoted and thrust the objects in the air at Odin and Sashi. Sashi twirled his blades in the air on the wrist straps of the hilts to create fans with his swords. Everything that came for them was deflected by the blades. Some objects were severed and everything else was thrown to the side. All but one.

A spear arced for Odin's heart. Odin couldn't see it through the twirl of Sashi's blades. Sashi lept over a small bolder and Odin was pushed back by the force. The spear was severed in half, but still managed to pierce through Odin's breastplate. Odin gasped in pain and lost his grip on Sashi. He fell off of Sashi's back and rolled to the ground. Sashi skidded to a stop and looked back. Odin wasn't moving.

The ogres attacked. Sashi flung his blades through the chests of two ogres, caught a club, and beat another ogre to the ground. He retrieved his swords and swung at another. Dodging attack after attack, Sashi jumped and slashed bringing down his enemies. Heran back to Odin cutting and attacking ogres as he past them by.

Odin didn't move when Sashi picked him up and threw him on his back. For a moment, Odin couldn't remember where he was or what he was doing. Odin's whole world faded into black.

*****

Jade sat straight up and gasped for air. She could still hear Odin calling out for her. Her eyes were wide open; the image of Odin falling and reaching for her had imprinted on her view. Her heart raced, the image of him falling was burned into her thoughts. She knew this was more than a dream.

She whispered, "Odin. Please, don't let go."

She lay back down and took a breath. Using the new connection Odin shared with her and the rest of his creation, she summoned aide from the woods. She closed her eyes and listened to the night outside her window. She heard a soft buzzing and looked up; a glow had come down from the window and sat next to her. A sprite landed on her hand. The wings were clear and glittered at the same time. The hair was long and gold, and the eyes were small and soft.

Jade brought the sprite up to get a good look at her. "You're so beautiful. Can you help me?" Jade asked gently.

The sprite nodded with a smile.

"I need your help. Have any of your friends seen a strong man riding a centaur?"

The sprite nodded again with a bright smile.

"That's wonderful. Listen, I need you to keep a secret from the other woodland creatures. Okay? I love that man. And the centaur is my best friend. Right now, they're both in a lot of trouble, and could die. The evil Lord Magnus" -The sprite balled a fist and punched her hand when she heard Magnus' name- "is sending all of his forces against the two heroes who are coming to save me from this awful cell. Odin, the strong man, needs protection. If he comes close to death at all, could you pour just little, teensy bit of your magical dust on him and save him?" Jade asked.

The sprite nodded and agreed to help.

Jade smiled. "Thank you. Sprites really are the best."

The sprite hugged Jade's finger and flew away. Jade waved the sprite goodbye, and lay back down whispering to Odin,

"Help is coming, Odin. Hold on for me, just a little longer."

CHAPTER 3

Odin awoke to the agony in his chest. He brought his hand up to find the maggots on his wound. Gritting his teeth, he wiped them out and shook them away from him. He groaned in pain, but they were finally out.

Sashi looked up and walked over. "I wish you hadn't done that. They were cleaning your wound." He handed Odin the spearhead to show how deep it had gone.

Odin looked at the spearhead and deemed it useful for a weapon. He cleaned it and lashed it to his wrist with the tip pointing out, all-the-while he fought against the pain. He looked up just in time to see a glimmer moving out of the trees towards them. A sprite flew out and hovered over Odin. More sprites gradually joined into a group. They hovered around Odin's chest as he stared at Sashi.

"Don't look at me, I don't know what to do," Sashi replied with a shrug.

Odin knew better than to anger sprites, so he let them do their work. A bright glow entered Odin's wound. Suddenly, he no longer felt the sharp pain in his chest, and became even more agile than when he began the journey. The sprites hovered around after they finished their work.

One lingered next to his ear and landed on his shoulder. "Your lovely Jade sent us to help. We hope to see you again," she whispered.

Odin smiled. "Thank you. Will you please send my love?" he asked.

The sprite giggled softly and flew away with the group.

Sashi looked at Odin's wound. It was completely healed. He was amazed and glanced up where the group of sprites had been.

Odin picked up his sword and sheathed it. "Where are we?" he asked.

"We're just beyond the ogres plains," Sashi explained.

Suddenly, a chill shot up Odin's spine. Eyes slammed shut, he saw the figure of a large person, heavily armed and staring up at the afternoon sky. Its hand was stretched up and lavished its full attention to its new advanced form. A large ax with a circular blade and a sharpened metal-tipped handle was firmly in his grasp. The abundance of metallic armor gave the Colossus the right to its name. The nose of the helmet spiked upwardly along its face and over the top of its head to form the Colossus' crown.

"He's freed the Colossus," Odin muttered.

Sashi almost smirked, "How?"

"He's given it a new form. It's even more heavily armored," Odin explained.

"How do we destroy it? Brute strength can't take it down," Sashi replied.

Odin nodded. "We need to find the Draco. He might help me again," Odin replied.

"Are you sure? The dragons don't like fighting the battles that don't belong to them. Not to mention the short memory span." Sashi warned.

"This battle does belong to them. If the titans roam free, they'll take over the entire world, including the dragons' lairs," Odin said and hopped onto Sashi's back.

"So, to the dragons lair?" Sashi asked.

"To the dragons lair," Odin replied.

They headed for the dark range of mountains ahead. The caves in them would hold the hiding places of the dragons.

*****

Jade opened her eyes and saw the sky. She heard the sound of the Ropens flying above and felt the breeze on her body. She lay in the grass and held someone's hand; it felt completely comforting. She looked and saw Odin there, laying with her, peacefully. His eyes were closed and he was safe. He rested peacefully with her by his side. She knew that this was what he wanted her to see, but what was actually going on? What was happening to her love?

"Why do you resist?" Odin asked looking at her.

"I want this to be real. I want to know that you're actually safe and we're here, together. Or if there's something that you're hiding from me," she explained.

Odin smiled. "This place is for us, and my love is for you. If I leave, you'll know where I go and what I do. For now, this moment is as real as we can make it."

"What do you face?" Jade asked.

"The first of the titans. The Colossus. I've dealt with him before, I can beat him again."

"Do you have to fight him?"

"He stands in my way. I won't be stopped. Not even by a titan."

"What if you don't succeed? What will I do if you take your last breath today?"

"I won't."

"But, what if …"

"Jade. I am Odin, the Eldest of elders, second to my father, and the symbol of good in the Dryad world. I will not lose to a mere titan. Death cannot have me, and life will not withhold me."

Jade couldn't move from lying on her back, she couldn't hold him, she couldn't curl up next to him. As hard as she fought, she couldn't satisfy her needs. Something was holding her back. All she could do was lay there with him next to her, hand in hand.

A tear fell from her eye, and the fear that she would never be able to hold him again was overpowering her.

"Jade, I have to go. Colossus is on the move. I'm getting help so I can fight him and defeat him. I love you." With that, Odin disappeared.

Jade closed her eyes and allowed the tears to fall at last. He really was gone. She felt his love, but not even a whisper of his voice was in her mind. Not a drop of rain to moisten her cheek when he kissed her.

No touch at all. Just an emotion that he sent her telling her that he was still alive.

"'You know I love you, Odin. Please, don't let me go," she whispered.

Then, like a breeze, she heard a small whisper in her mind say, "Never."

*****

Sashi and Odin entered the caves of the mountains and heard the rumble of dragons. Sashi drew his swords and followed Odin, who proceeded calmly through the caverns. Light filled the caverns from the tops of the mountains; their way was well lit.

A roar echoed through the caves, followed by the sound of a flame engulfing a large object and a tremor stretching through the caves. A thunderous wind chilled the mountain and was suddenly melted by a hot draft.

The small cavern finally bled into a main chamber, a huge space in the middle of the mountain where the two dragons battled. One was light blue and the other was a hard shade of crimson. Where the red one spat fire at the blue dragon, the blue one would shoot ice at the red dragon. Flying around the room, hocking their differences at each other, and clawing at each other's armored skin, the pile of treasured gold and pearls and jewels glittered on the ground.

Dodging a blast of fire, Odin climbed up to the top of the pile of precious stones and grounded himself.

"Dragons! You've received a challenge on your territory! Will you not protect what is yours?" he boomed. His voice was so loud that the dragons more than took notice. They both landed laughing.

"D'Argon, that was fun!" the blue one said.

"Don't push me," the red one replied, his skin now as peaceful a shade as a rose.

"Draco," Odin began, "I humbly request your help, once again."

Draco, the blue dragon, sniffed him cautiously. "I know your scent," he said, "I've helped you before. We did the impossible together for one day."

The red dragon, D'Argon reared its head and pointed his nose at the blue dragon, "The impossible, you say?"

Odin continued, "The same fiend that we contained at one time has broken free from his prison, and now Magnus has given the monster new power. I seek your help so that I might permanently neutralize it. I know that with your strength we can end this villain for all time."

D'Argon looked down at him. "And what spoils from the victory will we receive if we participate in this battle?"

Odin opened his hands at them. "Your territory is being taken from you. Is that not enough?"

The dragons glanced at each other, then back to Odin.

"And what would you have us do?" Draco asked.

Odin replied coldly, "His armor is his only strength and his only weakness. Melt him first and on my command, freeze his liquidated body."

"You're certain that he will be subdued by this one final effort?" Draco questioned with an icy fog escaping his lips.

"I'm no smith, but it's the only logical strategy." Odin explained.

D'Argon nodded, "All right, I'll go with you. But I want something in return for the fight."

Odin frowned. "Name your price."

"I want the weapon: the ax of the Colossus. You can keep whatever else he has of value. The ax is mine."

Odin nodded thoughtfully. "It is done. The Ax of the Colossus shall be yours once you pry it from his gods forsaken hands."

Draco smiled. "Then let us take to the skies. We have defeated Colossus before: we will do it again."

Odin jumped on the Blue dragon's back. "Sashi, ride out in front to the battle field of Denarra. We'll be right above you."

Sashi nodded and galloped out of the cave.

D'argon glanced at Odin and the Draco. "Stay close."

Odin drew his sword, "We'll follow your lead. Now go."

The dragons spread their mighty wings and ascended through the caverns of the mountains. They swiftly accelerated through the mountain, twisting and turning with the caves, and not letting the darkness have any meaning to them, they raced out of the caverns, shooting into the sky. Odin held tight to the blue dragon's neck as they soared over Sashi to the battle field of Denarra.

The ride was short. Denerra's territory was just beyond the limits of the barren mountain range. The terrain was easy for Sashi to navigate and no opposition stood between the heroes and their target. Now the battle with the Colossus was at hand. They could see him off in the distance. He was walking away from the Denarran Village. He must have already started plaguing the land, demolishing the homes, and poisoning the land. Now he was on the move for the village of the Dryads. D'Argon roared and darted forward as Sashi slowed down, and ran at an even pace. The red dragon came down and spat fire everywhere, surrounding the Colossus with flame. Then he filled in the circle, melting the armor. The Colossus retaliated by swinging its ax around and grabbing for D'Argon's tail or wing; anything it could grasp to bring the dragon to the ground.

D'Argon swooped his tail in from behind, knocking the Colossus to the ground. The dragon rested his weight and bathed the back of the Colossus in fire. The Colossus rolled over trying to get up, but was pushed back to the ground by the dragon's breath.

Suddenly, the Colossus reached up and grabbed D'Argon's neck. The dragon recoiled, but couldn't break free from the grip of the Colossus. The Colossus brought D'Argon's head up and looked him in the eye, then he lifted the ax ready to slice off the dragon's head. D'Argon took a deep breath and blew all the fire he could into the Colossus' face. The fiery current was so strong that it melted the crown off of the helmet and welded the eyes, mouth, and nose shut.

The Colossus let go and the dragon finished him off, melting every bit of him to a liquid metal. Then he twirled his way up and spat fire towards the sky.

"That's the signal," Odin said.

Draco nodded and came in next to the red dragon. He blew his frost all over the Colossus, freezing him to the ground. Ice shards formed on the back of the blue dragon's throat and shot out, pinning the Colossus in place. When the Colossus stopped moving, the blue dragon sat on the ground and caught his breath.

Odin hopped down next to Sashi. "Thank you, both. These people are now in your debt."

The red dragon stamped his claw. "Well, that was quicker than I thought it would be."

Sashi looked at Odin. "The Colossus is the first of a deadly series of titans. This journey will take more than two dragons to get Jade back. The next titan will be a far worse threat."

Then the clouds rolled with thunder and collide in the sky. Rain poured from the heavens, but the feeling wasn't refreshing or inviting. Odin received a vision. Birds of fire circled a village, scorching it and burning the inhabitants. They were massive, and all water from above and below could not kill them completely. Cold made little difference and wind was their friend. All that they did was burn village after village, without reason, without purpose, for nothing other than pleasure.

"The battle will be vast and all of the inhabitants of this world could use your help," Sashi said to the dragons.

"Where will this battle take place?" Draco asked.

"Magnus' lair. He wants us to meet him there. We'll bring all manner of hell with us," Sashi replied.

Odin turned to Sashi. "He's freed the Phoenixes. They're tormenting an entire city. We need to move."

"Which city?" Sashi asked.

"All I saw were towers, and domes. The Phoenixes were destroying them all," Odin replied.

The red dragon tilted his head. "That sounds like Centurion. It's a day's walk from here. Keep your course, head south, and you'll find your city."

Odin nodded. "Will you join our cause and fight with us?"

Draco nodded back. "We'll go ahead of you and wait. When you've reached his lair, we'll be ready for battle."

D'Argon tromped to the Colossus and wrenched the ax from it by breaking off the monster's hand from the wrist up. They lifted into the air and set off for the south-lands.

Odin mounted onto Sashi and roared "let's ride."

Without another word or thought, Sashi hastily rode toward Centurion.

*****

Jade was brought before Magnus in his throne room filled with demons. She fought against the arch-demon's grip and pried their claws off of her arms. She now wore a green gown to compliment her other features.

"What is it you want?" she asked with a glare

Magnus grinned. "Odin has taken down the first of the titans." He paused for her reaction. "Does it please you to hear?" he asked when she didn't answer.

Her expression didn't change. "I'm overwhelmed with joy," she replied blandly.

Magnus brought his hand up and glanced at the tips of his fingers. "You don't seem pleased that your lover is risking his life to become your rescuer."

Jade didn't move. "He's only my rescuer because you put him to the test."

Magnus looked at her and froze and replied in a cold voice, "and I will continue to test him, until he has cleared his transgressions against me."

Jade scoffed, "What sin, exactly, has he committed?"

Magnus placed both hands evenly on the rests of his throne. "Well, you're his love; his obsession. So, obviously, you are his sin."

Jade slightly shook her head. "I fail to make the connection."

Magnus stood up and paced around her from a distance.

"You know that Odin was once the eldest of elders. The story that you haven't heard goes like this. One day, he fell in love with the one creature in the universe that is forbidden to all powers and forces. and by no means would he be allowed to pursue this passion. He fell in love with a soul. One that he had known for ages. A soul that he himself had brought to the afterlife. It took him a hundred years to forge a deal with our father, but eventually, the father gave in to Odin's wishes. They both broke the vows of the elders and brought a soul back from the afterlife before its time had come.

Completely ignoring the words 'Observation only', they took the soul that was rightfully mine, gave it a body, and hid her away from me on this putrid little planet. When I tried to take that soul back, he sought to destroy me so that I would never be able to claim that which is mine."

Jade froze. "So, how will you reclaim that soul?" she asked.

"If Odin doesn't settle this score, I'll kill you myself. If he fails to meet me, I'll have you at rest once again. And if he dies, I'll have his soul instead of yours. Either way, the debt will be repaid," Magnus paused. "Only one thing remains to be answered."

Jade tilted her head in a sarcastic gesture of interest. "Do tell."

Magnus snapped his fingers and appeared in his throne.

"Why? Why does he go to the trouble of saving you? Why did you catch his attention so many generations ago? That answer eludes me," he said snapping his fingers again.

Suddenly, her gown fell completely off her body. She knelt down to pick cover herself, but the arch-demons stopped her, holding their claws up to her neck. She stared back at Magnus, as a melody from a music box echoed through the great hall. Like a dream, the music transformed the ambiance to a more peaceful nature.

"Dance for me." Magnus softly commanded.

Angered by his wish, she got up, and slowly moved her body into a Dryad step. Magnus never took his eyes away. He instantly saw what Odin saw, when he carried her through the worlds. She was passionate and tender. Her moves were caring and gentle, yet vigorous and pleasing. Magnus brought a hand thoughtfully up to his mouth, and watched carefully as he enjoyed seeing through his brother's eyes.

She danced: spinning, twirling, stepping, wrapping her arms around her chest and moving her hips. She looked absolutely angelic and as she continued, Magnus became envious of his brother. The obsession was deeper than a lust for the body Odin had shielded her in, or the soul that dwelt in it, but in both combined. Everything that had made the act of love forbidden called to Magnus, in this moment more than ever.

Through and through, Magnus could see that she truly was perfect. The love she felt for Odin only made her that much more appetizing. She slowly spun, and looked at Magnus to see if she was pleasing him. He was satisfied to say the least. She closed her eyes and twirled again, holding the anger back. Her majestic hair flew in her sudden spin, but she flogged her own soul in doing so. Tears filled her eyes.

"Enough," Magnus called, having had his fill of sensation.

She curled herself up. It felt more comfortable to conceal herself, than to stand there for eyes to gaze and judge. She wept, wanting so badly for Odin to hold her. The arch demons stepped in to force her to her feet. Magnus jumped up angrily, and with a wave of his hand, the demons fell to the ground. He turned his head away from the little Dryad, snapped his fingers and she reappeared in the tower with her clothes intact. Her sobs echoed in the tower, and her sniffles only fed the depression.

"Odin, where are you?" she cried.

CHAPTER 4

Odin closed his eyes, trying to comfort Jade. Leaning forward, he focused as much energy as possible into being where she was. The rain lightened up, but was still drizzling on the hills.

Sashi kept his arms down and back. "Whatever you're doing, it's working," he called, but Odin didn't hear. "I think the storm is diminishing."

Odin smiled knowing that he could comfort his love. He didn't know what was going on, but he was confident that she would be all right, and that his touch was helping. He focused on holding her, counting every detail of that one moment: how her skin felt against his and how her hair lay against his chest. How her neck felt on his lips, and the way she touched his face. Now only the clouds remained. Sashi rode over the hills, splashing through the puddles and hopping over the ditches. The highest tower of Centurion was just barely visible on the top of the hill they were on. Once again, the only sound was the beating of Sashi's hooves on the ground.

"We're here," Sashi said.

"Centurion," Odin sighed, "at last."

They entered the gates and slowly walked through the city. Everything was quiet and still as the dead. Buildings were scorched and towers were knocked down. Debris littered the streets. Odin and Sashi slowly moved around the broken buildings and shattered stone. Suddenly, the screech of a bird howled in the distance. They both searched the skies and found the legion of Phoenixes flying from the distance. They surrounded Centurion and swooped in to finish the city off. Then, piles of rubble were thrown aside, revealing the hiding places of a centaur army. They brought catapults from the ground and water-hoses that fed through the streets. As the Phoenixes attacked, the centaur army counter-attacked, catapulting water into the sky and spraying down the birds of fire.

Each Phoenix that was caught in a spray would burst into a lifeless flame and the ashes would fall to the ground. Through the ashes, another Phoenix would emerge, continuing its course.

Then the centaurs launched the catapult and a huge liquid mass engulfed a majority of the group of Phoenixes. They all took the same death and burst into flame. The ashes of all the birds created a giant cloud of ash. In an instant the mass burst into flames releasing a giant phoenix, screaming so loud that it shook the remnants of the city, causing everyone to cover their ears in agony.

Odin and Sashi stared in both amazement and dismay. The army of centaurs fighting and carrying on the battle was an incredible sight. But the error of their tactic was something to be later dreaded, if not now. No matter what they did, the Phoenixes would not die. No amount of water would bring the birds down to defeat.

One centaur came up next to them. He had a helmet like the rest of the centaurs, but the decorated breastplate and gold-hilted sword were signs of high military stature. "Are you a citizen of Centurion?" he asked.

Sashi shook his head. "We're travelers passing through. We've come to help with the fight against the Phoenixes."

The other centaur looked Odin up and down, searching for an identity. Odin returned the gesture.

The large Phoenix perched on a building and began picking it up. When it reached the desired altitude, it hovered over a portion of the centaur army and released the building. The centaurs all jumped away and dodged the painful death. A group of centaurs hosed the beast down, and it died once again.

Odin watched the event and glanced at the commanding Centaur. "I'd like to contact the commanding officer. I think I might have an answer to this problem."

The Centurion stared Odin down. "In case you haven't noticed, we're at war. The general has enough to deal with. Try a couple days from now when we're all dead and you might be able to voice your opinion about this 'problem'."

Odin slightly grinned. "Obviously, water isn't working to defeat them. You need to find a way of containing them without killing them."

The Centurion didn't take too kindly to Odin trying to make military decisions, but decided to take him in for questioning. If Odin couldn't prove his worth as an adviser, he would make a fine captive or slave. The Centurion led the way to a small building in the center of the city. A centaur with gold armor was at a table getting battle statuses from a lieutenant. They both observed a map.

"I want all water pumping out of the rootstock going to the hoses. As far as I'm concerned, the main valve is completely useless now," the general ordered.

"Sir, the problem has just gotten bigger, literally," the lieutenant added.

The general nodded and muttered to himself. "Water won't kill them. What will?"

"Nothing will," Odin replied walking into the small dome. "There are plenty of ways to douse a fire, but in some cases, water just makes things worse."

The general looked up at the new intruder. "Who are you and what do you want?" he asked firmly.

"I am Odin, and my friend is Sashi, and we offer you our help."

The other centaurs rolled their eyes or scoffed at his presumption.

Odin's eyes didn't wander. The General didn't move.

"We are barely holding our own ground with our entire army at our disposal. What good is one more centaur and a Dryad?" the General replied coldly.

Odin stepped up to the table. "Are the Phoenixes staying here in Centurion, or are they moving on?"

The General put both hands on the locations on the map. "The Phoenixes have been alternating back and forth between Centurion and Ferron. They've only left here because we fight back. They've already completely conquered Ferron. We expect this will be their final effort to wipe us out."

"We've fought them before," Odin explained. "We can tell you how to defeat them."

The general opened his arms, inviting an answer to all questions. "Pray tell, what secrets do you have?"

"Do you have any chain-linked harpoons?" Odin asked.

The General looked at the Lieutenant. Lieutenant nodded. The General nodded at Odin.

"Many?" Odin asked the Lieutenant.

Lieutenant nodded again.

Odin circled Centurion on the map with his finger. "Would a perimeter set-up be safe?"

The General looked over Odin's plan. "You want to harpoon the Phoenixes to the ground?"

Odin nodded. "But, one step further. We must not kill them." Odin took a candle from the table and covered it with a bowl, cutting off oxygen from the flame. In a matter of seconds, the flame died out.

"Once we contain them, suffocate them. That way, they won't be able to come back."

The General cocked an eyebrow at the plan. "Indeed."

The Lieutenant was irked. "We can't afford to lose that many of us, especially if you're planning a diversion to go with this plan. If we spread too far across the village, we won't have enough numbers to man the hoses or take the creatures down."

The Lieutenant looked at Odin, "Your plan has merit, and it's probably the best I've heard so far, but under the circumstances, we cannot make it happen."

Odin frowned. "Give me five of your soldiers, and all of the harpoons you have. I'll do this myself."

The General's cheek twitched. "You can do it?"

Odin glanced at Sashi, then back at the General. "We're going to do it."

General nodded again and looked at a group of Centaurs in the room with him, "You five, do as he says."

Odin glanced around and looked over his requested army.

They all had decorated armor, so he expected complete obedience from each of them. Odin balled his fists and walked out of the room. The five at his command followed him out.

He turned to the two on the right, "Bring all of the harpoons on a cart up to the ridge." He pointed at where he wanted them.

The two centaurs nodded and galloped away.

"You three, follow me," he commanded walking to the ridge.

*****

Jade lay on the ground in the tower. The morning star shown through the window and woke her up. When she looked up, the door to the tower opened and she saw Odin standing at the door. Jade jumped up and ran to him, and he wrapped his arms around her.

"Odin!" She screamed as she threw her arms around his neck, "I couldn't feel you! I got your message from the sprites, but you were gone!"

He held her tighter, "I'm here, Jade."

Magnus' heart boomed as he held her and kissed her. She didn't move from his touch, but she noticed something foreign about it.

"Are we leaving now?" she asked.

"We will soon. The elders are dealing with Magnus. They've come all this way just to condemn him. We'll be safer in here."

She closed her eyes and pressed her lips against his. As he kissed her back, he searched for a reason as to why he hadn't noticed her before? How could she not have captured his attention? Inside of her, she only thought of how she had missed him. The passion that burned inside her was enough to cover up any suspicion of a change in his manner. When his passion mixed with hers, they were inseparable. Intoxicated, infatuated, Jade pulled Magnus to the floor, kissing him with every ounce of passion inside her.

Love was something that Magnus longed to understand, but something he would willingly throw aside for justice. Love no longer had a meaning to him. It was something he was told he would never know ouside of family, and yet, it was being made there in the room of that tower.

*****

Odin handed all of the harpoons to the five centaurs and watched as one flock of Phoenixes flew passed the ridge where they were hiding. The hoses sprayed the flock and they all burst into flame. Just as the first time, the giant cloud burst into one giant phoenix. The two large Phoenixes could now do more damage to Centurion, and they took that to their advantage. Odin saw this error and quickly remedied the problem in his mind. The last flock of small Phoenixes was about to pass. When they were sprayed and merged into the third large Phoenix, Odin ordered the harpooners to fire. Five chains pierced through the Phoenixes limbs and wings.

Odin turned his head to Sashi. "Change in plans. You take command."

Sashi grimaced as Odin gripped one of the chains and climbed to the Phoenix. It yanked free from the Centaur's grip and flew out to continue laying Centurion to waste, just as Odin was half way up the chains. The Phoenix twisted and twirled around the towers and domed buildings. As Odin, swung below, he passed by the second phoenix. He capitalized on his momentum towards the fiery beast and sliced its belly with the spear-head lashed to his wrist. The spear-head broke off of his lash, leaving him without that option of a weapon. He saw that the Phoenix was coming up on the side of a long tower. He planted his feet on the wall and ran up, swinging onto the back of his flaming transport.

Regaining stability, he took the daggers from the sides of his boots. He drove them into the chain links and pinned the chains to the back of the Phoenix. Then, he pulled on the chains and maneuvered the Phoenix, aiming for another enemy. The fiery-bird screeched in pain, but submitted, all the while screaming to the other two for help. When the other Phoenixes noticed that the third was being hijacked, they came in for the rescue. Sashi watched as Odin stumbled on the Phoenix's back, but regained his balance and kept the Phoenix on course, down the street, straight to the harpooners. The other two would meet at the intersection of the street in front of the ridge.

Odin signaled the hose-liner as the three huge Phoenixes smashed together. He grabbed his daggers and leapt straight into the air with the whip-lash of the collision enforcing his flight to the sky. The three phoenixes were hosed together, then burst into flame, and as Odin came back down, he landed on the back of a giant, Phoenix whose wing-span doubled that of the dragon's put together. Odin tightened his gloves and planted his boots firmly onto the back of the Phoenix. Without a second thought, he gripped the chains that flapped from the Phoenix's wings and pulled them back as hard as he could. He felt them beginning to tear, but only inches at a time. As he did, the Phoenix lifted its body. Odin wiped the sweat from his brow to his shoulder and screamed angrily, "Sashi, now!"

Sashi shouted, "Fire! Fire! Fire!"

Twenty harpoons fired and speared through the limbs and wings of the Phoenix at the same time. It screamed in agony as more centaurs with harpoons surrounded the beast and shot the chains into the sides of the Phoenix, dragging it to the ground.

Odin hopped off of the Phoenix and landed in front of Sashi.

"You are the craziest Dryad I've ever known," Sashi chuckled.

"As we have already established," Odin replied with a smile.

"Yes, but I always make sure you haven't forgotten."

*****

Magnus and Jade held each other on the ground. She was happy to be reunited with her love, but Magnus was busy thinking of how he would convince Jade that all this made sense. She smiled at him and kissed him. Then, Magnus slowly waved his hand over her face, putting her into a deep sleep. He held her close and whispered to her.

"Jade, when you wake up, you'll believe that this was all a dream."

Magnus got up and quickly clothed himself. He, then, snapped his fingers to clothe Jade as she rested. He left the room of the tower and stormed back down to his main chamber. He suddenly realized what

Odin was fighting for. Odin would meet Magnus. He would confront him. He would fight him, just to have what was left back in that room. He grew covetous of Odin, now that he knew a fraction of what Odin felt. He couldn't let Odin have this. He couldn't let them get away with this relationship. Why should Odin have this privilege when Magnus could just as easily please her in his realm? So, Magnus would fight Odin to the death to have this perfect creature in his keep. Even if it meant taking on his brother's form forever, he was was going to take back what was rightfully his, and keep her as his own.

CHAPTER 5

The General shook Odin's hand, "You have my thanks. Not a single one of us could've done that," General said.

"It had to be done. Sashi and I are taking this fight to Magnus on his occupied ground. He has set the Phoenixes loose on these lands, among other horrors. I can assure you, it will be a battle of such a likeness that Magnus has never seen. Will you join us in this fight? Will you join our cause?" Odin asked.

General nodded. "I have ten legions training to fight in the secret army of Centurion. We would be happy to join your cause. Together, we will make this a battle worthy of songs and celebration for generations to come."

The centaurs poured load after load of clay on the Phoenix, starting at the tail, which was the hardest part because it never stopped swaying.

Sashi gripped his battle belt buckle. "I fought in the sieges of the Skord a century ago. They retreated, and I believed that I was the last of our kind. How have I never heard of Centurion or this army, or even how it came to be?"

The General frowned. "When the Skord retreated, they had already taken me and a few others captive. We escaped their world fifty years later and vowed that we would remake our army. An army of centaurs formed by our children, and their children, and their children's children. We are an army of ten generations of centaurs, and we have all but survived in this secluded valley."

The Phoenix screeched as the centaurs covered the tail completely and started on its legs. Odin smiled at the numbers mentioned by the General.

"Take your army and fortify it at the gates of Magnus' lair. Sashi and I will continue the fight against the Titans and meet you there. Dragons and centaurs will not be enough. The next time you see me, we will have allies enough to make us such a force to be reckoned with."

The general nodded. "Fight hard. Die well."

The centaurs now covered the wings and started up the neck. The Phoenix fought hard against the centaurs and the chains that held it down, but it was no use. Half of its neck was consumed. Most of the concrete had dried, and double layered. When the concrete reached its neck it started shooting fire from its mouth, but most of its body had been doused. Concrete was poured on its head and seeped down in its mouth. The fire instantly dried it, and the Centaurs finished the job.

The General added, "if you are willing, our neighboring city has had a visit from one of these titans. The fish are now few, and the beasts that live there lay siege on the waters every day."

Odin agreed and with that, the General signaled his troops and they all left Centurion. Sashi looked at Odin.

"So, where are we going?" Sashi asked.

"To the sea. West," Odin replied, mounting on Sashi.

A faint voice called from inside one of the domed buildings. "Are you Odin?"

Both Sashi and Odin turned to the voice. "I am," Odin replied.

The darkness inside the dome concealed the voice within.

"If you fight for your love, you will surly fail. Love will not save you, nor give a reason to finish your fight."

Sashi drew his swords as Odin got back down. "Who are you? How do you know this?" he asked.

"Tell me, can you feel your love now?" the voice asked. It almost sounded tender.

Odin stopped just outside the dome. He focused on his love for Jade, but he never felt a reply. Where had she gone? What had happened to her? Had Magnus broken the rules and killed her already? Did she simply lose her feeling for Odin? Why couldn't he feel her?

He boldly stepped into the dome. "What has happened?" he demanded.

A figure could just barely be seen inside. "Her heart has been blocked, taken." The voice paused. "Ah, I also see a great ancestral line in you. Your father, he is going to play a part in this story as well. His army is preparing. He sends his entire celestial force to your aid. And your sister, Lara, she has given her armies to your father for this single event in history."

Odin knelt down at the table. "Who are you?" he whispered.

"I am Andromeda, and I only see what everyone cannot," she answered, "and if you fight for your passions and obsessions, then you will fall. The demon now lives in heaven, and you have been cast out. If you fight, you will fail."

Odin got up and walked away. "I will not be told to give up. My love for Jade is stronger than any force of dismay," he said as he left.

The oracle stood up. "No. Go to the dune-sea. You will find the rest of your army there. But only you will be able to see it. Then accomplish your goal and finish this fight," she said.

Odin hopped onto Sashi. "You've said enough. Now, I continue my fight. Live in peace, oracle," he said and they rode away.

*****

Jade sat up and looked around. Odin wasn't there. She stared out the window. Something was wrong. Why couldn't she feel him? What was guarding her from the feeling? Had he given up? Was he still alive to fight for her? He was closer. Much closer in proximity.

She gazed out the window, searching the horizon for Odin and Sashi. She adjusted her focus up a few miles, then back a few miles, stretching her sight, straining to see. She found the figure she was looking for. Odin and Sashi were both walking across a desert. They headed towards the castle, but going a long way around. Then something shifted the sand. The sand curled in the air then fell to the ground. Another scoop of sand splashed in the air and sifted back to the ground.

*****

Odin tried to keep from falling into the sand. With each drop of sweat that fell from his brow, he wished he'd taken some water from Centurion with him. Sashi, too, had only enough strength to keep himself walking. He kept going on the water he stored from the mountains, but the heat was having its way with Odin. Odin staggered forward, smiling the whole time.

"Is that rain?" Odin asked for the fifth time, pointing at a wisp of sand.

"No. It's not," Sashi replied. "There's no rain here, Odin."

The heat pinched at Odin's skin and Sashi was on the lookout for plant life in the desert. Hearing Odin asking if the mirages were springs or rain was grating on Sashi's nerves. His patience ran very thin with the heat, Odin, and absolutely no wind. With an endless desert, there seemed to be nothing worth going on for.

Odin strained his eyes through the brightness of the blaring star and saw another wisp of sand jump from the ground. He turned around to Sashi. "Did you see that?" he asked.

Sashi looked up to please Odin. "There's nothing there, Odin."

"It's water. I know it," he cried running to where he saw the sand jump. He saw another leap of the sand to his left. He turned and followed where the sand jumped next.

Sashi tried to keep up. "Odin, slow down! You might be walking into a trap."

Odin chuckled in joy. "I'm a mortal looking for water and I've found it," he called back.

The sand shot from the ground right in front of him. He stopped and watched it rail to the sky. Sashi stopped too, but what he saw was Odin being completely surrounded by a sphere of sand. Odin looked all around and drew his sword. Sand was shooting from the ground and encasing him in a structure. Then it all moved and fell into a hollow ball of sand with Odin inside, and in a second Odin could see what was bringing the sphere into shape.

Large, circular organisms with spiked tales flew from the sand and dove back down as if the sand were water. Hundreds of them would follow each other and intertwine until they hit the ground. They all carried the sand up and each one would catch the falling bits of sand on their backs so that not one grain fell to the ground without them knowing it. They worked together as one to keep the sphere of sand constructed.

Sashi trotted up to the wall of the sphere and touched it with the hilt of his blade. He felt the sand eroding the hilt and pulled away before the damage was unchangeable. Odin watched the formation closing in.

In unison, the creatures spoke in one voice. "We are the Ralligins. You are the one called Odin."

The bands of Ralligins revolve around him and he responded, "I am. Are you the army that was foretold to me?"

"We are. We have served the elders since the time of our creation. The ancient vow to ever protect the creation of the elders has been passed down through us for a hundred millennia. We will follow as you order and keep our oath to your father and to you, our protector," they replied.

Odin shouted to Sashi. "Sashi! They want to help us!"

Sashi frowned. "Who's they?"

"The Ralligins! They're going to be our army!" he replied with a chuckle.

Sashi looked at the sphere of sand and reasoned that was what he was talking about. "The sand wants to fight?" he asked.

"No! The Ralligins! They're carrying the sand! Can't you see them?"

Sashi looked again and shook his head. "No!"

Odin sheathed his sword, "Will you be our front-line for the battle against Magnus?" he asked.

"To serve your purposes, we need freedom."

And with that, they disappeared back into the ground.

Then the sand started to twirl in the air surrounding both Sashi and Odin. It died back down to the ground and they looked around to see where they were. They had teleported to the underground of the desert. Water flowed from the side of the rock and dropped to a waterfall through the caverns. The entire cave was lit with lanterns and lamps along the walls of what looked like mines. Odin and Sashi looked up and found the light shining in through the mouth of the cave. Sashi ran to the side of the waterfall and drank his fill. Odin happily joined him, but kept wondering what they were doing in there. The voices of the Ralligins were inside his head now.

"We are being held captive in these desert lands. The Skord have forced their armies into these caves and fortified themselves under the deserts. In the center of their fortress is the Uniroth, the very mind of the Ralligins. It has been taken from its home in our world and contained in these caves. Without its freedom, we too, cannot roam free. Take back the Uniroth, and bring it to safety and we will be free to join your army," they explained as Odin drank.

"The Uniroth," Odin repeated.

Sashi turned. "What?"

"That's what we're after. The Uniroth. We'll be fighting off the Skord to get it."

Sashi spat out his water to one side and turned to Odin. "The Skord?" he asked in distress.

Odin nodded, closing his eyes "Yes. I cannot tell how many. The Uniroth is surrounded and guarded by them. The Skord are enslaving the Ralligins."

Sashi rolled his eyes when Odin spoke of the Ralligins,

"Are you sure you're not just crazy?" he asked taking another drink.

They heard clanking in the distance. A row of Skord marched right passed them. Odin and Sashi didn't move, but watched them march.

Sashi gulped his water down. "Okay, what's our plan?" he asked.

Odin took another drink and held back against the wall.

"We need to take them all out in one clean strike," he whispered.

Suddenly, another shiver ran up Odin's spine. He closed his eyes and watched as the next vision of the coming titan. The rocks of the walls bulged out of the walls and clung together, forming together. It never made a clear shape, but it rolled around crushing all in its path. Another joined it, and another after that. There were ten in total.

Odin opened his eyes. "The Stone Titans are here as well," he explained.

Sashi widened his eyes. "First the Skord, and now the Stone Titans. What's next? The Ragnarok?"

Odin backed against the wall. "Do you have all the water you'll need?"

Sashi joined him against the wall. "It should do. I'm just worried about how we're getting out of here."

Odin turned to Sashi. "Alive?" He looked back toward the cavern and looked for a stealthy way of attack. "I'm sure it'll be easier said than done."

Skord were everywhere, training, sparring, preparing their armor. There was absolutely no way to get around them without being noticed. Odin couldn't see where the Uniroth was, but he was sure he'd know it when he saw it.

He turned to Sashi. "There are two ways we can go about this. Option one, we split up and try to sneak in. It'll be tough, but I'm sure you can make it. Or option two, we ride out straight to the Uniroth and slay as many Skord as we can on the way."

Sashi drew his swords. "I am in favor of the second option. We will fight with honor. And if this is our last fight together, then we'll die covered in the blood of our enemies."

Odin nodded, mounted on Sashi and they leapt from the ledge, landing near a group of Skord sparring. When they looked up, it was as if all of the Skord knew of their presence and rushed for an attack. The heavily armored soldiers came from all directions. They slashed and lunged, but each blow was deflected. Odin and Sashi rode quickly through the caverns and shallow waterfalls. The Skord that they passed followed closely after and chased through the mines.

Odin jumped off and took down ten Skord, swinging and slashing his long blade, blocking their blows, and then knocking them to the ground. One of the Skord managed to keep a fight up with Odin. It blocked two swings, then a lunge, but as Odin moved forward, he brought his foot around the Skord's foot and punched it in the neck, tripping it to the ground. Then he pressed his foot into its face and crushed the skull under his boot.

Sashi twisted and twirled cutting anything within reach of his blades. Not one stayed on it's feet and the excitement brought flashes of war into his mind. He used some of the same moves as he had in the army and all of his training was coming back to him.

Smashing the hilt of his blade into a face and hearing another one squeal like a pig when he ran it through, he remembered what a painful venture it was being among the centaur soldiers. Odin took the dagger from his left boot and drove it through the chest of one of the Skord he knocked to the ground. He guided the soldier down, felt for the blade to go all the way through and he knew when it hit the ground. Suddenly, the ground erupted and the Stone Titans spurred to life.

When he looked up, he saw another group of Skord coming in to fight him, but then, they were all crushed when the Stone Titan charged after their target.

Odin finished off another and jumped out of the way as the Stone Titan crashed into the wall, shattering into smaller rocks.

"The Stone Titans have awakened!" Odin shouted, his voice echoing through the cavern.

Sashi groaned, "I hate this part."

Another group of Skord charged after him throwing their spears and shouting in their strange orkish language. Another Stone Titan crushed that group and continued through the mine. Odin dragged his blade in the ground as he began an attack on a lone Skord. Suddenly, one of the Titans changed its course and accelerated on for Odin. The Skord attacked high and Odin ducked, flanking away as the Stone Titan squashed the Skord.

Sashi picked a Skord up with his blades and threw it back into another. He ran a Skord's blade through them both together and left them on the ground. Then he sliced another into thirds and they slowly fell to the ground as another Skord attacked, leaping into the air. Sashi spun his blades into fans and the Skord's body splattered everywhere.

Sashi wiped his face of the meat and exclaimed in disgust.

Odin ran for Sashi and mounted on. "Ride. I don't care where you go, just ride. I'll take care of the Skord."

Sashi charged through another group and sliced all of the Skords heads with one clean cut. The veins in Sashi's biceps bulged and throbbed. Odin looked back and saw the Skord following once again. He smiled and leaned into Sashi's ear.

"Move closer to the walls. I think this might work."

Sashi carefully moved to the side. Odin brought his blade out and reached for the wall as far as he could without falling off. He could just barely reach it, but it wasn't enough, and the Skord were surrounding them.

"A little more," he called and again Sashi moved closer.

Odin leaned over and dragged his blade across the wall. Keeping his blade along the wall, he glanced back and saw three of the Stone Titans charging for them. They crushed all of the Skord that followed, but once that was done, they didn't stop. They were now gaining on Odin and Sashi. Odin looked up ahead and saw the trail getting very narrow from the ground to the ceiling.

"Hey, are we going to make that?" he asked.

Sashi sheathed his swords and leaned forward. "Keep your head down!" he shouted. Sashi brought his legs up, and his body forward.

Through the break of the wall, the awkward structure bled into the hall of a great temple. The Titans that were chasing them crashed into the walls and small stones that made it through slid on the ground. Sashi looked up and saw the shape of the temple. Three of the walls with giant windows in the centers, rode up to a dome. At the center of the dome was a glass window letting the star shine down upon them, beaming their only source of light in that hall. The forth wall was the wall of the caves. It wasn't as jagged or natural as the caves, but kept its color.

They both glanced down at the floor. The entire floor of the temple was made of glass, and they realized that they were on only a second story of the great structure, and a great distance above the first floor. Through the glass, saw an army of Skord in a lined and columned formation: one hundred by one hundred. At once, they hurled their weapons at the glass floor. Sashi closed his eyes and braced himself as Odin watched.

The ear-shattering crash followed every spear piercing the glass and the entire floor broke away. From the stain-glass windows, the Ralligins poured into the temple, shrieking. They circled the temple just below Odin and Sashi and the circle filled into the center. Soon, one giant plate of Ralligins hovered over the Skord.

"Odin, have you failed?" they all asked in unison.

"No. We've only begun," Odin explained as the disk levitated in the air.

"The room above you is their armory. The Uniroth dwells in that room. When it returns to it's resting place of our world, we will be free. Only you, an elder, can go in and bring it back." They all explained finally reaching, the top of the dome where the top window was. Odin stood on top of Sashi and sliced a hole through the glass window. When the afternoon star shown on them, Odin could see how the Uniroth resembled it. He climbed up and stood on top of the dome. He was outside, overlooking the entire world of Hajun. The Uniroth was a large orb, about the size of a melon, and it erupted in flame like the star. Odin brought his hands up and could feel the heat sink through his gloves before he even attempted to grip it.

The Uniroth blinked, and in an instant, he appeared in the world of the Ralligins. All of the creatures were surrounding him, flowing in lines in a hallowed formation. Just ahead of him was a road made of glass with a ruby staircase leading to a small pillow on a stand. He stepped lightly for the staircase and placed the Uniroth on the pillow. He took in his surroundings and watched his footing, wondering if the glass road would break under his weight. He stepped just as carefully on the ruby staircase. Everything he did was with precision and delicacy.

He lifted the orb over the stand and paused. It hovered perfectly over the center of the stand and beams shot from its center. A pulse rippled from the Uniroth and all of the Ralligins began joyously dancing in their formations. Odin stepped down the stairs and stood back on the platform that he was brought from. In a flash of light, he was back on the glass roof above Sashi, who was still on the disk of Ralligins. Odin jumped down and mounted back onto Sashi. "That was quick," he said.

The Ralligins closed the disk into a sphere and when they opened again, they were back at the edge of the desert. Sashi and Odin stood on the sand, remembering the scorch of it.

"Odin, we have been faithful to our oath, and still have found ourselves in your debt," the Ralligins voiced in unison, hovering in front of Odin and Sashi.

"Then you can repay me this way. We need you to fight for us in our battle against Magnus. As our ally, we will gladly defend you as you would defend us," Odin replied.

The Ralligins didn't move. "If that is your only request, we will meet you at the battle field in front of the stronghold of Magnus."

"Go forth. The day comes upon us like lightning. We will be there and gone before the gods even take notice," Odin replied.

The Ralligins disappeared into the sand.

"We need to take care of the titan at sea. Then we head back to the oracle in Centurion before night fall. She has more knowledge than she allows us to know."

They rode out of the desert and for the sea. It was only a mile out, but far enough to make a good ride. Sashi kicked sand up under his hooves as he rode towards the sea. They saw the long stretch of water now. It lined the horizon. When the small line of black spread to a strip of blue, they saw their way to the sea. A long dock stretched outwards. The spot of activity started leaping from the water. Odin could see giant fish jumping over and tackling each other. Their jaws stretched wide and snapped with such a force that the spray of water reached far into the air. They jumped out of the water so high that the only evidence to say that they couldn't fly was that they couldn't breathe for too long out of the water. These had to be the titans that the General had warned them about.

They rode on the long dock that stretched out to the sea. Odin dreaded this coming task. The sea was threatening and filled with anger. It was untamable: unrelenting. The waves crashed all around them, forcing the sea to churn. It was almost beautiful.

Odin looked out to the sea and watched the beasts jump from the water and crash back down to the waves. They were massive creatures, showing obvious signs of power and aggression.

Sashi stopped and Odin dismounted. "Stay here. I'll need someone to pull me out," Odin told Sashi.

Sashi glanced at him. "Are you sure?"

Odin gave Sashi a look. "Can you swim?" he asked.

Sashi shook his head with a small smile.

"Then, I'm sure," Odin replied.

He stretched his arms out and dove in the water with his full armor on. Using the weight of his armor to keep him held under and hidden, he swam with all his might to keep himself as close as he could to the surface. The water was cold, and more harsh below than it was above. He came up for air, gasped it all in, and went back down. He could see each wave roll over him, and the monsters were just barely visible in the distance through the dark sea. The waters fought hard against his body as he tried to move through it, but he proved to the water that he was stronger. He paddled hard to get to the monsters, but as soon as he got there, he almost wished that he hadn't.

He caught the whiplash current of a sea beast's tail and was thrown deeper down into the ocean. He fought hard to get back up for the fight, but another beast swam under him, the suction of its current pulling him further under.

Odin was losing air. And as deep as he was, having his armor on didn't help him at all. He took a dagger from his boots and latched onto a sea beast's dorsal fin, letting it take him to the surface. But instead of going up like Odin had planned, the beast dropped deeper, dragging Odin through the blackness of the waters. The water pressed hard on Odin and popped his ears, threatening to crush him completely. While helping to equalize the air pressure inside his skull, the oppressive water did little to help him survive this endeavor. Odin pulled hard against the dorsal fin and the current that the beast shoved up back pushed Odin up into another sea beast. He struck again and caught the tail of another beast. The tail jerked him from side to side through the water, making it excruciatingly painful to grip without ripping his arms out.

He relinquished his grip and the tail threw him out of the water. He soared in the air, caught his breath and was immediately snatched up by another beast. In the darkness and through the stench, he drew his sword and sliced through the inside of the monster. The scales split with the skin and the wound spread open like a second mouth. Odin slid out of the creature with the flow of the sea creature's insides. Again, he was swimming along the side of another sea beast and dragged through the current. The great fish quickly turned away from Odin, leaving him spinning through a funnel. He pushed himself up and caught his breath again at the surface. He sheathed his sword and was again swallowed by another sea beast.

Odin jabbed his dagger into the roof of the mouth of the beast and dangled as the water in the mouth flushed down the beast's throat. The tongue came up and smashed Odin against the roof, but Odin only stabbed harder against the tender skin. Fluids started gushing out, pouring into Odin's face. It was sticky and slimy, and it clung to his armor. The beast opened its mouth and water rushed in, knocking Odin back and washing him off. An ear-piercing screech threw him forward, and bones and phlegm hit Odin as they passed through the mouth. He relinquished his grip and flew out of the mouth covering his ears as he swam with his feet. Gritting his teeth, he came up for more air and waited to be swallowed by another.

Bobbing on the waves, the inevitable happened: he was gulped up, and swallowed. He tried not to inhale the internal gasses of the monster. He took his daggers, and once again sliced through the stomach wall. The gash opened up painfully as scales parted with the wound. He leapt out and brought his sword up over and behind his head. Then he slammed it forward and drove his blade into the head of another sea-beast, right in between its eyes.

Four were down, now he had eleven more to go. Falling to the water, a mass moved under all of the commotion, shifting the dark shades of blue. Odin saw the titan that he had come to destroy. The large mouth emerged from the waves and was slowly followed by its neck. Then came broad shoulders and muscular arms. The chest bulged with form. The entire body was blue. The shark-headed monster gripped two of the sea-beasts and devoured them. The water splashed against its body as it moved and joined once again with the rest of the sea. Odin could feel himself beginning to move closer to the titan as the water sucked him in. The titan took little notice to the small Dryad as it ate the larger fish. Odin looked on in distress. How could he possibly hurt this monster, much less destroy it.

Sashi looked around the dock to find some sort of spear. The sea around the dock gave very little options. A rusted pipe and a tree branch. Sashi shook his head in disappointment, drew his swords, aimed them at the larger titan and threw them as hard as he could. The swords flew high, and came down, singing in the wind with the speed, and drilling through the air. Odin was almost in the mess around the titan's sides, when he saw one sword pierce its side, and another punctured through its thigh. Both swords stopped with the hilts touching the flesh, and neither one brought any attention to the titan. It was if they were insignificant splinters on skin too tough, they couldn't even be felt.

Odin grabbed the bottom one and pulled himself up, out of the water. He stood up on the hilt, drew his daggers, stabbed the thigh with one and reached higher to stab in the other. He climbed for the next sword and reached for the hilt above him. He gripped it in both hands and swung his feet up. Squatting on the hilt of the next blade, he looked up to see how far he had to go. It was a long climb. When he got up and around to the shoulder of the titan, it began to take notice. Odin saw the magnificent hand reach up and swat at Odin, just missing him. The titan's shoulder rumbled and Odin clutched the daggers as he dragged forward through the air. He lifted himself up and could stand on the titan's shoulder.

The giant head of the titan reared up and its huge eyes were wide. Its mouth opened and the thousands of teeth were waiting to crunch Odin's bones. It quickly struck and Odin jumped back, reached up and stabbed the titan's arm, dangling from it's bicep. The titan released its shoulder and brought its arm up, squealing in pain.

As Odin was lifted, lying on the arm of the titan, he saw the gash that the titan's teeth left in its own arm. His head could easily fit in any one of the teeth-holes. He carved his way back to the shoulder again.

"You're annoying," he grunted.

He got up and ran for the titan's neck as it struck again.

The neck arched, giving Odin the perfect position to climb up. As the titan's head moved forward and erected up, Odin was just able to hang on the top of its head. The strong winds nearly knocked him down, and he knew that if he fell, the force of the sea alone would kill him. He pulled himself up, sheathed his daggers and drew his sword. The titan reached up, trying to crush him. Odin brought his sword up, jumped and put all of his weight into piercing the titan's skull. Fluids squirted, the titan's hands dropped, its head went slack, and Odin bobbed with its head. It almost seemed as if everything that was inside of the monstrosity now poured out into the water below. Odin flipped around so he could drop to the titan's shoulder. He sheathed his sword and dove down its arm to Sashi's swords. He gripped them both, and strained hard to pull them free of the titan. He dove into the sea below and swam back before the titan came crashing down.

He got to the dock and Sashi reached down to pick him up. Odin was half way up when he heard the deep splash and saw Sashi look up with horror written in his stone face. Odin took Sashi's swords and stabbed straight through the dock. He closed his eyes and the wave swept over them both. Sashi took Odin's boot and was nearly shoved away into the sea. The wood cracked under the pressure of the wave. They both dropped to the ground and everything was calm again.

*****

She was back on the beach, holding Odin. Feeling his arms once again was so relieving. But feeling him let go took it all away.

She looked into his eyes and saw only sadness. "What's wrong?" she asked.

"Jade, I can't feel you." he answered.

Thoughts raced around in her mind. What had she done? What was he talking about? What had torn them apart? She shook her head knowing something was wrong, but not knowing exactly what.

"I honestly don't know why that is," she replied.

He kept his hands lightly embracing her arms. "Have you been unfaithful? My keeping you here as a mortal is based on your faithfulness. Everything hinges on your love for me."

"We consummated our love. I though it would make us stronger."

His eyes burned when she said that. "You've been tricked."

Jade rapidly shook. "No. No! We are one flesh! You and me! No one else!"

Odin's heart pounded and fed the fire in his eyes. "It was not me."

Jade was now crying and clutching Odin's shoulders. "Yes, it was! Yes, it was!" she cried. "It was you! It's still you! I gave my heart and my body to you and you alone!"

Odin looked her in the eyes, and repeated "It wasn't me." He placed a hand on Jade's cheek.

Jade didn't blink. "Search me," she replied hoarsely.

He paused thinking of what exactly it was that she wanted.

"Search me, Odin. See who it was that I was with. If not you, who, then?"

He slowly nodded and brought her head close to his. He touched the tip of his forehead with hers and entered her mind.

Everything she saw, he saw, and everything she felt, he felt. He saw her memories and felt her emotions. He searched back through time to where she was last with him, until finally, he found the memory of hers that he did not share.

She was with Magnus. They were both in the tower of his castle, and they were both genuinely happy. Odin watched in pain through the vivid memory she had, but the face was as clear as Odin's heart. She was with Magnus. Only the memory on Odin's side revealed the true identity. To Jade, the picture was of them. He finished watching the memory and parted from her mind. Keeping his eyes closed, he whispered, "It was Magnus."

"No! I would never give my heart to that monster!" she cried.

He quieted her with his hand, "He took my form. You couldn't have known, but it was him that you gave your heart to."

She let another tear fall. "But, I was certain it was you," she whispered.

With the sadness shared by both, Odin wrapped his arms around her and held her. "Jade. I can't be joined with you, ever. I never could."

She looked up with questions in her mind.

Odin looked down and explained, "I am an Elder. Part of the code of the elders says that I cannot act on impulse and join with any other being of lower dimension. It is counted as impurity and that is intolerable in the Elder court. I can be here with you and love you, but I cannot become one with you." He sat down with her and held her.

"Why?" she whispered back.

"I am not the eldest," he said softly.

She grimaced. "Then, who is?"

"He was a nameless son. The first of the elders. I was second to him. We were all born of a Galaxian mother; a being of lower dimension from the father. With this heritage, none of us can come close to matching the strength and power of our father. The nameless son despised the father and envied his power. So he took it upon himself to train himself and fight the father, kill him and take his power with the father's own blade. Obviously he failed. With no one to rescue him, he was banished to the underworld."

Jade thoughtfully asked, "But, couldn't he break free from that prison?"

"Not on his own." Odin replied, "Anyone who is banished to the underworld cannot return from it. The only beings that go there are those that are impure and sinful spirits. Only corrupted spirits go there. So, when my father defeated him and banished him, none of the other elders dared oppose him. When the nameless son died, I became the Eldest of Elders. After my father saw the error of his ways in acting on impulse, he formed the protocol that any elder that joins as one with a lower dimension is risking the very extinction of the elders, and thus, the universe."

Jade nodded in understanding and looked down.

"Jade, the power of the elders still lives in me. I have not forsaken my right to the elders. I've kept my power so I can keep you safe, and if you ever fall into peril, I want to be able to bring you back out of it, safe and sound."

"So, we'll never be one flesh?" Jade asked.

Odin shook his head. "I'll always love you. But I must remain pure." Odin stood up. "Magnus will pay for what he has done. I will not let this go unpunished," he declared.

Jade stood up with him. "Odin. I'm sorry. I honestly thought it was you. If I had known …"

Odin turned to her. "Jade, Magnus is responsible."

Jade grabbed Odin's arm and turned him to her. With the fire now in her eyes she said, "forgive me."

Odin hooked her hair around her ear and touched her cheek. "I forgive you." He kissed her and whispered, "I love you."

"I love you, too," she replied.

He hugged her one more time and disappeared.

CHAPTER 6

They arrived back in Centurion, returning to the small domed building where the oracle was.

"I knew you'd come back," she said as Odin entered.

"I'm sure you did," Odin replied. "Confirm what I've seen. Jade's testimony that she has been with Magnus. Is it true?"

Angelica didn't move. "Yes. Magnus has sinned and it has brought an uproar in the Elder courts. You will want to go there next, if you want a part in it," she warned.

Odin nodded. "Are you coming with me, or will you stay?"

Angelica shook her head. "I have already seen it. My presence makes no difference."

Odin sat down and folded his legs. Sashi laid down to rest as Odin drifted into meditation. Closing his eyes, Odin relaxed and cleared his mind. His heart slowed and everything in him became calm. He slowly drifted off of Hajun and soared passed the moons and stars and galaxies to the courts of the elders.

He arrived at the gates and walked to the courtroom. The giant hall with pearl white walls had upper balconies that aligned the two side walls high above the ground. Each balcony had a staircase leading to it from the outer circle of the center of the room. At the very front was the throne where the Father mediated his house and watched his quadraplex of the universe. On his throne, his height portrayed his stature above the rest; as high as three quarters of the courtroom. On the floor level was the table: the meeting place of the Elder representatives. The eldest of every ten siblings was appointed representative of that set, so that all ages of elders were spoken for.

All of the elders were in the balconies shouting across the court at each other, their own arguments. The Father sat silently and patiently through the clamor.

Odin slowly stepped onto the ground floor and walked to the table. At the foot of the table he waited behind the Subjects chair until the clamor ceased. Finally, the courtroom became silent.

"Mighty Father, worthy brothers and sisters, I have come before you to request your help and allegiance," Odin boomed.

Instantly, the right half of the room began shouting at Odin, condemning him. They accused him of their doom and stated that he was the cause of this conflict. The Father lifted his hand and every single elder silenced. The Father nodded to Odin.

"I ask to meet with the representatives of the house, and with our mighty Father," Odin requested.

At once each representative stepped from the balcony down the staircases and joined together at the table where they sat in their assigned chairs. Then the Father's figure faded from the court and faded back at the chair in front of the table. Now he was only two head lengths taller than Odin, but still maintained the recognition of his stature with his height. He sat at the head of the table as Odin joined them.

Odin began, "Mighty Father, you would justify our actions years ago in bringing a soul back from the afterlife to this universe. Would you not?"

Odin's father nodded.

"You agreed to bring that soul back for me in my favor so long as I honored the code of the elders. Is that not correct?"

Odin's father nodded again.

"Brothers and sisters, many of you are enraged in this action of long ago, only because our Father and I brought life from that which was dead. Others of you believe that even in love, I could be trusted with this responsibility. I will say this; my actions with my obsessions have brought no harm nor any risk to our existence or extinction." Odin paused letting them all know he would make his point blunt and clear. "Magnus has." he finished.

Without letting Odin say another word, the elders that opposed him stood and shouted at him. Pointing their fingers and pounding the table, they shouted their accusations.

"You are the threat!"

"You have doomed us all!"

"This is favoritism!"

"You have no right to condemn!"

Again, the father lifted his hand. The elders all sat down.

"I reside." Odin declared and rested.

The first of the elders that opposed Odin stood, "By bringing this soul back from the grave, your actions are identical to those of Magnus. You have doomed us all! Reside." he sat back down.

The second elder that opposed him stood. "Magnus justly owns all souls journeying to the afterlife. If anyone has sinned, it is you for stealing the rights of Magnus' stature! You cast the first stone with your lust for this young girl! Reside."

The third stood. "As far as I'm concerned, if Magnus is found guilty of disobeying the code, you will be found guilty of treason for forsaking your place among your people, family, and leadership for this love affair. My vote will show you as much mercy as the Father's decision shows Magnus. Reside."

The first of the elders that sided with Odin stood. "I have known Odin for as long as I have lived. I've seen his works and passions. With the greatness in his abilities, he has also shown great restraint on his pleasures. He has found love, and a way to maintain that love without risking us. The only true threat to us is Magnus and his passions. Reside."

The second stood. "The souls that Magnus has in the afterlife are infinite. Surely he can find the maturity in him to spare one life so that Odin could share his love. If the Father has deemed this course of action worthy, then my actions rest with the Father. My faith and trust lie in both of you. Reside."

The third stood. "You've gone to great pains to bring your love to life, care for her, and rescue her. Your courage and passion combined are being used to not only save the lives of Hajun, but of your love as well. And now you seek to keep us all from extinction. If no one else will recognize that, I will. I believe your recent actions and your actions of the future will keep us all from certain death and right whatever wrongs anyone holds against you. You have my faith and my allegiance. Reside." She sat down.

Odin stood again. "I make this case for speculation. If anyone of you holds a grudge against me personally, please do not fear to speak now. But if anyone can prove your cases against my blade and armor, let them speak and I will surrender all points and my campaign." He finished drawing his sword and sticking it in the table.

The hilt of his blade shown like the morning star and the blade itself was as clear as glass. His armor was completely polished and clean. When the elders saw that there was not even a speck of dishonor on his armor, they were immediately silenced.

"I have remained pure, and I will honor the code to my death. If anyone has a case against that, please speak." He turned his eyes to every Elder, even the ones in the balconies that looked on. The elders that opposed him looked down in foolishness. The ones that sided with him smiled in awe.

The Father grinned. "You have, indeed, remained pure in your time with your love. You have no sin on your armor. My armies are for the righteous. You have everything that I can offer."

The elders that sided with him stood and faced the elders in the balconies and called in unison, "Brothers and sisters, will you offer your armies and allegiance to your eldest brother, Odin?"

Together all of the elders on their side agreed. "We will."

Odin turned to the opposing side. "Will you fight? Not for me, but for your own existence?" He looked at all of the elders in the balconies. "Will you fight this battle against Magnus?"

In unison the rest of the elders replied, "We will not!"

Odin turned to the table. "Then, let this day be a declaration of war. On the day of the battle, our armies will meet at Magnus' occupied land on my creation. When we destroy Magnus and his armies, we will reclaim our harmony with each other."

The Father tilted his head. "Odin, his transgression effects the fate of us all, and so we are sending our armies against his. But his transgression was against you. Only you will decide Magnus' fate."

The elders that opposed Odin turned to the Father complaining and begging that he change his decision.

The Father stood up and shouted, "I have spoken!"

Every Elder was once again dead silent.

Odin didn't move. "I accept this duty. I will go to his lair and fight him myself. When I bring him back here, I will make his fate known to all of you. Magnus will be tried as a criminal of the quadraplex in our court."

The Father cocked up an eyebrow. "Are you sure that this is what you want? To banish your brother to the underworld?"

Odin thought and replied, "I want to maintain peace and protect our existence. As long as Magnus remains in this universe or any other than the underworld, he will remain relentless."

The elders that sided with Odin nodded in agreement.

"Go, then," the Father continued," we will do battle on your command. Council adjourned."

Odin nodded once, turned around and left.

He opened his eyes and found Angelica there casting lots and listening closely to them.

"Your Father loves you, Odin. But he also loves Magnus. Losing either one of you would pain him immensely. That is why I tell you, if you fight for your love, you will fall. But, if you fight for Hajun, you will succeed. We all depend on you. Now go. The rest of the titans come straight from Magnus' lair," the oracle finished.

Odin stood up. "Thank you," he replied.

He and Sashi found a sturdy dome around the street corner and they rested there for the night.

*****

Magnus stood at the battle plans. To one side, he placed all of the conquered titans. In the middle, he had a place setting of all of the northern continent of Hajun. In a row directly in front of him was the last of the titans he had to send. He brought the piece that resembled Odin down a few more units and placed a piece that resembled the next cluster of titans in front of him.

"It is time to end this," Magnus whispered. He turned his head to the messenger. "Free the Skrulltan Jackals! After them, I want the giants awakened and the griffins in flight," he called.

"Yes, my lord!" the messenger replied.

In a court yard towards the back of Magnus' complex, portcullis gates lifted, opening cages containing the jackals. The huge creatures in the shadows of the seven cages slowly and aggressively pounded their first paw on the ground, then the next one. Their long noses were the first feature to be revealed to the light, followed by their lower jaw. The quadrupeds revealed their full form, howling in delight of their freedom. The leader of the pack leapt from his cage and took the lead, dashing from the castle, now on the hunt for their prey. Tails low, heads forward, and legs moving as fast as they could, they nearly flew through the air, heading north on the trail for Odin.

*****

Odin and Sashi had slept that night and rode out the next afternoon. The trees had thickened and the road was more narrow than the others they had traveled. The sky seemed too bleak and cloudy. The air had a harsh chill that stung their skin. But it was better than the dune-sea. Odin saw Sashi glancing around at the scenery. Sashi never did that unless he was tracking something or extremely bored.

"You all right, Sashi?"

"I have a bad feeling?" Sashi cautioned riding a little slower.

"More ogres?" Odin asked.

Sashi shook his head. "Worse."

"Should we stop?," Odin replied.

Sashi looked on. "I'll decide when I can tell what direction it's coming from."

To break his mind from the worry, Sashi began to sing a fun chant he learned in the centaur ranks. He started holding out the first note. "Oh, once I met a lady. She asked me for my name. I asked her if she'd marry me, she said I was insane."

Odin began to join in. "Another girl came forward, a smile on her face. I offered her to dance with me, she left without a trace. A big girl wiped my table, a shocking little lass. I knew that I was desperate, but this time I would pass. The dancing girl was teasing, some candy for the eye. I gave her my whole wallet, but she would not go for guys. This went on for a long time, I never had my chance. No lady would stand next to me or share in my romance. And so the hours left me by, and had no stroke of luck. And all that night I cried because I would not get to-"

Sashi suddenly stopped and turned his side to the road.

Odin leaned forward, then caught his balance and shifted his weight.

"Why are we stopping?" Odin asked.

"You didn't hear that?" Sashi sniffed the air.

"No."

"It was a howl."

"What is it?"

"I don't know. I've never encountered this smell before. It's coming down-wind."

Odin looked up to the sky. The evening star was setting once again. "How much further to the castle?"

"About a day's ride," Sashi replied.

Odin looked around at the landmarks. "Any allies that could be won over around here?"

"I don't think so." Sashi watched a herd of unicorns run north. They had picked up the scent as well and were evading it, fast. "Whatever it is, it's big and intimidating."

Odin dropped to the ground and bent down, touching his ear to the rocks. The ground told nothing of the coming danger.

"It's light. They make no tremors when they move on the ground," he said, getting up. "It could be one of three things. Either they're too far for me to get anything, they are small, or they're built for stealth. And something tells me it's not the first two." Odin noted and looked at Sashi.

"Odin, I don't like it. The smell is getting stronger," Sashi replied, all of the hair on his back stood straight out.

"What do you want to do?" Odin asked.

"I don't know if my skills will be of any use with this beast. I've battled monsters my size and succeeded, but this smells like more than I can handle," Sashi worried.

Odin nodded. "Then we wait. Let's take separate sides of the road. If we have the element of surprise on our side, we'll use it wisely."

Suddenly, the ground around them exploded and dirt and rock flew in the air. They both took cover and waited for the explosions to subside. When the dust settled, and the debris fell, Odin looked up and saw a figure standing in the smoke. Sashi drew his swords and prepared for the worst. The cloud of dust blew away revealing a circle of nine men in long flowing robes wielding staffs and holding their palms out to Odin and Sashi.

Odin drew his sword and backed against Sashi. "I have no quarrel with you. My fight is against the beasts that plague these grounds."

The men lowered their guard and held their staffs in front.

The leader on the road stepped into the circle. "Who art thou, trespasser?"

"I am Odin."

"Art thou friend or foe?" the leader asked.

Odin lifted his head to show no fear. He knew the customs of the older cultures. "If thine enemy be mine, then be it so, thou art my ally," he replied mimicking the leaders accent in an attempt to befriend him.

"Dost thou affiliate thineself with the traitor, Magnus?" the leader asked.

Odin frowned. "I do not," he replied.

"Then, thou art our friend."

Odin held his hand out to the leader. "My friend."

The leader shook his hand. "And what be the name of yonder beast that thou art taketh with on thy quest?"

Odin boomed, "Yonder beast be Sashi, the Centaur of old!" Donning the booming nature of the native accent seemed to endear Odin and Sashi to these new acquaintances.

The leader held his hand out to shake Sashi's. "Welcome, Sushi," he said.

Sashi shook the leader's hand. "It's Sashi," he corrected.

The leader ignored Sashi's correction and turned to the circle. "The evening star doth forsake these sacred lands and these foreign beings quest to protect these grounds from a questionable doom, this night. Be it so, we shall join them in endurance of whatever battles they seeketh to defend this land from." The leader turned to Odin. "Pray, tell us the identity of this threat that thou doth prepare'st to fight."

"We do not know," Odin replied.

Suddenly, Odin was snatched up by the jaws of the Skrultan Jackal. Odin screamed in pain, drew a dagger from his boot and stuck it into the dog's nose. The Jackal crushed Odin's bones and dropped the pieces of him to the ground while the men lifted their staffs together. A beam of light burst from the tips of their staffs and a bolt of energy stretched from their staffs and pierced through the Jackal that had snatched up Odin. The first Jackal disappeared into nothingness.

Six of the nine men were snatched up and fought hard against the grip of teeth that held them. The leader and two others stood on the road and held their staffs up, trying to bring the Jackals down with their strength alone. The beams that shot from their staffs touched a Jackal, but weren't strong enough to pierce it.

The leader turned to Odin. Odin was still lying on the ground in pieces. Then, he looked at Sashi. "Whilst thou fight if we augment thine power?" the leader called.

Sashi drew his swords. "What do you want me to do?"

"Simply fight. My brothers and I shall assist you in ways of the old kingdom!" the leader replied.

Sashi ran up to the first Jackal as the three men held their hands straight out at him. As Sashi swung his sword, sparks flared from each hilt and fire stretched from the blades. Sashi reached up and sliced through the belly and cut off the legs. As he moved away from it, it fell to the ground, yelping in pain. Five remained.

Sashi leapt up and caught his hooves on the back of the next Jackal. He crossed his blades over the Jackal's neck and when the metals touched, electricity sparked endlessly and he severed the Jackal's head. The heat of the blades cauterized the open wounds to a crisp.

As the Jackal fell, he dove forward off of its back to the head of the next. But when he should have been falling to the ground, the power of the wizards kept him in the air. He hovered to the side of the next Jackal. He bent his body down so he could drive his blades into the side of the Jackal as he came over it. The swords punctured the side and when the hilts met the Jackal's flesh, fire spurts shot from the other side.

The Jackal cried in pain as Sashi dropped to the ground on the other side of it. He rode for the fourth Jackal that jerked the man in its jaws to death. Sashi twirled around its front leg and reached up stabbing both blades into the Jackal's belly. The men kept their hands out and tapped the tip of their staffs to their outstretched hands. The swords exploded inside of the Jackal's body and vaporized the entire Jackal.

The other three Jackals had dropped their prey and turned to Sashi, who took a stance in the middle of the three of them, reaching both swords straight up in the air. A bolt of lightning came down from beyond the sky and stopped just above his blades. The bolt divided into three other bolts and engulfed all three Jackals. When Sashi looked up, he saw that the bolt was a long trail of the Sprites that had rescued Odin before. They cleared away and nothing was left of the last of the Jackals.

The Sprites flew away. The men stood up and grouped together in a circle. They joined their staffs together in the middle of the circle and their injuries were healed. Sashi trotted over to Odin. Odin's broken body lay flat and dormant on the ground. Not a breath entered his chest. Sashi touched Odin's forehead, and couldn't sense any life in him at all. Odin was completely dead.

Then, thunder rumbled in the clouds and the rain began to pour. Sashi knew it was Jade, mourning for Odin. Then the ground began to shake, and all of the trees were nearly knocked down by the winds. Sashi turned to the men in the circle.

"Can you heal him?" he called.

The men circled Odin and each lay their staffs down on the pieces of his decimated body. The power that flowed through them was shared with the wind, and the rains eased until they stopped. Odin began to glow. His body was adhered back together and his strength was restored. He gasped for air and sat straight up and looked to the skies.

"Jade," he whispered.

"How did you do that? How is anything that transpired here possible?" Sashi asked.

The men picked up their staffs and aligned in front of them both. The leader stepped in front of the line.

"We are the Light. The nine descendants of Throth," the leader explained.

"You're wizards?" Odin asked.

The leader frowned. "Our abilities are hardly paranormal, but indeed, you may call us that."

The second in line spoke. "Dost thou contain the power to summon divine beings to thine aide?"

"The Sprites are my friends. They have saved my life in prior times of desperate need," Odin explained.

The second in line spoke again. "Then why did these Sprites not rescue thee?"

"They must have known that you were going to. But battle is hardly ever in their agenda. Speaking of which, we're going to confront Magnus in his courts, and fight him to the death. Will you join our cause?" Odin requested.

"Good sir," the leader continued, "thou art not in the company of an army. We are but a lowly brotherhood; however, we will watcheth over the battle and help in whatever way possible."

Odin nodded, "Fair enough. In that case, I bid you all farewell, and you have my thanks."

"Fare thee well, noble sir, and that which would be a mammalian being called Sushi."

"Sashi," Sashi quietly mumbled.

"Until the fates decide to have us meet again." They all bowed and disappeared in a cloud of smoke.

*****

Jade slept peacefully now. The monsters had left. The nightmare of the little boy's death had subsided and she, a small girl, found a certain comfort in the arms of the little boy that she had saved. She smiled whenever the boy would speak in his innocent voice, but with a heart full of love.

"Jade, I'm not letting go," he said, holding her.

"I love you, Odin," she replied. The smallness in her voice made the boy smile back.

She looked up and played with the boy's short blond hair. Then, his hands came down her sides, and he lightly tickled her ribs. She laughed and shook her hair all around. He stopped and hooked her shoulder-high hair over her ear and brought his hand down her cheek. Her hand dropped and took Odin's. Odin leaned in and his small lips touched hers, and innocently pulled away. She looked at him with smiling eyes and giggled happily.

"I love it when you laugh," Odin replied.

"Then kiss me again," Jade replied, silently giggling again at the smallness of her own voice.

Odin cupped her cheeks in his hands and pulled her in and kissed her passionately. When he didn't pull away, she slowly brought her arms around him and held him there so that he couldn't let go. Then, his hands came down to her shoulders and around her bare arms. She pulled away and giggled again.

"I liked that one," she replied.

He couldn't stop grinning. "So did I."

Magnus appeared far behind them and called Jade. She turned her head, but kept her arms around Odin. Odin looked and saw the full grown threat there, wagging his finger at Jade. She leaned her head on Odin's chest and listened to his heartbeat one last time.

She turned to Odin. "I have to go. It's time," she replied, now with an even smaller, and more pitiful voice.

Odin wasn't smiling anymore. "I'm not letting you go. You're mine," he whispered.

Jade let go of him and backed away. "Are you going to fight him?" she asked.

Odin reached up and drew a wooden toy sword. "I will. He won't have you," Odin's little voice roared.

She slightly giggled at his valor. "Bye, Odin. I love you," she called, and ran off hiding her laughter.

Odin put his toy down and stood. When Odin turned around, the monsters of the world seemed to close in on him and take the small boy to a place he never wanted to be. But then, anyplace without Jade was a place he didn't want to be.

She woke up with eyes wide open. One word echoed in her mind. It wouldn't go away no matter how she directed her mind. Giants! It meant something. Giants would be three times the size of Odin. Jade sat up and looked out the window. The morning star was shining down on the land and illuminated the hills on the outer ridge of Magnus' lair. She strained her eyes to see along the road leading to Magnus' realm. She couldn't find Odin. The giants, however, she saw, clearly. Four of them were stomping from the hills and guarding the gates to the lair of Magnus' structure. If Odin was not there by sundown, they would have their traps already set.

CHAPTER 7

Odin and Sashi rode for the gates of Magnus' lair. The evening star was on its way down. Sashi had doubled his speed and was ahead of schedule. They rode all day without rest, without water, without food. They didn't speak, and were

determined. If anything stood in their way this time, it would have to be very powerful. They could see the gates just beyond the hills. The ground was welcoming and fed the hills their base. Odin could breathe easy because he was almost at the end of this journey. He wondered how Jade would look when she saw him. And somehow, he felt her already, watching him. They slowed down and Odin hopped off. He turned to Sashi.

"You doing okay?" Odin asked.

Sashi panted, "No. I need water. I can feel my energy draining."

Odin looked around, "These people are landlocked. There has to be a water source somewhere."

Sashi knelt down and listened to the ground. Odin didn't move. He let Sashi do what he needed. When Sashi was in stressing conditions, his body's senses would heighten to, what soldiers called, survival mode, so he could do exactly what he was doing: search for what he needed.

Sashi closed his eyes and followed the flow of water underground. He could hear it getting further up to the surface. But when he got just close enough, the ground changed, and the sound disappeared. He opened his eyes in frustration and looked up.

Suddenly, he was slapped to the ground. His body slid to the side and knocked against a tree. Sashi didn't get up. Odin drew his sword and saw the four figures tower over him. Just then, his hand was tackled by a rope and he couldn't break free.

He turned to slice whatever had him, but his other hand was tied down before he had a chance to react. Both hands now restrained by ropes, he was lifted up and his body stretched in the air. The ropes were wrapped around trees and each rope was held by a giant. Then, one grabbed his legs and pulled him down against the ropes and the other one brought an arm back ready to punch him.

Odin watched in horror as the giant let his fist fly and impale Odin's gut. He groaned in pain as the force of the punch made his body fight itself. He swung backward, then came forward. The giant hit him again, throwing a sharp pain through his breastplate, spreading through his chest. He squeezed his eyes shut and fought hard against the pain. Just as he had forced the pain out, it hit him again. This time, the giant grunted with his swing. The other three laughed as Odin let out a cry of pain. Then, the pain stopped.

Odin looked up and saw the giant bending down to the ground. When it came back up, it held a large plank. Odin shuttered with the pain he already had, but could only imagine what this would be like. He bit his lips and waited, holding all his breath in his chest. The giant grinned holding the plank in front of Odin's chest and brought it back for the swing. Odin closed his eyes and imagined Jade smiling at him.

Then Odin's face moved like a rag-doll. He pulled hard against his restraints. He felt the sharpest pain he had ever encountered before every rib in his body cracked. Fluids drooled from his lips and everything was spinning. He brought his head up and looked at the giant as it swung again. Again, his head bobbed back, and everything blinked to darkness, then back to reality. He turned his head to Sashi, but Sashi wasn't there. The ropes that stretched his arms stretched the pain through his ribs.

His head shook uncontrollably and he couldn't breathe anymore. His wrists were chafed but didn't bring any of his attention from pain. The giant swung again. Odin could feel his body beginning to tear in half, and he would not care if it did.

He swung forward, and opened his eyes. The giant swung again and knocked his ribs again, breaking them and popping them through the skin. He screamed in pain again, and the giant swung again, pouring more power into the plank. Ignoring all of the pain, he fought hard against the ropes, pulling his body into a curl. His other bones popped and his body trembled in pain. With every last breath in him, he picked up the giant that held his feet, and the other two giants that held the ropes dragged towards the trees. His breaths were sharp and quick, and all of the pain just gave him more stimulation.

Shaking even harder, he shouted as he brought his body into a ball, sobbing in agony. The ropes were so tight that he could feel them beginning to snap.

Finally, he saw Sashi below him, twirling his blades everywhere and slaying the giants with lightning speed. He stabbed his blades into one giant and slashed at another. When one got back up, he'd go back and slash and stab again. The rope holding Odin's left hand went slack, and he dropped to the ground, swinging towards the tree that kept its hold on him. The other giant let go of his rope and jumped in to attack, but was jolted back by a sword that pierced all the way through his heart. Odin lay next to the dead giant and didn't move.

With all the giants dead, Sashi walked up to Odin and looked down at him. "Are you dead yet?" he asked.

Odin groaned about to answer, but Sashi cut him off.

"Good. I need water." Sashi grunted moving on.

Odin stared up at the sky. The evening star beamed down on him, but the first star shown in the sky. Odin blinked and saw the star grow brighter in the sky. He squinted his eyes at it, trying to see if his eyes were lying to him. The star got brighter and larger, and it looked like it was falling straight down to the planet.

He focused on it and waited for it to do something. For a moment, it just twinkled, then, it flickered, then it intensified and grew.

Odin saw little sparkles all around it now, and the object was spiraling its way down. Odin got tired of watching the orb, so he closed his eyes and waited for it to do whatever it came to do. Nothing happened. He imagined Jade. Could she see him lying on the ground like this, at his weakest point, unable to move? He heard buzzing all around him. He opened his eyes and found Fairies surrounding him. They were sprinkling their dust all over him and he felt his ribs slowly mend back into place. The shooting pains in his arms left and his head was strong and focused once again. He could move again and felt like he could win the battle himself. He stood up.

"Thank you," he grunted. "I am in your debt, once again. Now please, keep Jade safe at all cost."

The Sprites and Fairies nodded and charged up over the hills to the castle.

Odin looked around for Sashi. He had to walk to find him. When Odin found him, he stopped and watched. Sashi had dug a huge hole and was drinking from the spring that shot up from the ground. Odin waited for him at the hole, but Sashi didn't stop drinking. Every drop was being used and he didn't start storing water until the ground he stood on started to crack. Sashi felt it and startled a little. He turned and jumped back on top of the hole as the ground broke away. The water shot up through the hole from the ground and Sashi did his best to salvage what water he could from the mighty flow.

When he was done, they started up the hills, and stealthily made their way along the side to find the camps of the Centurions. They found the camps on the west side, just inside the realm. They rode on, to the biggest tent, where the battle would be planned. Thousands of tents surrounded the battle tent, making their way unclear and longer than it should have been. They wove around the tents, hopping over camp fires and armor, dodging unaware centaurs. The tents, however, were the most annoying obstacle between them and the battle tent.

Finally, they found the battle tent. It stood tall and full, containing the strength of the army inside. They entered the tent and the crowd of centaurs parted for Odin to reach the table.

When he met the General, the inside went silent. They shook hands and took their seats. The General explained his basic plan.

"We'll spread out over these seven points. One legion for each point. They will come down the hills attacking the Skord at the point just at the bottom of the hill. We're expecting his demons to join the battle, so that'll bring his army to about twenty thousand militants. We have also discovered the winged horses he's training. They will be carrying an air combat unit of what we can only assume will be Skord, and joining with a couple hundred Griffins. We're letting the dragons handle the air combat but if they need a back-up plan, we'll have harpooners ready."

Odin nodded watching intently.

"If all of us have taken down the army, we will empty out Magnus' castle of any spoils that might be left. We have our plan. The numbers are frightening at first glance, but we've been through worse with the Orks and Skord soldiers," the General finished.

Odin rubbed his chin. "I have added to our numbers. An ancient race called Ralligans are with us." Odin worked his fingers over the map. "Keep the positions the way you have them, but only send in your front-line as the first wave. The Ralligins will go ahead of them, and will take down about half of the Skord, and most of the demons with a single wave. When they fall back the Ralligins will stay. Send everyone else in at that precise moment."

The General thought, then continued, "We wanted the element of gravity on our side. If the ... Ralligans- was it? Don't hold up their end of the deal, I will lose my entire first wave of centaurs."

Odin countered, "The Ralligans will remain faithful. This will lead us to a sure victory."

The General gave Odin a questionable look. "You have assurances that the Ralligins will be fighting?"

"More than assurances, I have an oath," Odin replied.

The General cocked up an eyebrow. "Very well."

Odin stood up. "Sir, there is a matter that you should be made aware of. Magnus has to be stopped, and I am the only one that can do it. Only an elder can make another elder answer for their crimes. This is my reason for being and I have every intention of accomplishing my mission before the evening star falls," Odin explained.

The General nodded. "Fine. We will fight to the end and repay to you our debt."

*****

"Great Elders, be with Odin. Keep him safe and let his blade fly true. Let not his armor fail, and let not this hero fall. Let the legend of Odin be spoken throughout history. And may my love be kept safe in his heart."

CHAPTER 8

Sashi stood in line with the General. Odin mounted on Sashi and mentally prepared himself. The dragons laid beside the first legion of Centaurs. The front line made its way up the hills and held position at the tops. The demons had already started on the battlefield with the army of Skord behind them. Their army spread all across the land. The Skord archers fired their first wave of arrows.

"Shields!" the General shouted. Everyone brought their shields up and blocked the arrows that fell.

A second wave of arrows soared in the air and fell on the shields once again. Not a single centaur fell. A third wave was shot and again deflected. Then, the army of front-liners charged for the bottom of the hill.

"Ralligins, you fulfill your oath this day," Odin whispered.

The front line of centaurs reached the bottom of the hills and a wave of sand came up from the ground and stayed in front. It grew bigger and bigger as it charged for the army of demons. The entire mile-long army of demons was picked up and dropped to the ground where they were trampled on or attacked by the centaurs. When the centaurs took down all of the front targets, the other demons and Skord had already started to stand back up.

Then the Ralligins came up and picked up another portion of Skord in the middle. The line of centaurs backed up, as the Skord fought their way to them.

Odin signaled the General and the General advanced up the hills. With every eye on the General, the army followed. When he reached the top, he charged down bringing the long blanket of Centaurs over with him. Sashi, Odin and the General all led the army and fought down their targets. Odin stood on Sashi, and leapt over a group of Skord and demons. When he landed, he tripped them all with his blade and everyone around them fell to the ground. He jumped again as a few centaurs trampled over the fallen evils.

Sashi was, once again, swinging his blades and twirling them into as many Skord as he could. He banged the helmet of one, and stabbed another. Kicking two down, severing limbs, he was almost untouchable. Then, every centaur's blade shot sparks from the hilt and fire surrounded the metal of the blades as they pierced their enemy's armor. Not wanting to waste focus on how it was happening, they kept fighting, accepting the new abilities. Sashi brought both blades together and swung them into the chest of a Skord. The Skord was picked up by the blade and a pulse of energy pushed it into the air and shot it across the battle field.

Odin looked up at the evening star, it was at the very top of the castle. Suddenly, he was kicked to the ground by a Skord, and held down by its foot. It brought its sword up ready to strike. Odin stuck his sword into the Skord armor and fire shot straight through. It fell to the ground burning on the inside of its armor, screaming.

Odin got up and saw another wave of Ralligans pick many Skord up high into the air and drop them to the ground. He ran in and fought off as many as he could.

Then, screeches from above echoed through the skies. An armada of Griffins and Pegasus' came from the tops of the castle and charged for the Centurion army. Sashi lit an arrow and shot it over the hills to the dragons. Immediately, the dragons lifted into the air and shot down the air combat unit of Magnus' army.

Some of the Griffins picked up a few Centaurs and dropped them from a fatal height, but they were soon scorched or frozen and fell to their own deaths. The Pegasus' galloped in the air, and stomped over the heads of other Centaurs. Again, they were soon remedied. Another wave of air combatants came out of the castle, and the dragons did their best to take them all out.

The clouds began to twirl in the skies above the hills of the Centurion camps. They grew darker with every twirl, and at the same time, a twirl formed over Magnus' castle. Then, from the center of each twirl, a great plethora of angels descended and conflicted with each other over the battle field. The sky was filled with celestial hosts, and all of them were battling in the air.

Some of the Ralligins took more Skord into the air, the dragons set more fire-balls and hail masses plummeting to the ground. But, from each exit of the castle, Magnus' forces kept coming.

Soon some of Odin's angel allies came down, and with one swipe, took twenty Skord out. Then, they would go back up to the skies and continue their battle. The dragons finished off the air combat, so they did what they could to scour the Skord that were still marching into the battle. Every centaur was fighting. All of the Ralligins were picking up their enemies and dropping them. Odin was letting his sword fly with sparks in the air and fire on the blade. He hit as many enemies as he could.

Two centaurs were working together, backing each other up as Skord would run in for attacks, and each would be thwarted. The little demons surrounded them and hopped for their faces, but every attempt was blocked. Finally, one little demon made it through. It started burning the Centaur's face off with its flaming body. The Centaur screamed in pain, prying it off only to have it replaced by another one. Then, they over took his entire body. They started crawling on the next centaur and clung to his face, and again, another centaur was taken down.

Then, the little demons saw Sashi battling a group of Skord. They skipped and hopped over to him. Sashi turned and spun his blades by the wrist-strap on the hilts, forming fans in front of him. The demons would jump for him, and burst into flame as each one was torn to pieces.

Suddenly, the ground around a group of centaurs exploded, and the explosions rippled out along the ground, taking Skord into the air and exploding them as they landed on their backs. Another group had the same effect. Both groups were stunned and watched as it happened again on another part of the battle field.

Odin found his way to Sashi and climbed on. Pointing his sword at the sunset, he shouted, "Bring me that light! The evening star does not fall slow enough!"

Sashi lifted his front legs into the air, kicking two Skord down, and rode as fast as he had ever ridden before through the army of Magnus to the castle. No dragon could match his speed and no Skord could hold him down. Spreading his blades out, he knocked down as many as he could until he reached the gates of the castle. Odin jumped off and ran into the giant open doors. Sashi turned around and fought his way back into the battle.

Odin entered the castle. Two huge doors stood between him and the courts. He shoved them both open and the light that shown over Odin cast beams around his figure, and let a long shadow fall on the red carpet of the courts. He stepped inside and found Magnus holding Jade, taking on Odin's form once again. Jade resisted and Magnus just kept taunting her until he saw Odin. He smiled keeping Odin's form and stood up to welcome him in.

Odin drew his sword. "I'm here, as I promised, and now I will do what I should have done a hundred years ago!" he boomed.

Magnus laughed. "You fool! Don't you know about the battle out there? I'm winning! Your pathetic excuse for an army is waning by the minute and you come in here ready to fight like a god! You are truly an imbecile!"

"Let her go and fight me, Magnus!" Odin shouted.

"Gladly, sir," Magnus sneered.

Out of thin air, a majestic blade appeared in his hand. He jumped in the air, and the two Odins crossed blades for the last time. Odin twirled and struck for Magnus' arm, but it was quickly deflected. He brought his sword up and hit for Magnus' other shoulder. It was blocked. Every move that Odin made, Magnus seemed to know what it was. Magnus struck above Odin's head, but Odin blocked his blow. Magnus quickly brought his foot up and kicked Odin across the court.

Odin knew Magnus would not fight fairly, and Magnus would keep using the power of the elders to counter Odin's hits. Odin got up and unleashed a flurry of hits on Magnus, unrelenting and unwilling to let

Magnus make a move. Magnus just kept blocking every stroke of Odin's mighty sword, hit after hit after hit.

Odin brought his sword down on Magus and then backed away. "Are you to afraid to fight me fairly? Are my attacks too good for you to keep up?"

Magnus brought his sword down to his side. "Odin, you have dared to challenge an Elder of my stature while you are in Dryad form. You have evaded me for an age and caused setback after setback in my plans," he growled. "If you force me to choose between a fair fight and just finishing you off, here and now …"

With a lift of his hand, Odin levitated in the air. Flying higher above the ground, he stopped and Magnus dropped his hand. Odin fell to the ground. He braced himself and landed on his hands and knees. Then, Magnus kept him there knelt down and brought Odin to his feet.

"Then I will have to weaken your resolve before I end you." Magnus smirked and threw Odin to the wall. "You want me to come down and fight you at your level? You'll have it," Magnus replied aiming his hand at a crystal ball. All of his power left his body and was stored inside of the crystal, leaving a heated aura around the ball. Odin stood up and charged at Magnus. Magnus picked up his blade and blocked Odin's attack. Magnus attacked Odin's arm, but Odin blocked. Magnus struck again, but Odin moved out of the way.

*****

Sashi made it back to the General and they defended each other. All of the demons had been slaughtered, the dragons had taken down every Griffin and Winged Horse and were icing or roasting the Skord that were left. The General was warding off a Skord, and finally knocked it down. Another one came in and attacked. The General threw the Skord up and slashed at it relentlessly. He finished it off by running his sword all the way through the Skord's neck.

"Take your pitiful screams back to your master!" the General growled. He turned to the Sargent. "Take a hundred troops and initiate the catapults. Let none survive."

The Sargent nodded and fulfilled the command.

Sashi continued to fight, blocking another blow. But when he looked toward the General, he saw a Skord running their way. He shouted to the General "Behind you!"

The General twirled around, but it was too late. The Skord sliced at the General's neck, forcing him to the ground. The Skord brought its blade up into the air as the General thrust his sword up and through the Skord's gut. The Skord fell forward, bringing it's sword down on the General. The sword in his hand ran the General through the lung, killing him within moments.

"No!" Sashi cried, enraged, attacked furiously, taking Skord down left and right. He came up on a few centaurs and took their targets down for them.

"You're not killing fast enough!" Sashi shouted at them taking five more down at once.

When all the Skord around him were dead, he turned to the centaurs around him. "Move!" he shouted. They instantly ran for another kill. Sashi continued in anger through his own massacre. Blood spattered on his face and ran down his fiery blade to his hand. He moved heavily and channeled his anger through his sword. With each Skord he killed, they would explode in flame inside of their armor and squeal in agony.

Then, the roar of a hundred Jorns came crashing from the castle. The bulky fiery figures stood twenty feet from the ground, and bellowed at the falling of the Skord. Each one picked up a boulder and threw it at the Centurion army, then they advanced forward, stomping over the enemy targets in their way. They'd pick up dead Skord or centaurs and fling them around as defensive weapons against the attacking centaurs. Then the angels came down and picked up a few of the Jorns and dropped them from the sky. The rest of the Jorns rushed the attacking centaurs, shoving them left and right by their shoulders and arms. Centaurs flew over the tops of one another and fell to the ground.

*****

Odin flipped over Magnus, holding his sword down on Magnus' blade, keeping it from going any higher. Magnus slid around and swung low, then high. Odin followed with his blade, and kept Magnus back.

Jade charged them with a dagger from an ornament from the wall. She repeated to herself inwardly that Magnus was mortal now. She could earn this kill.

Magnus blocked a blow from Odin and slapped Jade to the ground. Odin's eyes burned and his heart pounded. He grabbed Magnus' neck and squeezed the breath out of him. Magnus slashed at Odin, but Odin moved his sword in the way and kept his grip on Magnus. Magnus coughed in Odin's grip.

"Jade, back away," Odin growled.

Jade stepped back and watched. Odin threw Magnus away, charged at him and swung his sword down on him. Magnus brought his sword up and held against Odin's weight. Odin smashed his sword down on Magnus, slamming it down again and again. He beat his anger through his sword on Magnus' blade and kept going until Magnus gave way. Magnus had to put his other hand along the side of the blade to support it. He brought his leg up and kicked Odin off of him. Odin staggered back as Magnus stood up. They faced each other and crossed swords once again. Odin attacked, and putting all of his strength into his final swing, he threw Magnus to the ground. Holding his sword down to Magnus' neck, he waited for Magnus to react.

"Beg for mercy!" Odin ordered.

Magnus spat at him and threw his blade into Odin's. He got up and blocked another blow.

"Is your resolve greater than mine? I have justice on my side," Magnus replied.

Odin swung again. "Justice will not keep me from killing you."

Magnus leaned into Odin's face. "Do you see yourself as a hero? You broke the laws of the universe! You rebelled against the code," he replied shoving Odin back. "You are the villain! You gave up your chance for reconciliation!"

Odin brought his blade up and sliced it down. "Reconcile with this!"

Magnus blocked his head and swung for Odin's side. Odin blocked again and continued swinging.

*****

The catapults lined the hills and hurled their stones, crushing the remaining Skord. The last of the angels came down and fought. They took down most of the Skord.

Now, with the Skord over half way gone, it looked like the centaurs were going to win. Then the Fairies and Sprites came in and took the other Skord. Sashi kept his fight clear and made sure he didn't get caught in any of the crossfire. Even the dragons were hard to dodge.

The battle sped up in Odin's favor and the Skord were almost completely gone. Most of the catapults aimed at the Jorns which were almost all dead. Sashi twirled around in a full circle and took all surrounding enemies down. The Ralligins took small pockets of Skord in the air and threw them around. Sashi threw a Skord to the ground and stabbed it under the helmet. Suddenly, a sharp pain pierced through his chest and he took a deep breath as he stretched his body trying to rid himself of the pain.

He looked down and saw the sword that stabbed through his chest. He gripped it, and tried to push it back out, but the Skord shoved its blade back in. Sashi submitted. His fingers fell to the ground and blood spewed from his hand. Sashi had fallen. The blade disintegrated inside of Sashi's body. Soon enough, his whole world turned black. He fell unconscious, and the only thing he could hear was a penetrating buzz and the screaming of the Skord that struck him. With one final sweep of the angels and another drop of the Ralligins, the last of the Skord and Jorns were destroyed and the centaurs rejoiced in victory, as Sashi drew his last breath.

CHAPTER 9

Odin dragged Magnus' blade back and slipped passed him. Magnus spun around and guarded himself. Odin kicked Magnus back and swung for his head. Magnus blocked Odin's swing, but staggered back from the force of his kick. Magnus charged in on Odin and pressed hard against his guard. Face to face, swords crossed, Odin pushed harder, brought a hand up, balled his fist and threw a left cross for Magnus' face. Magnus staggered back, regained his composure and brought his sword back to thrust through Odin.

All at once, they grabbed each other, brought their swords back and ran each other through. They both trembled in shock and stared at each other, watching the blades shake through their backs. Hands still clutching the hilts, and gripping each other's shoulder, they waited for the first to fall.

Jade screamed in horror, "Odin!" She ran up to them and pushed Magnus away. Odin fell to the ground as everything went black. He could feel his life slipping out of his grasp, and everything seemed to slow down for a moment. He could only hear dull noises of Magnus and his sword falling to the ground, and Jade screaming. And there, in her arms, he died. Magnus turned to the crystal with his power inside. It had already evaporated to the Elder Courts. He closed his eyes, giving up and let his soul ascend.

Jade cried endlessly over Odin. She kissed him and held him, begging him to come back. She dropped her head on his cheek.

"You promised me you wouldn't let go!" she screamed. "Don't let go, Odin." she continued whispering to his heart. "Don't let go."

Feet clanked on the floor coming up behind her. One last Skord was left in the castle. She didn't turn to it. Even when it was right behind her, she kept holding her love, longing to join him. She heard the sound of metal slowly rubbing against leather. She waited fearlessly for what was coming and accepted the harshness of the cold steel through her heart. She fell on her love and waited as her world faded into night. Slowly, a sneering smile grew on Magnus' face. He could feel her soul returning to his realm. His armies had fallen. His castle would be destroyed. He could feel the world spin away from him in death; but he had finally won.

*****

Odin and Magnus were side by side in the courts of the elders. The Father sat in his throne and received the final report of the battle. He turned his head to Odin.

Lara stepped next to Odin and whispered to him. "You have done well in this war. You will be happy to know that your faction won. The Skord no longer plague the lands of Hajun," Lara said.

Odin nodded to Lara in thanks as she stood next to her seat at the table. Then he looked at the Father. "I ask to meet with the representatives of the house, and with our mighty father," Odin requested.

Magnus turned to Odin with a questioning look on his face. Once again, each representative stepped from the balcony down the staircases and joined together at the table where they sat in their assigned chairs. The Father's figure faded from the court, and faded back to the chair in front of the table as he did before.

Both Magnus and Odin stood at the table. Odin began as Magnus listened patiently. "Mighty Father, you have given the fate of the elder, Magnus to me, only if I defeat him in a battle. Is that not correct?"

The Father nodded.

"Would you agree that my sword slew him in battle, thereby making our agreement binding?"

The Father nodded again.

"Then, if the court has no objection with the Father's' decision, I would like to make Magnus' fate declared for all to hear." He paused and silence fell across the courtroom, waiting for Odin to finally banish Magnus from his ranks as an elder, and as a fallen soul, descend into the underworld, to join the souls that he had put there.

Odin continued, "Magnus is to remain an elder in these courts. Hopefully that will settle any differences within our ranks. I gave him the position as Keeper of the Souls. It is my right to take it away so that he may find a new challenge and title. The title of Keeper of the Souls," Odin hinted, "is mine to give to whomever I choose." He turned to Lara the third elder that was for Odin. "Will you accept it?" he asked.

She nodded. "I will."

Odin turned to Magnus and said strongly, "It is by my mercy that Magnus is not banished to the underworld for the sin he has committed, as our nameless brother was, and he will remain in our heavenly courts. I Reside."

Magnus closed his eyes and nodded in gratitude of a fate far better than what was promised.

The first elder that opposed Odin stood. "I see that in this battle between Odin and Magnus, not one but two souls were claimed. The score of this fight is even. If Magnus is stripped of his status as keeper of the souls, then Odin should be stripped of any status he carries. Reside."

The second elder that opposed Odin stood. "Having mercy on our brother makes no difference to me. You made the first sin, and if Magnus must pay for his sins, then you will pay for yours. Reside."

The third elder stood, "The armies of the elders are all but destroyed. Only the Father's angels came back alive. The only one that still has an army at hand is you. The only one that remains relentless is you. You are the true threat here, now. With Magnus no longer to oppose you, there is no balance in the family. If you ever sought to conquer us all, I believe that, now with our armies obliterated and other forces demolished, you are the only one with that power. No single elder should have that kind of access, no matter how loyal he is. Reside." He sat back down.

The first elder that was for Odin stood up. "The covenant struck in our last meeting was as follows: Magnus directly transgressed against

Odin, Odin controlled Magnus' fate. Odin decided on his own that in the moment of Magnus' death, Odin would decide what would happen. There was never a claim made on Odin's death. What Odin does is legally binding to the courts declaration. Reside."

The second elder stood, "Odin has shown us his blade and his armor. He has no sin to be paid for. He asked us to send our armies to help him in battle, and we did, knowing there would be casualties. When we agreed to help, you sent your own armies to counter ours. If you did not expect to be the losing side, you should not have sent your armies. As far as Odin's own fate is concerned as a super power, he has the right to it, and my house will trust in his loyalty. Reside."

Lara stood up. "Odin, you have the right to the elders, so you may reclaim your place as a representative of the house. Jade, however; is a soul now. She was killed, and is following her path to the afterlife. She is now mine, as you have appointed me the keeper of the souls. I cannot let a soul leave for a second time without giving something to the other souls. If you wish for her to be brought back so you can be with her, it will cost you something more. Keep that in mind as you decide your fate. Reside." She sat back down.

The Father turned to Magnus and signaled him with a nod.

"I accept this fate with gratitude, and thank Odin for his mercy. I Reside," Magnus breathed out and sat.

The Father stood. "Odin, consult with Lara and decide your fate with her. Bring your decision to me. I will write it in history. This council is adjourned."

The elders left the table and Magnus joined the Father. Odin stood with Lara and discussed with her the payment.

"I'm sorry, Odin. I cannot justly let Jade go without giving something. I trust you on Hajun with her, and you have my loyalty. But you gave of yourself when you took her the first time. The universe will not have it the same way a second time."

Odin nodded. "What must I give?"

"What will you give?"

"Anything I can," Odin replied.

Lara considered. "Then, give this a thought. After you have decided your fate, the elders are moving the Courts out of this galaxy. If you stay on Hajun as you did before, you will not have any contact with us, and your right to the elders will have little worth on that planet. Nothing opposes you, but you will not join the afterlife with Jade if you keep your right."

Odin nodded. "Then, my right to the elders is the bargaining chip?"

"If you give your right, you will be with her even to the afterlife. Can you accept death as your bargain for love?" Lara asked.

Odin thought and answered, "I can."

Lara nodded. "Odin, Magnus will succeed you as the representative of the house if you do that," she warned.

Odin smiled. "But I won't be here to care." Then he looked in her eyes. "What do you think about it?"

Lara tilted her head. "I think he won't be as good as you as the Eldest of the Elders. But if you think he will fill your place, then I trust you."

Odin closed his eyes. "Justice is a fine virtue for the Eldest. As long as the Father keeps his watchful over him and his ways, I think you'll be fine. Divide my armies amongst the elders. If they are so threatened by my power, then they can share it and fight for it themselves," Odin said.

Lara glanced at Magnus, then back to Odin. "You know, there was a project we worked on before you became a creator god. The elder gene?"

Odin kept his hand away from his pocket and thought. "We had decided it was better off scrapped. To have that kind of power coursing through a mortal's lineage is just too problematic."

"But it would ensure that your powers would be in the care of your descendants, even after you died."

Odin knew she knew he had perfected it.

"None of your power can pass down unless you've made it possible," Lara said with a slight smile.

Odin nodded. "Something tells me a lot is going to change when I become a mortal."

She hugged him and they headed confidently to inform the Father. The Father agreed with Odin's decision and allowed Odin to prepare for departure.

The Father summoned Jade to his presence. "You have been brought back from the afterlife for the second time. But, it has cost your lover a heavy price. This will be the last time you are brought back; the last time your death is hindered. From this moment forth, your life is determined by fate," the Father declared.

Jade nodded and her soul faded from the heavens.

The Father turned his head to Lara. "You planned this, didn't you?"

Lara smiled and simply walked, knowing that the Father had watched the whole time.

*****

Jade woke up in her bed, in the village of Hajun. She remembered holding Odin's dead body, and dying herself, but nothing after that. She got out of her bed and left her hut. Everyone was there in the streets and happy to see her. They hugged her and welcomed her back. But Odin and Sashi were nowhere to be seen. How had she come back? Was Odin coming? Would she see him again? Was Odin held captive in his own courts?

She smiled at the other Dryads and searched the village for Odin's face. No one mentioned him, or spoke his name. She found herself in the fields, just outside the village. If Odin was nowhere else, he would meet her there. She waited for hours. The Ropens were soaring above and the evening star was setting. A tear fell as she got up, giving up the hope she had in seeing him. She walked away from their spot, and trudged back to the village, and one last time, she whispered, "I love you Odin."

She turned around and glanced at their spot. And there was Odin, walking up the hill. He smiled at her and joined her under the sunset. She didn't move until he was with her. Then she latched onto him and just held him in her arms, not letting him escape or be taken away. His arms wrapped around her, and he kissed her hair. The Sprites and Fairies flew in bands around them and the wind softly blew around them as their passions mixed and their hearts pounded together.

"I'm not letting go," Odin whispered. "I promise."

Book II

SINS OF THE FATHER

CHAPTER 1

"The power of the elders in the palm of his hand, and he wished it all away."

"That power rightfully belongs to you. Our house has always believed in you."

"With such power, I could escape from this madness and rival our father on any realm."

"What conduit is there that could grant you all of our power?"

"There is only one tool of such destruction in this quadrant of the universe."

"Name it, and I will see it in your hands."

"The Chevron. The sword of Orion."

*****

Lara ran for the Table. The last of the Representatives of the house would be meeting in the final hours it existed. She stood at the table and turned to Magnus and Stratus.

"Our armies are all but decimated," Magnus reported. "Every elder has attempted close combat with him and fallen."

Stratus let a smile cross his lips as he quoted the prophesy. "The harbinger of your doom will bring down your house, and in three days, the new kingdom will rise."

Lara shook her head. "There is more on the line than our lives. Omega has reconstructed his system with our brother's help. The entire universe will feel this shift in power. We must survive and counter the imbalance." She turned to Magnus. "Magnus, follow behind him.

Make sure you report his every move. Stratus, you know what to do," Lara finished.

Stratus nodded. "What's the boy's name?" he asked.

"Decimus. He lives on Hajun," Lara said.

The building began to shake, and the courts crumbled. "Valefor is here," Lara muttered.

The last three elders glanced at each other in fear and faded from the court room as it shattered and every bit of rock fell to the ground. The entire structure drifted into space. Valefor hovered in space over the debris and stone. Without a word he left and headed for the nearest star system to find the Galaxians.

*****

In the land of dreams, a Dryad girl no more than eighteen years of age, floats alongside the souls that have not decided their own fates yet. The river of souls finding their rest at the end floats on, and she watches, waiting for the one. The one soul that knows her. The one with the same purpose, the same inspiration and stimulation to search the world of dreams for her. The twin souls that were destined to be together from the beginning of time. They knew each other, as they had been with each other again and again. Born together, drawn to each other, across galaxies and times and planes of dimension, they would find each other here now.

She knew him as soon as she saw him, and at the same time, floating down this river, his eyes darted to where she was. He strained across the souls to the shoulder of the riverbed, reaching and stretching as if fighting time itself to cross over and be with his love.

But just as he reaches the shoreline that separates the certain land from the undecided river, his grip slips and the current drags him forward, away from his love. She gets up, dashing forward to slow his departure. She reaches out to take his hand, and when his hand meets hers, it passes through as if there was never anything there to hold on to.

The Dryad woke from her dream, panting. Taking in each breath with a desperate will to calm herself, she lay back down and stared at the ceiling of her small hut.

"It was just a dream," she whispered to herself. Repeating the phrase over and over, she closed her eyes and felt herself drift back into unconsciousness.

*****

It was midday when Stratus appeared on Hajun. The peaceful planet had very little in the way of inhabitants, making his journey that much easier. Many of the Dryads were running through the streets to one giant temple of Ferron, and Stratus quickly joined them to enter the loud arena. Everyone was shouting and cheering for the champions in the middle, but Stratus only had eyes for one. He watched for Decimus, hoping that he was already one of the champions.

The bell rang and the champions turned to regard each other before beginning the battle. In unison, the crowds chanted one name, Gorin. Obviously the favorite of the champions, but could Decimus be in there somewhere? Blades swung, armor clanked, and in the first few seconds, a champion had already fallen. Stratus prayed that the fallen one was not Decimus. The crowds cheered even louder as the victorious champion moved on to fight another. They continued chanting for Gorin.

One of the Dryads approached Stratus, "You're not from around here, are you?" she asked.

Stratus shook his head and watched the game. The Dryad turned to the game as well but continued talking. "What's your name?" she asked directly.

"Stratus," he replied.

"I'm Valkyrie," she said.

"Do you know of Decimus?" Stratus asked.

Valkyrie looked at him. "No. I've never heard of him."

Stratus frowned and walked out of the coliseum. Valkyrie curiously followed.

"Hey!" she called, "What do you want with this particular Dryad?"

Stratus stopped and turned around. "The fate of the universe rests in his hands. If I don't find him, train him, and take him to the courts of the elders, we will all be dead."

"What's so special about him?" she asked.

"Do you know of a Dryad named Odin?" Stratus asked.

Valkyrie's eyes widened. "Yes! Everyone does."

"Decimus is going to help me find Odin," Stratus replied.

Valkyrie tilted her head. "Odin is dead. How will you find him?"

Stratus smiled, "No, he's not dead. He just moved on."

Valkyrie stepped forward and lead Stratus along the City road. "Odin died with his wife in their hut. They left about eighty years ago. Their hut became their tomb so that no one would forget."

They stopped in front of Odin's old hut. Stratus continued the story. "They entered the afterlife together, and the old elder's legend went on forever." He turned to Valkyrie. "But did he have a son?"

Valkyrie's cheek rose. "I don't know. Wait, you're saying this "Decimus" is the last scion connected to Odin?"

Stratus closed his eyes. "Myself and others believe so. We have not watched over this planet for the last hundred and fifty years, so there is no guarantee. But that is why I'm here."

Valkyrie paused trying to make sense with what he saying. "Keep watch? Are you an -"

Stratus quickly stopped her from speaking of his origin, "Yes. I am. Speak of this to no one. I need to find Decimus as soon as possible, or Valefor will take the universe for himself and destroy all that oppose him."

"But, wouldn't the Father …"

"The Father is dead. Valefor murdered him." Stratus answered.

Valkyrie didn't speak.

"If you know where the last scion is, then you would be of great and very much appreciated help. If you don't, then there is very little you can do."

"There's a city just north of here. Odin and Jade lived there for a good portion of their life. They might have raised their offspring there if you think they would."

"What is the name of the village?" Stratus asked.

"Centurion," Valkyrie replied.

Stratus nodded. The name sparked a memory, but he couldn't connect it to anything. He turned north and looked at the falling star. "Will you lead the way?" he asked.

"It's a couple day's walk. We'll need to leave in the morning," she replied.

Stratus turned back around. "You don't have horses?" he asked.

"Do you really want to go, now?" Valkyrie curiously questioned.

Stratus considered. "It's a better idea than sitting here getting answers that won't help."

Valkyrie looked slightly offended. "I can get horses and we can ride to the mountains. But they won't be much use once we get there."

"Good idea. Can we leave tonight? Time is of the essence," he said a little more gently.

Valkyrie thought. "Maybe. It'll be dangerous, and tiring, though."

Stratus nodded. "Danger means very little to me. If you can make it, then we'll go."

Valkyrie grinned and left to find horses.

*****

Magnus faded onto a small moon. He followed closely to Valefor and watched the dark elder enter the holy temple of the Galaxians. Magnus heard the women scream as he barged in. Magnus quickly ran to the temple and watched Valefor pick up a Galaxian by the neck and stare into her eyes.

"Where is Lara?" Valefor's deep and raspy voice growled through his gritting teeth.

"Not here. Your quest is thwarted once again," the Galaxian replied. Her feet swung under her dress, but her face remained impassive.

Valefor grinned. "My quest is only beginning. But first I need to rid the elders of all attachments. Sever their ties to the past."

She choked under his grip and her body dropped and dangled in his hand. Magnus trembled. He was powerless to help the Galaxians. He could not confront Valefor without being obliterated in a moment. He just waited. All of the Galaxians in the temple were killed and Valefor took the throne at the front of the temple.

"This will do for my place of worship. With the courts of the elders demolished, none will oppose my will," Valefor roared.

Solaris faded into the temple. "Now, the plan will be complete. With the majority of the elders dead and their power dwelling in us alone, we can rule the universe as ours, shared by brothers in arms."

"Yes," Valefor replied, "ours for the taking. For the changing. But, there are flaws with this plan of yours."

Solaris turned around to face him. "What flaws do you speak of?" he asked cautiously.

"The remaining elders. Have you brought any of the three to their knees?" Valefor questioned.

"The elders have separated. Spread across the galaxy. I've only tracked one to Hajun," Solaris said.

"Then Lara remains invisible?" Valefor presumed.

"A flaw that will be easily remedied," Solaris said.

Valefor stood up. "Find her. I want her brought to me alive. I will kill her myself."

"Lara? She is but one Elder. Surely we can rule the universe without her power," Solaris replied.

"I want her, now!" Valefor shouted.

Magnus turned around and faded out.

"Yes, Valefor," Solaris replied and faded off of the moon.

Magnus followed Solaris' trail through space across galaxies and nebulas. Never losing track of where he went. On the moon of Tyrannus, in the Galaxian temple, Valefor closed his eyes and watched Magnus follow closely to Solaris.

Through thought, he communicated with him.

"Magnus, it has been a long time. You may follow Solaris as long as you like, but when you try to intercept him, you will fail. I promise you, you will fail."

Magnus didn't stop or even pause. He shoved Valefor' words out of his head and moved on. But knowing that he was being hunted sent an uneasy discomfort through his body. Solaris crossed through an asteroid field and dove through one of the craters.

"Lara!" Solaris called. His voice echoed through the vacuum of space. No one answered, so Solaris moved forward.

CHAPTER 2

Stratus and Valkyrie walked down the mountain. Resting on top was good for the night, but the light of day would show their location to all that looked on. Valkyrie carried a short sword at her side and a shield on her back. Her battle shirt kept her completely free to move and fight. The trees were still and silent. Even the wind on the mountain could not move them. Stratus touched his hands to one of the tree trunks.

"These are not native here," he said.

"They were alive once, moving with the planet. They migrated up the mountains and stayed here until they died," Valkyrie explained.

Stratus closed his eyes. "Treants," he muttered. Valkyrie looked up. "It's as if you know the planet, intimately."

Stratus smiled and touched the ground of the mountain. "I do. I helped Odin make it."

Valkyrie stood and looked to the horizon. "So you put the plague on it?"

Stratus opened his eyes and clutched at the ground. "What plague?"

Valkyrie pointed. "That plague."

When Stratus looked at the horizon, he saw the rolling clouds bringing in the darkness. He stood up and stared into it trying to feel its presence. It was not natural, and it was not a storm.

"What is that?" he asked.

"It strikes the ground with fire and ice, and blows down the houses and crops. It covers our village for days and nothing escapes it," Valkyrie explained.

Stratus turned his eyes to her. "How far away is Centurion?" he asked.

"Two day's journey. That storm will be here in a few hours though."

Stratus cut her off. "Point!" he shouted.

Immediately, she pointed in the direction of the city. He looked at where she pointed and fixed his eyes on that spot. He grabbed her and picked her up. He squatted down and jumped from the mountain, but they did not fall. She latched her arms around him and tried not to scream. As they ascended and accelerated, her ears pounded and her heart raced. They began to fall. She felt his grip on her slowly let go, and she feared the feeling of free-falling.

The wind blew her hair up into Stratus' face and he lost sight of the ground.

"Valkyrie, I can't see," he grunted.

She pulled her hair down and shouted, "Don't let me go! Are you insane?"

The ground got closer and was coming much faster than he anticipated. He slipped her around his neck so she sat on his back. Then he spread his body out to catch whatever up-drafts he could to slow his fall. He counted his heartbeats to time how long it took for him to finally reach the ground. He placed one hand below him and braced Valkyrie with his other arm.

He landed on the ground, shaking the area around them. He stood up and waited for Valkyrie to let go. He turned his eyes to her and saw her frozen panicked expression.

"Valkyrie, we're on land. And you told me it was about a two day walk." They looked where she said Centurion was supposed to be. "It's a little longer than a two day walk, isn't it?"

Valkyrie didn't move, but she slightly nodded.

"Okay," he sighed gripping her arms. He squatted down again and jumped back into the air, getting much higher this time. He looked around and saw the highest tower of the city. It was beyond the reach of his jump alone, but he could make it if he changed his trajectory.

"Hang on!" he shouted.

She tightly wrapped her arms around his neck, but he ignored her choking him. He pointed his head down to the tower he saw, locked his arms to his sides and kept his feet together. Valkyrie's hair flew straight back and the wind chilled her skin. She wanted to scream, but her voice was frightened away.

The frost of the storm captured their skin in the last few seconds of the fall. Stratus smiled and landed softly on the ground inside the City. He pried her off of him and shook off the frost from his clothes. He turned to her. Her hair was knotted and her cheeks and eyebrows were covered in frost. The horrific expression was chiseled on her face.

"You okay?" he asked.

She didn't move, but just managed to squeak out, "Uh-huh. Yeah."

He dusted the frost off of her and explained. "We would have walked, but I needed to get here and get some answers before anything else tries to stop me."

Her stiff body was shaking as she got all of the frost off. "Yeah. Okay," she breathed out.

He looked around at the pristine towers. Everything was beautiful and peaceful in Centurion. But the clouds that loomed above had the residents hiding in their homes. Stratus moved to the large dome next to the tallest tower.

Valkyrie followed, straightening herself with every step.

"You're okay," she whispered to herself. "You're okay."

Stratus opened the doors and stepped inside the great hall. Everyone was quiet and the Admiral of the Centaurs sat on a pillow at the head of the hall. A guard stopped Stratus and asked what he needed.

"I am looking for a certain family member. Decimus. Have you heard of him?" Stratus asked. The centaur guard shushed him and led him to the admiral. "This traveler is the one you've been expecting. Would you like to speak with him?" the guard asked.

The admiral took off his helmet and stood up. "Finally. Come with me," he ordered.

They stepped into a private room. "You've been expecting me?" Stratus asked.

The centaur turned to him. "Let's begin from the beginning. My name is Sashi. I fought with Odin and was appointed Commander of Centurion when I entered the army. Odin was my best friend and we still keep contact."

Stratus' face contorted. "Wait, that would mean that you're over two centuries old."

Sashi nodded. "Three-hundred thirty-seven planetary cycles, to be exact. I'm almost starting to lose count."

"But it was always told that you died in the second battle of the Skord!"

Sashi smiled. "I did. The sprites revived all of the centaurs and we flourished back here in Centurion. As for Odin and Jade, they did have a daughter. Lara died giving birth to Decimus. Decimus knows nothing of his legionary grandfather."

Stratus nodded satisfied that he got some answers. "Where is he now?"

"On a quest." Sashi answered.

"A quest?"

"He does that a lot. He wanders the world trying to find his place. He's never at peace with himself until he's on the move. He knows he's destined for something more and he's trying to find out what it is," Sashi explained.

Stratus smiled and rolled his eyes. "Just like Odin. Where did he go?"

"Back to the ruins of Magnus' realm. Like you, he's trying to find the answers for his life. He's catching on to his grandfather's legacy, and soon he'll fully grasp it all."

"Why didn't you just tell him?"

Sashi considered. "I was going to. But I figured if he wanted to know bad enough, he'd find it for himself. I haven't said a word concerning Odin's previous whereabouts and he's tracked his grandfather as far as he could. The story of Jade, and why they came here. The dangers of old that Odin and I faced. Decimus has gained his own skills and knowledge and he's well earned them all."

Stratus stood up. "So, he wants to know what happened to his grandfather?"

Sashi grinned. "More than anything. Can you give him that?"

Stratus turned around. "I'll give him what I can. But, I'm sure he'll be happy with what I have."

And with that, he met Valkyrie outside and they left.

*****

Lara faded next to Magnus. "What happened?" she asked.

"He killed her," Magnus replied.

Lara put her fingers to her mouth. "Did she suffer?"

"She suffocated. It lasted a couple of minutes, but it was so cruel," Magnus explained.

"What else did you find out?" Lara asked.

"Solaris was working with him the whole time. They both have the power of the rest of the elders. We can't defeat them alone and I don't think even the last Scion could face this evil. Not Solaris, and certainly not Valefor. With all that power combined, their objective is clear. They want the universe," Magnus explained.

"So, why are they after me personally?"

Magnus shrugged. "My guess is they want the afterlife. Which would make sense because Odin is in there and he's the only other relic in the universe that Valefor would fear. Beyond that, the afterlife and underworld would be his and that alone makes him unstoppable."

Lara concurred. "Okay, I will stay out of sight. But, if he seeks total universal control, then he'll be after you too. So be careful yourself."

Magnus grinned, "Don't worry about me, I'll be fine. You just stay invisible for the time being."

Lara hugged her brother and faded out of the galaxy. Solaris passed by Magnus faster than a ray of light and followed closely to Lara. Magnus grit his teeth and chased after Solaris to keep him away from Lara. Valefor's voice entered his head again.

"You'll never reach him. He's much too fast for you with the power of the other elders giving him his speed. Lara is now mine."

Magnus grinned. "Remember the quantum leaps you taught me to use? I've been using them to fix what we destroyed. And now, I'm going to use them to destroy you."

Then, Magnus slipped into a parallel universe. None of the colors had changed, but a black hole had formed next to him. He aimed for it knowing every risk he put in his actions. He felt the heat intensifying as it crushed in on him. For a second he could feel all of the debris being thrown at him and clinging to him. It was dark for a millisecond but the jet-stream of the black hole shot him out just where he needed to be. He blinked into another parallel universe where he caught an asteroid flying through space. He gripped it and shoved himself forward, slinging himself back to his universe.

Solaris was just ahead. He was gaining on Lara. Magnus came over Solaris and silently flew above him. Then, he reached out and wrapped his arm around Solaris' neck. They instantly stopped and Lara took her chance to escape. Solaris fought against Magnus and tried to break from his grip, but Magnus wouldn't let go.

"Father would be so disappointed in you," Magnus said.

Solaris was still prying Magnus' arm off of his neck. "Father was an evil monster that sought to capture the universe off its guard and take it for his full control with his twisted ideals for rules and laws," he choked.

Magnus brought his chin out and empowered his grip. "You've said enough. Our family didn't plan for your corruption to go this far."

Magnus took his knife and drove it through Solaris' chest. Through the blade, he could feel the power seep from Solaris into his blade and drain into his own body. Magnus apologized to Solaris, letting his body drift away. Once he had released Solaris to the galaxy, he flew off to catch up with Stratus.

CHAPTER 3

Stratus and Valkyrie walked through the storm, down the road to the gates of the ruins of Magnus' kingdom. They had walked for miles across the long pass to Magnus' realm. Stratus turned and saw a figure move through the dark forests. He stopped and waited for whatever it was to emerge. Valkyrie stopped with him and looked around for whatever it was that Stratus searched for. Stratus got ready for a fight as Valkyrie pulled out her sword.

Stratus turned to look at her, "What beings reside here?"

Valkyrie looked deep in the forest, trying to reason what it could be out there. "We're obviously not alone. And it's huge."

She turned to Stratus trying to read what he was thinking. "I think it's an Azhi-D'aki."

Stratus stayed his guard. "The what?"

"A three-headed dragon."

"Evolution. I hadn't expect it to get this far so soon," Stratus replied quietly.

Valkyrie lifted her cheek. "It has been over a hundred years. Inbreeding and such may have caused mutations like this."

Stratus got down on one knee, turned his body and looked toward the Azhi-D'aki. "This isn't a mutation. It's an advancement."

He watched the figure move in the dark. It was skinny, but long. Its front hung low and it almost slithered its way around the thick forest. It was quick, and camouflaged well in the dark. Through the wind, they could hear it hissing and growling.

Valkyrie watched Stratus's moves. "I know it's not a very good time, but, do all the elders look like you?"

Stratus never looked away from his predator. "No. I took on the form of a Geonite. It was the second most powerful being I could think of."

"You couldn't keep your Elder form?"

"Not if I wanted you to see me. I had to manifest myself in a physical form to join you on this dimension."

"So the agile body and the somewhat bulky biceps are just a front?" Valkyrie asked.

Stratus thought and paused trying to construct an appropriate answer. "Pretty much. Yeah."

"So, how can you jump so far if your leg muscles can't give you that kind of power?"

Stratus turned with the Azhi-D'aki as it moved. "I still have the power of the elders in me that allow me to move like I do. Can we please get back to this hunt?"

Valkyrie shifted her shield and her sword as her eyes darted everywhere with the sounds of the forest and the moves of the Azhi-D'aki. Then everything went silent. The trees stopped moving, the wind stopped blowing. All the animals were gone, all the sounds left, even the dragon.

Valkyrie and Stratus faced opposite directions to make sure that they could see every edge of the forest that surrounded them. Everything about the trees seemed to eerily close in on them. Stratus heard something above them but didn't make any sudden moves.

He whispered, "Valkyrie. Don't move, keep your guard up."

He closed his eyes and sensed the Azhi-D'aki grip the tops of the trees with its claws, holding it silently above them. The three heads of the dragon loomed above them, ready to snatch Stratus and Valkyrie into its jaws.

Stratus concentrated on the metal molecules of the sword. He became one with each and helped the sword to expand. The blade stretched high above him and curiously attracted the Azhi-D'aki's attention. It hissed at the blade and Stratus focused on getting the monster out of the trees. The tip of the sword twisted and wiggled like the head of a worm, and wove back to the ground. The sword didn't seem threatening at all to the Azhi-D'aki, so it followed the blade. Its feet boomed on the ground and pounded as it stepped closer.

Stratus smiled at his distraction and divided the blade into three that wiggled around at each head of the Azhi-D'aki. He looked at Valkyrie, but she had moved to the trees and was making her way to the dragon. He looked up and found her climbing up one of the trees behind the Azhi-D'aki, climbing down a vine. Her sword hung next to her, and she gripped the vine tightly. She lowered herself until she hung just above the Azhi-D'aki. She silently took her sword out and readied it above the three heads.

Stratus did his best to keep the dragon occupied while communicating with Valkyrie. "Is that really a good idea?"

Then, the middle head of the dragon smiled. "It was a bad idea from the start." All three took a huge bite out of the sword, then turned to Valkyrie.

"They can talk?" Stratus shouted.

Valkyrie swung on one of the dragon's necks and kicked one of their faces. "Of course they can! They were charming you to make you think you were charming them," she shouted, warding off another strike. Stratus fought two of the heads that struck at him.

Valkyrie rolled on the ground dodging a bite, and held her sword out so this head would come down on it. But, the head only attacked around her blade. Stratus held an energy force-field against two of the heads and tried to surround them with it, but the third bit at him, taking his mind off of the energy field, and more towards defending himself.

Valkyrie had the perfect chance, and she took it. She leapt in the air, over the Azhi-D'aki, and cut the loose head off from the neck up. It wiggled on the ground and finally died. She landed on the other side of the dragon, next to Stratus, just as he had let the energy field go completely. The Azhi-D'aki shrieked in pain and its wings flapped, lifting it into the air.

Stratus quickly sheathed his sword and lifted his hands into the air at the Azhi-D'aki.

"What are you doing?" Valkyrie asked. "It's gone."

"Not for long," Stratus replied. "I'm creating a fluctuation in the gravity. I'm going to pull it down."

"Don't do that. We've scared it off," she begged.

"No, we only made it mad. Instead of letting it get its chance to attack again, we'll catch it off guard and finish what we started," he said.

Valkyrie sheathed her sword and watched the dragon come back down in front of them. It crashed into the ground and rock and dust flew into the air. Valkyrie ran for it and watched the tail come up as its heads dug deeper into the ground. Gaining speed, she ran up the neck and back, jumping for its tail. The two heads darted around at her and hissed loudly. The fins on the sides of their head stretched out and their tongues flicked.

Valkyrie latched to its tail as it lifted back into the air. Stratus held out his hand, doing his best to keep the dragon close to him. Valkyrie stepped up the dragon's back to its neck. She gripped her sword and ran it all the way through the neck on the side. She jumped off the dragon, swinging from the sword she had wedged in it's neck, letting the inertia bring her back up to its other head, completely severing the second head.

She was about to carve through the last neck when a gust of wind blew her off. Stratus watched her fall and concentrated his power on her. She stopped over the trees and levitated back to him. She landed on her feet and looked up at him.

"Thank you," she gasped.

"You're welcome," he whispered back looking for the dragon.

Suddenly, the Azhi-D'aki screamed at them both from behind. They jumped around and held their weapons up at it. They backed away as it slashed its teeth at them and hissed loudly. Its jaws chomped as it struck at them, and they could only watch it step forward biting at them. As it slashed at them once again, a fireball came from above and impaled the dragon to the ground. Rock and dragon meat exploded. Valkyrie guarded herself from the explosion, but the entire wave was blocked by Stratus's energy field.

Valkyrie looked up. "Please, tell me the fireball was you."

Stratus helped her up and looked at the clouds that loomed above. "No, it wasn't me," he replied.

She saw the fireballs raining from the sky and the ice that blanketed the updrafts. "The plague," she muttered.

They ran as fast as they could through the forest, dodging the fireballs and pieces of hail, ignoring the heated chills that bit at their skin. Above the castle, the sky was covered in the dark cloud and only a small beam of light could be seen on the inside of the cloud. It was not a fireball. The castle would have been their safest place to rest.

They opened the doors and ran through closing up behind them. Valkyrie caught her breath and Stratus looked around at the giant court room. He could smell the presence of someone else in the castle. He looked all around for Decimus. He found the young Dryad stepping in the moves of a fighter in battle. He jumped and leapt and dodged as if he were fighting an invisible swordsman. All the while staring at the floor and at his feet.

He followed the ground in a trail where he stopped, turned around and got back to a fighter stance. He hopped a little, moving his feet quickly. Then, he ran back to where he was before, jumped into a flip, turned around, lunged, and fell. Stratus walked up as Decimus stopped.

"Decimus?" Stratus asked.

He looked up. "That's me. I heard you coming from outside. You and a girl." He caught his breath and sheathed his sword. "Did I do something? Trespass on sacred ground? Desecrate a tomb? Vandalize a holy artifact?"

Valkyrie glanced at the tracker that they had been following and knew in an instant who he was.

Stratus smiled a little. "No. But, I expected you to be younger. You're needed to save the universe," Stratus answered.

Valkyrie instantly recognized Decimus from her dream. Her heart fluttered at the memory. But then, Decimus returned the feeling.

"Do I know you?" he asked.

Valkyrie didn't know how to answer.

Suddenly, the doors of the castle shattered and Magnus flew in with a beam of light surrounding his figure. He smiled at the three in the room and the light dimmed.

Stratus met him in the middle of the courts. "Magnus, finally," he whispered.

Magnus gripped Stratus' forearm. "You miss me?" he asked.

"If you're here, then that means Lara is safe," Stratus replied.

"For the time being. Valefor had help," Magnus said.

Stratus gasped. "Tell me."

"It was Solaris. He had about half of the elders power in him. Valefor must have the other half including that of the Father," Magnus explained.

"Solaris. I never would've guessed that. It makes sense though." Then Stratus looked into Magnus's eyes. "That means that you killed him. Which means ..."

"I made the decision. I know very well what it means," Magnus replied.

"You should not have done that. He can't fight for it now," Stratus said sternly.

"Lighten up. Now there's one less thing to worry about."

"He is the last Scion! Nothing more! He's not a trained fighter, or skilled in meditation, or a fireball thrower, or anything that we need. And now, he's been deprived of the one battle he needs to defeat Valefor," Stratus started to shout.

"So, I'll train him!" Magnus shouted back, but only to show that Stratus was over reacting.

Stratus paused. "You'll train him? Do you think your teachings alone are going to help him defeat Valefor?"

Magnus ignored Stratus for a second and looked over his shoulder at Decimus and Valkyrie. "Who's the girl?" he asked.

"Her name is Valkyrie. Do you understand at all what you've done?" Stratus urged.

Magnus shook his head. "No. Do you think she'll be of any use to train him?"

"Of course not! She ..." Stratus thought about this new idea. "She's a great fighter. She know some advanced moves." He turned to Valkyrie and saw the connection that Magnus was making.

"The prophecy. You don't really think it's them. Do you?" Stratus asked.

"Why not? The last scion, the unknown fighter, and a storm of terror all in a place of holy abundance. Forces collide, and bleakness is great. The never ending chaos is overwhelmed in time and space and energy. Darkness consumes the light and the light in the distance prevails. The fact that they look about the same age doesn't connect the dots for you? Stratus, you and I get to train the new order." Magnus explained.

Stratus smiled at the connections. "This has to be the most insane event I've ever taken part in."

Decimus and Valkyrie stepped up to the two elders. "What's going on?" Decimus asked Stratus.

Magnus held his hand out and his blade appeared. "Let us begin." he said to Decimus, "Have you atoned for your sins lately?"

Stratus drew his sword and pointed it at Valkyrie. "Defend yourself, or I will part your head form your body."

*****

Lara watched again and again as Valefor put the image in her head. The Galaxian choked and dangled in his hand. She shook her head trying to free herself of the disgusting image. But Valefor would not let her go.

"Get out of my mind," she shouted.

"Tell me where they are and I shall let you free," he replied.

"No, I'll not give you the universe," she replied.

Then the image of her Father came to mind. Lara was taking control again, using the memories to keep him and the Galaxian alive.

The Father looked into her eyes. "Keep fighting. We'll help you," he whispered.

Lara tightly balled her fists and fought hard against the depression Valefor had on her.

"Save her. Father, save her. Please," Lara begged.

The Father attacked him. Valefor lost control over Lara's mind and they both left her. She opened her eyes and saw that she was completely safe in her solitude. Valefor wasn't moving for her. He was going to wait for her to come to him. She quickly connected to her brothers. She closed her eyes and their images faded into her mind.

"Are you ready to fight Valefor?" Lara asked.

"We need to train them and then they'll be able to travel with us," Magnus replied.

"You may join us if you like. The three of us working together will be quicker to teach them," Stratus suggested.

"I'll be there soon. I just need to make sure Valefor won't follow," Lara explained.

"Good." Magnus replied. "We'll be waiting." And their images faded away.

A harsh tingle shot up her back. She gasped in surprise and searched the souls. Down the dark funnel where the souls were spiraling, sleeping, oblivious to each other or anything around them, towards the bottom she watched another soul slip through the funnel. She searched for the alert that was sent to her. Both Jade and Odin were holding each other and close to the end of the funnel.

"It's only been little over a century. How can they be there already?" she asked herself. "They're not ready. Their souls should be slower than the others. They've lived two lives already." But no matter how she reasoned, she could not change that they were sliding back into the living universe, ready to be reincarnated on their planet of origin.

CHAPTER 4

"Have you atoned for your sins lately?" Decimus asked.

Magnus woke up instantly and guarded himself as Decimus sliced his sword down on top of Magnus' blade. Magnus pushed him away and got up returning the fight. Decimus quickly rushed Magnus and shoved him back to the floor.

Magnus gritted his teeth and waited to ward off another attack. "I hope that you fight with some semblance of honor. If not, then I have no reason to give you a fair match."

Decimus allowed him to get up and ran up to him, leaping in the air, keeping Magnus' blade down and flipping over his head.

Magnus spun around and guarded again. "It seems that move runs in the family …" he commented swinging low.

Decimus placed his hand on the side of Magnus' blade and pushed away while swinging high for his head. Magnus jumped away trying to hide the surprise.

"Did you ask for something original?" Decimus snickered.

Magnus tilted his head. "Creative, but dangerous. Are you sure you're ready for dangerous?"

Magnus twirled his blade and Decimus struck. Their blades crossed high and Magnus shoved Decimus back. He swung for Decimus' feet. Decimus jumped high swinging his sword over Magnus' head. Magnus sliced for Decimus' stomach and leaned back as Decimus swung for his face. After hearing Decimus' blade slice through the air, he became threatened. Magnus shook his head. "You asked for it."

Two identical images resembling Magnus appeared at either side. "Let us begin," they all said.

Decimus flipped backwards above the blades of the other two figures and lined them up in front of him. They all attacked differently and he could easily block them as long as there was diversity in their attacks. He lunged for one, but the other two blocked it and shoved him back to his stance.

"Ah, ah, ah, you stay on the defensive. Leave the attacking to one better suited for it." they all ordered.

He jumped over them again and backed them against the wall. In one swift move, he sliced through all three of them at the gut, but his blade went right through as if they were nothing.

He backed away at a guard and stared at all of them. "Okay, that's not fair," he said.

They all drew their swords back, ready to strike if he moved. "It's original," they all replied.

"Magnus!" Stratus called.

They all turned to him. "Busy here," the one to the right called back. Stratus smiled. "Breakfast," he ordered.

The other two disappeared and the Magnus on the left dropped his stance and made his way to Stratus. "Do you want some dragon or unicorn?" Magnus asked mocking Stratus' creation, and walked out to hunt for food. Decimus sat next to Stratus and waited for food to arrive.

Stratus stretched his fingers over some sticks and a small spark ignited the sticks into a flame. "You have a great deal of skill to keep the Eldest of Elders on his toes," Stratus commented.

"Is Valefor going to be as unfair as Magnus?" Decimus asked.

"He'll take advantage of your weaknesses. But we're training you to control that."

"Why me? Why of all people would you ask for a tracker like me? I can't be that special," Decimus replied.

Stratus sat back. "Are you ready to hear this?" Decimus nodded.

Stratus smiled. "Okay, your tracking abilities are only a portion of the potential you have in your blood. The skills that live in you are much more than for the use of a simple fight. You are the last Scion. Your mother was named Lara after the elder that helped Odin live peacefully in purity here on Hajun. Your Mother's father was named Odin, and in the story of the Elder himself, Odin rescued a Dryad named Jade from 'a dark being with magnificent power'. Your grandfather was married to Jade."

Decimus had already put the pieces together. "So the elder that descended to Hajun and rescued his love from the dark being was a real person? And in my bloodline?"

Stratus nodded. "He was your grandfather. And the dark being with magnificent power is the very one that's been training you. For a long time, Magnus was jealous of your grandfather for finding a life outside of the Elder Courts. A life with love, which is something no elder has ever had until or after your grandfather did. It was forbidden to do so. Our father's firstborn was the one that made it forbidden for that kind of relationship between one of my kind and a mortal being.

When our father fell in love with a Galaxian, she bore us, his children. The firstborn son of our father was jealous of the Father's power. Because our mother wasn't of the same race as our Father, we could never equal to his power as a substantial portion of his power would be lost in mingling with the blood of our mother. And, as powerful as we are, our father was beyond us. When the Eldest grew jealous of our father's power, he sought to destroy the Father with his sword and inherit his power through his murder. The Father thwarted his move and banished him to the underworld. After Odin had his life on Hajun, it enraged a majority of the elders and they began a revolt against the Father. The Father was forced to wipe them out and banish them as well. But one managed to evade the Father's attention. As far as we know, Valefor escaped the underworld and took it under his control. I believe that the one elder that kept the revolt going was the one to free Valefor, and together they killed the rest of the elders and inherited their power. I'm absolutely sure they killed our father together."

Decimus' heart was pounding as he reasoned the ending. "So, Valefor has the power of a majority of the elders and the power of the Father, and I have to kill him. Exactly who is Valefor?"

Stratus closed his eyes. "This is where things get complicated. In order to contain a Power, they can only exist on a certain plane of existence of space-time. The Underworld is one such containment field for out of control Powers, as punishment for their lack of responsibility. When a Power, no matter how great, is in this state, they are highly vulnerable. All that exists is their consciousness and a shimmer of their power."

"They're a soul?"

"Exactly. That shimmer of power is known as their essence, and that can be absorbed by other Powers if they have the right tools."

"You would need a conduit of unlimited endurance to take the essence of every soul from the Underworld."

"Valefor didn't need all of them. He just needed enough to escape and conquer my family."

"But how? He can't just do that."

"The sword of Orion is the only tool he would know about that would have that kind of power."

"How did he get it?"

"Let me fill in the gap. Orion is the name or my father."

Decimus looked at the fire and connected the dots. Solaris kept the revolt going. He could steal the sword and send it to Valefor.

"When the eldest had absorbed enough essence of other Powers, he became overwhelmed with their power and life forces. They had added to and altered his personage. He became Valefor."

"So you knew Odin for most of his life?" Decimus asked.

"I'm the second youngest elder. I was with your grandfather when he created this planet. I liked to help him with creations and such. This world was actually one of our greatest successes. It's lived peacefully without our presence for a long time," Stratus explained.

"How much power do you have compared to Magnus?"

"As of now? I can't even compare. He killed the elder that was helping Valefor. Whatever power that particular elder held would have been willed to Magnus."

"So, Odin was the Eldest at one point?" Decimus asked.

Stratus nodded. "After Valefor was sent to the Underworld as a soul, Odin inherited the position. Then he moved to Hajun, giving the position to Magnus."

Suddenly, a gust of wind blew into the court and Lara appeared in the doorway. "Stratus, don't you know that fire inside is highly hazardous on a rescue mission?" she asked.

Stratus rolled his eyes.

Lara scoffed and sat next to Stratus, "So, you're the last scion?" she asked.

Decimus was so captivated by Lara's youthful and beautiful image that he couldn't speak. He just waited for something to happen.

Stratus answered for him. "Yeah. He's definitely it."

Lara smiled and leaned into Stratus's ear. "He has our brother's more attractive features, to say the least," she whispered.

Stratus noticed Decimus staring at Lara and quickly reacted. "Hey."

Decimus looked up and woke from the trance. "Yeah."

"You know she's only a couple million years older than you, right?" he glanced at Lara, then back to Decimus. "And she's technically your great aunt," he finished.

Magnus walked in carrying a dragon-skin full of rabbits. "Breakfast is served," he said sitting next to the fire.

"Trying to burn my kingdom down, are we?" he asked Stratus. Stratus stuck a rabbit on a stick and held it over the fire.

"Magnus, the walls are mostly gone, the ceiling is weak, and the rest of your castle has been destroyed. If there was anything left to burn down, would you even care?"

Magnus shook his head in discontent. "You should have seen this place in it's prime. It truly was a universal wonder."

Lara silently gawked at Magnus' ego.

Decimus cooked his own rabbit. "So, how does this story end?" he asked.

Lara and Stratus glanced at each other, and Stratus finished, "You and Valkyrie rise up as the head of the new order, and reign over all that is ours. After that, the universe is yours to change."

Lara placed her hand on Stratus' shoulder. "We need to talk," she whispered.

They stood up and walked away as Magnus continued in the other room.

"What's wrong?" Stratus asked.

"Valefor killed our mother. Both our parents are dead. And on top of that, both Jade and Odin are about to be reincarnated," Lara explained.

"So, plan "C" is going down the abyss," Stratus said.

"Worse than that, if Odin gets reincarnated, the last scion loses its right. With Odin back in the world, there will be no scion. We need to act before every hope of winning this battle is lost. As for our original plan, Valefor is still a dead Elder. He's just acquired the power of the elders and is living as a soul without a body. We can't send a living being to kill the dead. Not unless the living being is extremely powerful," Lara finished.

"Then how is getting Odin back in the world to fight Valefor going to affect the power of the last Scion?" Stratus asked.

Lara tilted her head. "I was thinking the same thing. How did Valefor get back anyway without turning mortal? That kind of thing shouldn't happen."

Stratus smiled catching onto the clue she was hinting at. "Another plane of existence. Odin is as much an elder as we are, just not on our plane."

Lara shook her head. "He gave up his birthright. He's completely mortal."

Magnus raised his hand. "We can break the rules for him again. I know how much this family loves doing that for him."

Stratus rolled his eyes, but Lara continued. "I'm inclined to agree. Maybe we could get Odin out of the afterlife, the same way Valefor got out of the Underworld. We give him the Chevron, he takes down Valefor. Problem solved." Lara suggested.

"Have you tried waking him?" Stratus suggested.

"Yes, but he's not listening. It's as if he wants to stay dead. So he can be reincarnated," Lara answered.

"You think the last Scion could help?" he asked glancing at Decimus.

Lara cocked up an eyebrow. "It's worth a shot."

"How long do we have?" Stratus urged.

"I'd say four days, if we're lucky," Lara replied.

"Then we have three. Two to train, one to fight. Do you think you can teach Valkyrie?"

"In that amount of time, it'll be tough. I'll need to contact the remainder of the Light. Maybe he'll help," Lara suggested.

"Valkyrie has great skills in fighting. She only needs to train in meditation, and she'll be ready."

"In that case, you teach Stratus all you know, and we'll make our move."

Magnus shook his head. "Even if Odin has the Chevron, it wont be enough. It's not just the power of the elders inside of Valefor. That's countless Powers and life forces. We'll need multiple outlets for that kind of power to seep into."

"We'll tear that fabric of the universe when come across it," Lara responded.

Valkyrie woke up and joined the others at the fire. She wasn't used to rabbits for breakfast, but she made due. When noon struck, they began their lessons. Stratus and Magnus taught Decimus how to fight, and in a day he learned everything he could. Lara and Valkyrie worked on meditation: the only way she could rise to another level of dimension and travel to the Galaxian world. Valkyrie could feel her soul leaving her body, sharing the power of the elders that she worked with, taking on different forms. She could feel herself becoming one with everything around her.

Soon, she could move objects and manipulate their form. Decimus could defeat each of the elders that sparred with him, but when they joined together in a fight, it was much harder. By nightfall, he had them both on the ground, desperate for a break. They rested that night, and switched the next day.

Decimus concentrated on meditation, and quickly learned everything he needed for the travel. He gained the knowledge he needed to enter minds and learn hidden thoughts, even those of the elders. They had plans made to leave the galaxy when all of this was finished. He saw visions of the future, and secrets of the past: how Magnus had made love with Odin's bride. Decimus learned everything Valkyrie knew, how to manipulate objects and change his own form. With a little more practice, he would be able to ascend to a higher plane of dimension. He was becoming the elder his grandfather had once been. He saw a figure outside the castle. It was coming in, and it looked threatening.

Magnus stopped his attack. Stratus and Valkyrie looked at the door holding their attack on each other. In the silence of the castle they heard a tapping coming from the entrance. Slow, intermittent tapping. A staff held by a figure in a dark cloak entered. Decimus kept his eyes shut and watched as the figure began to glow in his mind. It stood up straight and removed the cloak revealing a glowing Dryad.

Valkyrie began to lose her balance and fell on top of Stratus, but they kept staring at the figure in the doorway. The figure stepped slowly to Decimus and its eyes could be seen when it sucked on its pipe and the fire reflected in its eyes.

"Thou art calleth me forth, did ye not?" the dark, raspy voice asked.

"I did. Are you the one that is called the last of The Light?" Lara asked.

"I am the final descendant of Throth. Thine call hath been answered. What be thine wish?" the voice asked.

"We need your help in teaching these Dryads to become immortal," Lara replied.

"The path to immortality is a long one for the unskilled. Hath thou any training?" he asked.

"I can see your true form, and I know what you are," Decimus said. "I know you will not be fighting for us."

The figure looked down trying to enter Decimus' mind, searching for an identity. But his plan backfired. Once he opened his mind, Decimus struck. "Obey my command." Decimus ordered inside the figure's mind. "Reveal yourself."

The figure fought hard against Decimus, but couldn't move. "If thou called me for my assistance, thou art placing much discouragement on my heart," the figure growled, leaning on his staff.

Decimus sat still concentrating on the powerful being behind him. "Take off your cloak and tell us exactly who you are and why you've come."

Lara wanted to intervene, but trusted that she had been deceived and waited for their battle to end. Decimus' body was tense but controlled, and the figure stood tiredly over them. Magnus, Stratus and Valkyrie stood around the figure and could almost see the battle being fought in their minds.

Then Decimus began to speak, intensifying his power. "Take off your cloak," he ordered.

The being fought his own move to obey and shook as his arms came up. "Thou art strong. Do not take advantage of my ageing. Not to serve thine purposes."

Then, Decimus' head dropped and a harsh pulse of energy erupted from the being's body, pushing everyone to the walls except for Decimus. The cloak flew away, revealing a scrawny and pale man. His tunic covered most of his form, but the cloak was to keep his face from being exposed. The man quickly waved his staff and the cloak covered his body again.

"You should not have done that," the man growled curling his fingers and creating a fireball in his hand and throwing it at Decimus' head.

Decimus didn't move, and the fireball was swallowed by an energy beam. The man roared in anger and tried siphoning the energy beam from Decimus into his hands. Decimus stood up and stretched his arms. His feet left the ground and his eyes never opened. His body flashed and blinked into nothing. He was completely invisible.

The man took his staff in two hands and raised it up. Every bit of debris levitated and collided on Decimus. But the rocks never touched him. They just bounced off and crashed to the ground.

Stratus and Lara stepped in. "Enough of this," Stratus ordered.

The man tapped his staff to the ground and the entire building rumbled as the debris crashed down. Decimus came back to the ground and gracefully landed. They were both out of breath.

Stratus hung Decimus' arm around his neck and carried him away. Lara and Valkyrie talked to the man. "We called you here to help us, not to demonstrate how powerful you are," Lara explained.

The man wheezed, "I only wished to show thee a way to immortality. He has proven that he hath training, but will he learn from me? Methinks not."

"He will learn. He must. We cannot destroy Valefor in our mortal state," Valkyrie pleaded.

The man sat down and Valkyrie joined him, "Let us begin. Ye may call me Ryuu. In order to accomplish complete immortality, thine focus must be on the energy that thine body emits. Thou must embrace it and control it so that instead of giving off energy as waste, thou useth it to bringeth new life. When thine energy becomes abundant, thou art regenerate it and useth it for healing and concentration." Ryuu went on.

*****

Stratus wiped the blood from Decimus' nose. "Why did you fight him?" Stratus asked.

Decimus felt dizzy. "In case you didn't notice, I was on the defensive. I only wanted you to see what he was."

Stratus tilted his head. "He's the last member of The Light. We all knew that."

"Not just that, he's part of the Plague. It's feeding off of the debris and resources of the planet and he's feeding off of it. Somehow it's giving him power. He shares his energy with the weather and this storm is compensating the lost energy with the destruction it lays on the planet," Decimus replied, his eyes still never opened.

"So, he's destroying the planet with this storm," Stratus reasoned.

"You didn't see the connection between him and the storm? There was a physical link between them feeding through the destroyed structures of the building," Decimus insisted.

"No," Stratus answered.

"How? I saw it as clear as crystal," Decimus replied anxiously.

Stratus tilted his head. "You didn't look at him once. How could you see that?" Then he noticed that Decimus still hadn't opened his eyes. "In fact, you shouldn't even see me."

Decimus shook his head. "I'm looking right at you."

Stratus stood up. "I'll be right back." And he went to get Lara.

Stratus quietly moved in behind her and tapped Lara's shoulder. "I need you to see something," he whispered.

Lara stood up and followed him to Decimus. They both stood in front of him. "What's wrong?" Lara asked.

Stratus created a small energy ball and tossed it to Decimus, who caught it and tossed it back with his eyes completely shut.

Lara was surprised. "How did he do that?" she asked.

"I don't know."

"I'm not a child. Playing catch isn't anything impressive. What is going on?" Decimus asked.

Lara knelt down in front of Decimus. "You've evolved to a point where you no longer need your eyes," Lara explained.

Then, both Stratus and Lara heard Decimus' voice inside their heads. "I have?" he asked.

Stratus was shocked. "Are we going to be able to fix this before we leave here?"

Lara was equally confused. "I can't say. Maybe this is supposed to happen."

Decimus got up. "You two are making me very uncomfortable. If I don't get some answers, heads will roll," he replied in their heads again.

Stratus turned to Lara. "He doesn't need his mouth either. This could get annoying."

Lara stared at Decimus. "Decimus, you're flying again."

Decimus pointed his head down. "No, I'm not. I'm ..." he tapped his feet in the air and didn't feel the ground. He paused. "That's strange."

Stratus turned to Lara, "I'll be right back. You stay with him," he said.

She nodded and watched Decimus rise higher in the air. She bit her lip anxiously. "This isn't good."

CHAPTER 5

Ryuu smiled at the success Valkyrie was making and he could see her feeling her own power give her life.

"Soon," Ryuu continued," thine body will no longer be the threshold of thine soul, and it will live only in the energy it emits, once it has enough power to store itself."

At the same time, both Valkyrie and Decimus were shining like the morning star, and their bodies had completely disappeared. In only milliseconds, Valkyrie and Decimus recollected all of the memory of every past life they had shared together. They could comprehend that their mortal minds could not store the memories of their own immortal souls, and the rush of memory that swept over them was intense and refreshing at the same time.

Decimus glanced at Valkyrie and remembered how many times they had been joined together, only to be torn by death. He remembered, once, tying a knot in a ribbon with her and vowed to hold onto each other to the end of time. He remembered how she had sat beside him when his mortal body was born with a mental defect, and still in another life, he had never moved on when she died early from giving birth to a son. Children; they had had twenty-two of those in total through their past lives. The assassins that attacked him when he became the leader of nations, they were destroyed by Valkyrie's sorceress's powers. Then she was thrown from the tops of a cliff by her father when he didn't approve of them sharing a life together. Decimus dove from those heights and caught her and found some way of keeping them both from dying there.

He was the one. Valkyrie looked through his soul and remembered him in her dreams. He was the one in her thoughts at all times.

They reappeared next to each other in the castle courts. The elders were obviously impressed and Ryuu felt his work was completed. Decimus' eyes were open again and Valkyrie felt freedom.

Decimus looked at Valkyrie. "I understand, now," he whispered.

She smiled and took his hand.

Stratus turned to Ryuu. "You're the one that's keeping the storm here, aren't you?"

Ryuu swallowed hard. "Thou art correct."

Stratus nodded. "Can you destroy it?" he asked.

"Not without destroying myself," Ryuu replied. He stood and declaired, "Omega will strike. Death cometh for all." He left, leaning on his staff as he walked.

All of the elders, including Valkyrie and Decimus, stood in a circle. Lara smiled. "Decimus, Valkyrie, keep your eyes closed and your minds on me," she ordered.

They nodded and ascended. They moved freely in place and followed Lara through space, across the galaxy past stars and planets and comets.

Magnus broke free from the circle and started drifting away to a planet nearby.

Through thought, Stratus asked, "Where are you going?"

"To Monon III. I need to make another deal with Dreadnought," Magnus explained.

"Dreadnought? You'll be taken prisoner there!" Stratus replied.

"Stay your course. I will meet you."

Lara looked forward. "We need to keep moving, Stratus."

Stratus took Valkyrie's hand and they continued to the moon of Tyrannus. Three spiraled galaxies joined at their outer rims and formed the triangle. The bright center of each galaxy converged at the center of the triangle. Just beyond this triangle of galaxies, there was a giant star that with every flicker and twinkle, it would flash a little brighter. The fifth planet revolving silently around it was Tyrannus, the gas giant. The rings around Tyrannus swung and crossed as if it were an atom.

The four elders rounded Tyrannus and faded onto the moon that the Galaxians thrived on.

Valkyrie and Decimus felt woozy from the travel, but overjoyed that they had proven their status as grown elders. Stratus looked around, and found the barrier that closed off the temple from the outside world. "Where is Valefor?" he wondered out loud.

Lara started for the barrier and saw the demon on patrol across the wall. "We don't want to attack him directly. Not until Magnus finishes his mission and meets us here. It'll take all of us to bring Valefor down."

The other three walked with her until suddenly, she stopped. Another harsh shimmer shot up her spine. She saw the afterlife, the souls spiraling down to the bright light at the end of the funnel. At the end of the spiral, Odin and Jade were next in line. Lara grabbed Decimus' hand and they disappeared. Tripling the speed they were before, they flew past galaxies and nebulas to the edge of the universe where stars ended and not a single light shown. There was nothing but black. Then, a door opened in the black and they flew into the doorway.

Lara growled at Decimus angrily, "Call for your grandfather."

He looked down the perennial funnel and began to shout for the dead elder to save him. Nothing happened.

*****

Magnus entered the tavern that Dreadnought was usually in. He opened the doors and found the old reptilian at the counter. Two of his arms were crossed on the counter, his head leaned on another, and the fourth held the cup that he drank from. The bar had a foul odor from the many species of revelers in the bar, all smoking, drinking, dancing, sweating, and more.

Magnus kept his composure and sat down next to Dreadnought. "I'll have a Tiki's revenge," he told the bartender.

Dreadnought looked up. "That's the voice of a homicidal maniac ordering the drink of crazed and depressed king." Then he turned to see Magnus staring at him. "So, they tell me immortality isn't all it's cracked up to be. You tell me it's all you desire. I've gotta know, where were you when I got my share of it?" his chopped voice whispered loudly and his words slurred.

Magnus took his order. "Fighting a crusade of my own, but now all that is done and over with. Now, I need answers," he said taking a sip of his drink.

Dreadnought laughed. "Answers? Magnus, if I had answers, do you think I'd be here making deals? I'd be living like a god if I had the answers I need."

Magnus touched his glass to Dreadnought's. "I'll drink to that. What I need to know is if you've made any deals to any elders. After that, I'll let you get back to your drink."

Dreadnought shook his head. "Didn't you hear what I said? I'd be living like a god!" he shouted through the noise in the room.

Magnus grinned. "Yes, and that's all well and good. And if gods existed, I'm sure you'd be one of them. But answer me: have you made any deals with any elders besides me?"

Dreadnought ignored him and continued. "The gods look down on these crummy little planets and feel no pain, no remorse, no regret, no shame in watching us in what we do. Sleeping on the clouds, drinking from the cup of pleasure, eating from the vine of freedom. I could have that right now," Dreadnought thought aloud.

Magnus took another sip of his drink. "Dreadnought, take it from one who knows, there are no gods. There are higher beings of dimension that create things in space as you would create a picture or a sock. One of these beings becomes just the slightest bit jealous or angry at the other, and suddenly they're the evil force of the universe. It's just how things work. Higher beings create lower beings, and lower beings create other lower beings. Pretty soon, the chain ends and here you are wondering how we did it. The whole 'god' concept came from one higher form that couldn't get attention from the others, so they took their desires to the lower beings who would worship him or her for their creation, or the creation of other things that the lower beings came in contact with."

"And shouldn't we give thanks to the gods that created us? Regardless of which one we put our faith in, they deserve credit for our existence, much as a painter would receive credit for his works of art." Dreadnought paused and said under his breath, "I could be that."

Magnus stopped and squinted, realizing that he was wildly digressing from his task, and defending his point to an intoxicated victim of alcoholism.

"You're drunk," he said more to himself than to Dreadnought.

Dreadnought stood up and staggered away. "You don't care. No one in this godforsaken place cares," he shouted heading out the door.

Magnus finished his drink and paid the bartender. "Gods don't exist, Dreadnought! If they did, you'd know." he called as he followed Dreadnought.

Dreadnought's body almost slithered in the most drunken manner, and he clumsily bumped into the street dwellers that crossed his path. Magnus followed closely and caught up to him.

Dreadnought hissed, "You've got a lot of nerve ..."

Magnus stepped in front of him and stopped him. "Okay, Dreadnought. I've been nice, but now I need answers."

Dreadnought's head bobbed as he looked at the ground.

"What happened to the fear I used to strike into you? I told you, I don't have the right answers we need."

Magnus stopped and tried to reason what he was saying. "What are you talking about?"

Dreadnought looked up. "I just gave the last of my supply to your oldest brother."

Magnus took a deep breath. "You gave him twenty-five trillion demons? And they still have the immunity to psychosis powers."

Dreadnought nodded. "I don't know why. The way he spoke and everything about him just made me want to give him more. In return, he gave me immortality. Everlasting life. But this was ten years ago. Now I've been dealing real-estate on planets that I don't even know the names of."

Magnus sighed in distress. "That means he's taken complete control of the moon on Tyrannus."

"Tyrannus?" Dreadnought laughed. "I've got so many complaints from the residents of Tyrannus that I had to throw the last of my permits away for that moon."

Magnus shook his head. "I don't need an express there, I just want to know, what more do you have other than real estate."

Dreadnought teetered back then caught his balance. Reaching into his pocket, he smiled, "I've got some tickets to Amphibious Laxitus opera, bonds and stock in moisture-evaporators, and a few hundred jelly-tots."

Magnus was frustrated. "Jelly-tots?" he repeated softly. "I'm about to face the most powerful being with the largest army of demons this universe has ever seen, and all you can offer me is real-estate and jelly-tots."

Dreadnought pulled out the plastic bag covered with reptilian symbols. "Why? Do you want to buy the jelly-tots?"

Magnus rolled his eyes and sighed, "How much?"

"About two-hundred in universal currency." Dreadnought answered.

Magnus gave an exhausted expression. "Fine, pull it out of my account. Now, when can we get another army of demons? We need it now!"

Dreadnought scratched his head. "Well, I can pull out the troops I sent with your brother if the price is right."

Magnus shrugged his shoulders. "Name it, toothbrush, breath mint, anything."

"My original deal with your brother was a universal credit per demon, but he didn't have it. I'll pull them out if you double it," Dreadnought proposed.

Magnus took a deep breath, "You want fifty-trillion universal credits on the spot so you can give me his army? I could sooner destroy them all with the jelly-tots than buy them off!"

Dreadnought tilted his head. "Your choice. I'm not the one going to the fight. I'm just saying, fifty-trillion credits would give me a better security plan for my immortal life. I could retire and be back on the job in three life-times."

Magnus squeezed his eyes shut and thought aloud,

"Where am I going to get fifty-trillion universal credits in the time it takes to pull the troops out?"

Dreadnought smiled. "How much have you got?"

"Maybe a million, but there's no way I can get even one trillion, let alone fifty."

"What about power?" Dreadnought asked slyly.

Magnus narrowed his eyes. "Why would you want that? You're already immortal. You couldn't possibly need an offensive ability."

Dreadnought smiled. "Well, neither do you, but you have it anyway. I just want to put my name on the universal map, that's all."

Magnus closed his eyes and shook his head, almost laughing at Dreadnought's reason. "You really don't want that."

"That's what your brother said about immortality, yet here I stand," Dreadnought replied dizzily.

Magnus considered. "Have you noticed how unsafe your deals get when you're drunk?"

Dreadnought smacked the remaining beverage in his mouth and continued. "Do we have a deal or not?"

Magnus rolled his eyes and held out his hand. "Deal."

Dreadnought chuckled and shook his hand. Instantly, Dreadnought could feel the strength entering his body. He smiled at the power he received and Magnus pulled away quickly.

"Now, pull those troops out. I need them gone by the time I reach Tyrannus," Magnus ordered and flew away.

Dreadnought smiled and looked over his body. "Well, it feels good. But, how far can take this?" he thought.

*****

Lara was left with little choice. The battle would wage on, with or without her. She let go of Decimus' shirt and watched him fall, fully trusting that his screams would call out to family members. Then she saw three figures coming up. Decimus was easy to see, and Odin carried him by one of his arms. But the third, she couldn't make out. It wasn't until they were hovering in front of her that Lara recognized Odin's daughter carrying Decimus' other arm.

Odin had a firm look on his face. "My time has come. Why are you keeping me here?"

"Valefor has escaped the Underworld. He has killed all of our family, save myself, Magnus and Stratus. He knows we cannot directly strike his immortal soul. Will you help us?" Lara pleaded.

Odin nodded, "Where is he?" he asked.

"In the temple of the Galaxians," Lara explained.

Odin nodded to his daughter who rejoined her peers in the rest of the afterlife. "Lead the way," Odin said.

CHAPTER 6

Stratus warded off the little demons mixing his sword skills with his powers as an elder. Valkyrie and Decimus appeared next to him and joined him. Decimus created an anti-magnetic field around a group of Demons. They bounced into each other and jetted out of the center through a miniature black hole. When Decimus let the field down, he observed what little damage he did. The demons stood back up as if they had just gone on a magnificent ride.

"My powers aren't working!" Decimus called to Stratus.

"Most of them don't on demons. We have to destroy them by the sword," Stratus explained.

"Who thought of the idea to make them immune to us?" Valkyrie asked.

"I don't know, but, their numbers are small. I'm sure we can take these down," Stratus replied.

Suddenly, the barrier of the temple ruptured open, and the rest of the twenty-five trillion demons flooded through the doors and over the wall. The three elders finished off the few that attacked and turned to the barrier. They could barely see one individual demon as they flowed over the wall, blanketing the ground they ran on.

"Valefor, what have you done?" Stratus muttered.

"For the love of everything holy, where did he get them all?" Valkyrie called to Stratus.

Suddenly, Magnus appeared next to them and drew his sword. "We won't have to fight them all," he said. "We only need to keep a fight up long enough for a plan of mine to work." He took the bag of jelly-tots and threw a few in the air. Instantly, they spread into flying cephalopods, squirting acid on portions of the demons that surrounded them.

Stratus turned to Magnus. "What are those?" he called.

Magnus popped a couple in his mouth and chewed as he answered. "Jelly-tots. Just think it and they make it come true?" he replied holding the bag out.

*****

Odin faded into the temple with Lara at his side. Valefor jumped up. "Impossible!" he shouted.

Odin drew his sword. "I have a message from the Father." He brought his sword up and aimed the tip at Valefor. "Vengeance is mine," he growled.

Valefor hid the intimidation and drew his sword. "You won't have much ease in this battle. I've grown more powerful than you can ever know."

"The prophets of time have predicted your doom. No matter how hard you try, you will not defeat me." Odin replied, strongly.

Valefor got down, ready to charge, "Skip the pleasantries! Fight me!" he shouted and rushed up to Odin.

Odin swung high for Valefor's head, but Valefor dodged and sliced through Odin's stomach. The blade went completely through and came out as if Odin wasn't even there. Valefor recovered from the shock and guarded an attack.

Odin stepped forward, backing Valefor against the wall. "You will not defeat me."

Lara disappeared to help the others with the battle against the demons.

Valefor shoved Odin away and glared at him. "Once I'm through with you, your sister will suffer a fate worse than yours."

Odin closed his eyes and entered Valefor's mind, "She is in the protection of the family that you sought to destroy. You will fail." Odin warned.

Valefor gasped when he felt Odin drain him of his power. He did his best to shove Odin out of his mind, but it was too hard. He quickly thought of a distraction to knock Odin out of his head. He sheathed his sword and in his hands, he formed a ball of ice and enveloped it in a shell of fire. He used what energy he had left to throw it directly at Odin. Odin didn't move, never looked, and resisted his urge to defend himself. And just as the ball was inches away from imploding his head, it reversed course.

The ball impaled Valefor's head and threw him back a great distance as ice shards surrounded him and fell on him, with the fireball burning through his skin.

"Did you forget that I am no longer a Dryad?" Odin's voice asked inside Valefor's head.

Valefor stood back up and his injuries healed. His lip curled as he drew back his sword and darted it for Odin's head. Valefor wasn't very surprised when it went straight through and caused Odin no pain. The surprise came when the sword darted back at him. Valefor caught the sword and held it out, reasoning why he couldn't hurt Odin as a soul. When he charged for Odin again, he was thwarted by a huge energy blast that pushed him up in the air. His body twirled uncontrollably and came back down. Just before, he hit the ground, he stopped, hovering over the floor. He looked at Odin, who still had his eyes shut.

"Now that you know that I'm using your tactic against you," Odin reasoned, "the obvious question is, how stable is your concentration compared to mine.

Valefor smiled and waited for Odin to make a move. "You think I want to solidify my manifestation?"

"Concentration makes me impervious to all of your attacks, both physical and mental. I would have expected you to have mastered that by now, brother!"

Odin took his chance. He opened his eyes, pointed his sword at Valefor and swung it once in front of him. A trail of electricity followed his blade, and exploded beneath his opponent. Valefor flew again to the ceiling and the entire roof of the temple erupted. The debris in the air crushed another great portion of the demons.

Odin jumped up and swung his sword again, fighting Valefor on the broken ledge of the remnants of the roof. Valefor's eyes locked with Odin's as they fought, shoving each other along the ledge of the roof. Each move of one being, blocked by the other.

CHAPTER 7

Stratus guarded himself from the debris and pushed some shrapnel down on the demons. Then, he noticed Odin and Valefor fighting on the broken roof. He kicked down the demon he was fighting and watched Odin in the intense battle.

Valkyrie glanced at Stratus and saw a demon attacking his back. She shoved away her attackers with her shield and shouted, "Stratus!"

When Stratus turned around, he saw Valkyrie taking down his attacker. Together, they stood back to back and defended each other from the demons that rushed them.

Decimus grew tired of watching the jelly-tots build a greater kill count than his. He closed his eyes and shifted his body into the figure of the Colossus. His sword grew and became the ax in his hand. The demons stopped in their tracks as Decimus grew and towered over them. Decimus stepped forward and crushed as many demons as he could in one step. He made every step count.

Lara destroyed a few that hopped for her face and shouted to Decimus, "Cheater!"

He turned his head to Lara and started crushing her quarter. Then the flaw to his plan took control of him. The demons that dodged his foot climbed onto it, and crawled their way up his legs. Lara sheathed her sword and jumped for Decimus. Flying in the air, dodging the jelly-tots, she latched onto Decimus' leg and kicked off the demons that tried to crawl past her. Decimus kept walking and Lara leapt from one leg to the other, peeling off the crawling demons. She finished the last one and saw the demons retreating. Magnus swung his sword and watched one demon scream,

"New orders! Into the temple!"

Magnus sighed and let his guard down. "Finally!" he shouted.

The brood of demons scurried away and flooded inside the temple. Decimus returned to his natural form and watched the last of the demons roll on the ground between his legs and run on all fours for the rest of the group. The grass burned under it, leaving a trail of death on the ground. Decimus looked around at the battlefield and saw that all of the grass was dead. They had burned it all.

Stratus and Valkyrie looked at Magnus. "What just happened?" Stratus asked.

Magnus watched Odin and Valefor as he explained. "I bought off the demons from the dealer that Valefor saw and I turned them against him."

The jelly-tots came down and shrunk back to their small bean-like form falling into the bag.

Lara watched the flood of fireballs crawl up the walls of the temple. "Does the word 'holy' mean anything, anymore?" she grunted.

They ran up to the barrier wall and watched the fight at a closer angle. The demons interfered with the fight between Valefor and Odin. One second they would be fighting each other, and the next, they would turn and defend themselves from the demons. Then they would go back to fighting each other.

Valefor shoved Odin to the ground and faded out, off of the planet. Odin stood up and threw the attacking demons aside. He followed after Valefor. Stratus and Decimus quickly faded out followed by Magnus, Valkyrie and Lara.

They all did their best to keep up with Valefor, almost racing each other to get to him. Magnus reached up to Stratus and handed him the bag of jelly-tots and Stratus gave them to Decimus.

Decimus opened the bag and held one in his hand. "What am I supposed to do with them?" he asked.

"You can eat them or tell them to be something," Magnus answered.

Decimus thought hard of what he could use to make the situation progress in his favor. He needed to catch up to Valefor and he needed to do it fast.

He chewed on one and thought, "I need speed."

Instantly, he accelerated five times faster than Valefor traveled. He drew his sword and aimed quickly at Valefor. With all he had in him, he lunged for Valefor, but just as he did, Valefor and Odin disappeared again. There in space, the elders stopped.

"Where did he go?" Stratus asked in surprise, "Where did he go?"

Magnus looked around. "I don't know," he replied panting.

Lara knew where she was, and she knew where they went. "He's in the underworld. They're both in the underworld. Who knows how many souls Valefor has won over and promised freedom. Odin might not come out of there."

Valkyrie sheathed her sword, "Well, we're going after them, right? We're not going to just leave Odin like this."

Stratus looked at Lara and saw that she really didn't want to go. They both knew what they would face and it frightened them both. Magnus almost agreed with them, but he remained loyal to the family.

"We'll go for him," Magnus declared. "Lara, you stay here. You have to stay alive no matter what. Stratus, I need you to help them with the plan."

Stratus concentrated his look at Magnus. "Are you sure? Do you really want to go through with this?" he asked.

Magnus handed Stratus his knife. "There's no avoiding it. Let's just get it over with," he replied.

Stratus looked the blade over. "This isn't star matter, is it?"

Magnus nodded.

"From the Eye of Serius?"

Magnus nodded again.

Stratus felt Lara place her hand on his shoulder and looked into her eyes. She whispered in his mind. "I'll watch over you four."

Magnus drew his sword and prepared for the worst. "Send us there." he ordered.

The four elders grouped together with Magnus up front, the Dryads behind him, and Stratus behind them. Without a word, Lara disappeared and sent them through space to the portal at the other end of the universe, sending them to the underworld.

Stratus opened his hands and blindfolds appeared in both of his hands.

"You two are going to need these." Stratus whispered to the Dryads as he wrapped the blindfolds around their eyes. He took their hands and had them both grip his knife. Valkyrie held the bottom of the hilt with her left hand and Decimus gripped the top of the hilt with his right hand. He took their arms and drove the knife hard through Magnus' back. Magnus lurched forward with the familiar pain of a blade straight through his chest. The Dryads froze in place as the power inside of Magnus flowed through them both. When Magnus was completely dead, the Dryads removed the blindfolds and saw the dead elder hanging from the knife that they held.

They both let go and Stratus caught his brother. He took the knife out of Magnus' back and let him drift into space to the afterlife.

"Goodbye, brother." he whispered.

Decimus and Valkyrie stared at Stratus, wondering what his plan was and how that had to be a part of it.

Stratus looked on to the underworld. "You two are now more powerful than I could ever be. This was your destiny. And now you two will rid the universe of this evil threat forever."

"Will you stay with us?" Valkyrie asked.

Stratus smiled at her. "Of course. I'm not going to leave you alone in this place. You need a guide and I need bodyguards," he chuckled, and subtly saluted his fallen brother. "I'll see you soon."

They landed on a cliff over a dark canvas on-looking the disaster of the prison the Underworld threatened to be. All that could be heard were agonizing echoes. Echoes of pain and suffering of the souls paying their debt for misusing their lives and corrupting their purpose. It was almost a game. Each soul needed more power to take on other, more powerful souls. They chased after souls with smaller power and battled the souls with greater power.

Thunder clapped from the clouded top of the underworld, unwilling to show any light from outside of this prison. There was no hope here. The elders stepped off of the cliff and strategically made their way into the prison of the underworld.

"Odin and Valefor are here somewhere," Stratus whispered.

Valkyrie pointed to the top of the center tower. "Look, he's there!" she called.

They were just inside the barrier of the underworld prison. Stratus drew his sword and watched a group of un-dead dwellers chase two victims along one of the streets of the prison. Cities were scattered across the span of the Underworld as battle maps. The Dryads stayed close behind him. They dodged all the attention that they could and found the entrance to the tower that Odin and Valefor were fighting on top of. Trying to use stealth to their advantage, they quickly and silently climbed up the cells of the prison and traveled over the roof-tops. Hopping from one small construct to the next, over streets flooding with un-dead dwellers, ignoring the screams of the corrupt souls that would soon join them.

Valkyrie suddenly stopped. She looked down and heard a small boy call, "Help me!"

The un-dead dwellers surrounded him and he reached out his hand for Valkyrie.

He stuttered through his pain, "I d … d … don't … want t … t … t … to die ag … g … gain." His speech was slow and proved his mind was not as mature as his age let him on to be. "Please … he … help m … m … me!"

Valkyrie looked at him with the most amount of pity she could give. The boy certainly didn't look like he belonged here, but somehow the universe deemed him worthy of everlasting pain.

A hulking soul darted around the street. It had just fed on a victim and still could not sate his need for more power. He found the boy and attacked. But the boy struck with his claws and ripped the brute to shreds, eating the body and in-taking all of his power.

Stratus stood next to Valkyrie on the roof of another cell. "His name is Icarus. It would be best to not attract his attention, even with the power you've accumulated," Stratus explained.

Then, they heard the screeching of an un-dead dweller that had chosen them as a target. The wailing of the un-dead gained the attention of the every other soul within earshot. Stratus and Valkyrie leapt again over the streets, across the gaps, and over the roof-tops heading quickly to the tower.

The street cleared and they saw their straight shot to the door at the bottom of the tower. Decimus was already there, holding the door open for them and watching out for anyone or anything that wanted them as a meal. Valkyrie and Stratus dove from the tops of the cells and ran down the streets where the riot of un-dead chased after them. They screamed and squabbled at each other, racing for the new meat.

Finally, Valkyrie and Stratus reached the tower door and ran in, locking it behind them. The dark tower had light towards the top where the windows began halfway up the tower. Outside, they could hear the clamor of the un-dead souls pounding on the walls and piling over each other to get in first. The three elders started their way up the spiraling staircase. They ran up the tall tower and aimed for the light. Their steps echoed through the tower and their breaths were sharp and muffled out any other sounds from the outside. Then, one sound rudely interrupted their run as they were halfway up. The door to the tower fell in and the barking and squabbling of un-dead souls rushed inside the tower. All of the souls followed the ones in front up the staircase, and a multitude of un-dead souls lost their balance and fell from the staircase. As the line of un-dead drew ever closer to the three elders that kept running, the staircase seemed to rain un-dead, even from the higher points of the tower.

The elders closed the top doors and were happy to escape the bombardment. Now they watched the fight above them. On the rooftop of the tower, Valefor and Odin were locked in battle. They must have killed each other numerous times already. Their battle was no longer limited to the pain their swords would inflict on each other. They poured their emotional power into their attacks. Where Valefor struck with anger and malice, Odin struck with passion and an undying need for justice.

Valefor knew that Odin wasn't powerful enough to destroy him, and Odin knew Valefor was losing power with each passing moment of the fight. They both reasoned that only one champion could possibly take this battle.

Stratus brought the two Dryads together and whispered, "It'll take both of you to bring Valefor to his demise."

Valkyrie lifted her shield and blocked an energy blast. "Is this the best idea you've got?"

Decimus drew his sword. "She has a good point. But the elders saw fit to call on us for a reason." He looked at Valkyrie. "We can handle it," he said strongly.

Valkyrie turned her head to Decimus. "I don't know that we can. Even then, when we killed Magnus we took on the powers of half of the elders or less. What happens when we take it all on. Can we handle that?"

Stratus placed his hand on Valkyrie's shoulder, "If he kills the last of the elders, the universe will envelop and explode within itself because of the unbalanced power. He is not the only evil of his kind, but we are the last of the good. If you two are destroyed and he inherits your power, then I'll be all there is. And I can't go up against him as I am. I do not have the power."

Valkyrie turned away and looked at Decimus.

Stratus continued. "Now is the best time. Now is the only time. He is distracted, and you have all the time you need. If you don't do it, and Odin fails, then who can? Once one of them dies, the one still alive will be able to banish them to whatever world and plane they want."

Decimus glanced at Odin slipping around Valefor and he turned to Valkyrie. "We can't let Odin be taken here. And we can't let Valefor become the source of ultimate Evil in the universe. It's up to us," he called.

Valkyrie thought and listened to the sound of the two spirits battling. Then the door to the ceiling started pounding. The un-dead had reached the top and were trying to get to the other elders. Valkyrie stood and faced the two spirits. They both attacked Valefor on either side of Odin. Valefor warded off Decimus and pushed Odin to the ground. Valkyrie flipped over Valefor and swiped for his back, but Valefor brought his blade over his head and down his spine, completely defending his back. Decimus got back to the fight and sliced for Valefor's gut. But before he could get his sword in full motion, Valefor kicked Decimus in the face, forcing him to the ground.

Odin got back up and wiped the blood from his lip. Completely free to attack, Valefor took advantage of the moment and drew back his sword.

Stratus jumped up. "Odin! Guard!" he cried.

Odin spun to the side and Valefor's sword lunged just next to Odin's arm. Valefor reached around with his other hand and took Odin's sword from him.

Valefor laughed. "You've lost your concentration, Odin. And you've given me full control. The battle is now mine."

"Not yet!" Odin shouted back.

The Dryads thrust their blades in on both sides of Valefor and Odin fought hard and fast to keep his front guard down. Stratus drew his sword and stepped in front of his foe, between Valefor and Odin. He handed Odin his sword and waited for Valkyrie to catch Valefor's flaw in his low guard. As soon as she noticed, she could have his entire arm off. Neither of the Dryads dared to risk letting Valefor have the upper hand by lowering their guard and using their powers of meditation. They all knew this fight would have to end by the sword.

Decimus jumped up and pressed down on Valefor, just as Valkyrie lifted her shield and was knocked to the ground by Valefor's side strike. Valefor pushed Decimus away, brought the two swords together and lunged for Stratus, stabbing the blades completely through Stratus and Odin. Both elders lurched and gasped in pain.

Then, the Dryads brought their swords back and severed Valefor's now solidified abdomen, spilling his organs onto the ground. All of the elders paused as the power rushed through Valefor, then, from his body to the Dryads. They could all feel the energy searching and finding the most powerful end of the fatal train of death.

Valefor was drained of power and in unison, the Dryads drove Valefor to the ground and chanted, "We banish you, Valefor, to eternal exile in the Underworld."

Valefor screamed in agony and his skin began to crack as if a tree under extreme pressure. Through the cracks of skin, dark blue and black light breached out of his body. As the cracks bled and stretched across Valefor's body, the skin broke away and shattered. Finally, Valefor's body burst, and all that was left was a shrieking lost soul dissolving to nothing.

The two Dryads sheathed their swords and looked back at the last elders. But where Stratus and Odin were supposed to be, all that was present were their swords lying on the ground.

Decimus picked up the Chevron and looked at Valkyrie. "We've done it," he sighed.

Valkyrie glanced back at him, "Yes, we have," she whispered back.

The door to the tower burst opened and the un-dead beings rushed to the outside of the tower. But when they searched for their targets, they found nothing.

*****

Decimus returned to the point in space that Lara was left waiting for them, but Valkyrie wasn't there. Decimus looked to see if she had fallen behind, but not even her trail was visible.

Decimus turned back to Lara. "I'm going back. I have to find her," he said.

Lara gripped his arm. "Decimus, no. Valefor has taken her. And if you try to rescue her, you won't survive."

Decimus relaxed and completely faced Lara, "What do you mean 'Valefor has taken her'? She and I both just killed him. We watched him die."

Suddenly, a ray of light flashed behind Lara, and in the harsh beam appeared the image of Odin and Stratus.

"I'm ready," Odin said.

Lara took the Chevron, turned around and took Odin's hand. "Come, I'll take you back as I promised," she said. She glanced at Decimus. "Follow me," she ordered. All of the elders dashed through space back to the afterlife, where the dark starless space devoured them and the portal to the afterlife opened. They all stepped on the cliff over the funnel of souls. Odin stood at the edge of the cliff and looked down.

"Jade, I've returned. We'll be together at last. Just guide me to you," Odin whispered.

Jade's ghostly soul rose from the funnel and met him at the edge of the cliff. "Odin?"

"Yes, Jade. I'm back."

"You're not the lower being that you were before," Jade replied.

Odin shook his head and turned to Lara. "Is that the truth?"

Suddenly, Stratus floated up over the elders and the funnel of souls. His arms stretched out and he lifted to the funnel where the souls of the elders twirled and twisted above the funnel of the lower beings.

Lara shook her head. "Complications arose. We had to break some rules to bring you back. You will live again," she told Odin. "When you live, your birthright will be yours again. A gift from us for your work today."

Odin smiled at Jade and stepped off the cliff. Together, they descended down the funnel and through the bright end of it to be reincarnated. Lara and Decimus left the afterlife and headed for Hajun.

They stood at the top of the mountain and watched the plague dissipate. They felt the gusts of wind pull on them and attempt to whip them off their feet.

Decimus looked at Lara, "You said that Valefor had taken Valkyrie. How could he have her if we killed him? And where has he taken her?"

Lara didn't waste time and began to explain "The very evil that took control of Valefor has passed along with the power trail to Valkyrie. She is now the new host for Valefor, and I don't believe she can be saved."

Decimus shook his head. It was something he could not allow. He wouldn't. His breathing grew deeper inside him and he tried his hardest to sense where she was. Spreading his concentration to the ends of space and searching every speck of dust in each nebula, he found her.

He could feel her struggling against the power. He could hear her screaming to be set free. She was hurting, the pain was immense. Then the discouragement overwhelmed her. The thought of there being no hope, no escape, it consumed her to the point of complete submission.

"I'm coming for you, Valkyrie. Don't you give up on me yet," he thought.

He stood up and faded out, off of Hajun. Lara followed. "Where are you going?" she begged.

"I'm going to rescue Valkyrie. She needs me, and I need her," he declared.

She caught up to him and looked into his eyes. "She's not the same, Decimus. She's conquering every evil source until she becomes the last one. She's feeding the parasite and making sure that she is the only source of evil in the universe. Once that happens, she will be unstoppable," Lara explained.

Decimus' eyes didn't falter. "I'll find a way to stop her," he growled.

Lara moved in front of him. "No, Decimus. You don't understand. You're on a very short time limit. When she becomes the only source of evil, she will be the only thing that balances the forces of the universe. If you kill her then, or destroy the evil inside of her, the universe will begin to unfold and we'll all die."

Decimus stopped and stared at Lara. "So, now there's too much good in the universe? Somehow that doesn't sound quite right. Meanwhile, the only person I care about is about to be brought to shambles all because some evil parasite stole ..."

"I know it's hard to take in all at once!" Lara didn't give him the chance to explain his emotions. She knew that he would just have to understand. "I know, it's harsh. But you need to think this through. You can afford one move. One play. If you go in on your own without a plan, you will have wasted your only chance to win. Take your time. Think it through. Don't fall for a trap of odds because you want to rescue the one you love."

Decimus leaned forward with a glare. "Have you forgotten who I am? I'm the last scion. Fighting for love and surviving against all odds runs in the family." And with that, he beamed out following Valkyrie's trail.

CHAPTER 8

Valkyrie stood on the planet Omega V searching for the enemy of time itself: Omega. It felt only natural to Valefor to search Omega out. If she was correct in her assumptions, Omega would either be here on this planet, or something very important to the Omega plan would be here in his place. Valkyrie knew what was going on here and felt that somehow, she would have to stop both Omega and Valefor at the same time.

"I'm not strong enough, Decimus," she whispered through thought. "I need you."

In her mind, she saw Decimus standing behind her, holding her. Through the ages, no force was powerful enough to keep them apart, and now he could see that he wasn't able to save her this time. Yet he let her know that he was still coming for her. But there in front of them, Valefor stood in the shadows. His glowing red eyes opened, revealing his position in her mind. His form was clouded, as were his intentions.

"Why are you doing this to me?" Valkyrie asked.

The cloud of darkness surrounded them, but those red eyes never moved. The deep, raspy voice spoke, "I have only recently discovered my true function. I am to do your job for you and destroy all other evil forces in the universe. I am finished waiting for you, the elders, the gods of time, to accomplish this for me. I am taking matters into my own hands, thus, holding the balance of the universe as one of those matters taking. My first task is to destroy the Omega Concept."

"What is the Omega Concept?" Valkyrie asked.

The red eyes blinked, and from the cloud extended a ghostly hand. The image of a planetary system appeared, revolving over his hand. The planets were scattered in their orbits around their star, and the planet closest to the star was pulsing an aura of energy that disappeared as it passed the outer plants to the rest of the universe.

"The system in the center of the universe. It is called the Omega system. This system has the only satellite in existence that, as a planet, was born instead of sculpted into existence, completely formed by the will of a deadly race: the Omega race. The other planets in the system are constructed of individual elements. The star being the element of fire by hydrogen. Omega I, completely made of every kind of stone, Omega II, liquid needed for most organisms to survive. Omega III, every kind of metal. Common molecules found in the air and atmosphere of all worlds supporting life is Omega IV. Omega V supports it's own resources as an ark for the most common fauna and flora in the universe. Omega VI is dead planet. At its hollow core is an outlet of the afterlife, the elements of life and death. The electro-movement and passing of the souls that leave the afterlife is the guiding light of this system.

Finally, the planet that was created by the Omega race: the igniter. It is the closest planet to the star. As the planets align, they strengthen and intensify the guiding track for the Omega concept's target." Above Valefor's hand, the planets that revolved over it slowly straightened to alignment. "When each planet is aligned on one side of the star, and the igniter is on the opposite side to the planets, its energy will spark the star and Omega will follow the radiated energy along its track across the planets, seeking out any planet in its way with the elements specified in its own planetary system. Once Omega's energy beam reaches the Omega VI, it broadens its reach, following the movement of the souls. Its target is every element the energy beam meets in its system. This makes it a universal threat and I must destroy it."

Decimus kept hold of Valkyrie in his arms, but his eyes burned at Valefor. "You can do what you wish with Omega, but you cannot take Valkyrie as a host to do your bidding," Decimus growled.

Valefor's hand recoiled and his eyes blinked. "She does not have a choice. She is now my vessel and I will do what I must to fulfill my mission. You cannot stop me." The red eyes closed, but only the dark cloud remained.

Valkyrie turned around. "Decimus, don't leave me here. I can't fight him alone."

Decimus shushed her. "I'm not going anywhere. I'm staying right here. We'll get through this together," he assured her holding on to her.

*****

Decimus tracked Valefor all the way to the Omega system. He could see that the last five planets had already aligned and the first planet had only about half of a cycle to join the other planets in alignment. He had to think of something, and he knew the answer was in the system's star. He quickly faded onto Omega V and sought out Valefor.

Trees were everywhere, on one huge mass of land that covered half the planet. The water that resided on this planet bled through the land and covered the other half of the planet. Although he had never been here before, his thoughts were always with her. His steps were demanding of the ground to guide him, and he would settle for nothing less than respect from the native dangers. His eyes that burned were fixed ahead of him, and they never turned away from Valkyrie's call.

He carried his anger with him through the forests of Omega V.

Valkyrie dashed through the woods and up the cold mountains. Somehow, Valefor helped her and guided her through all the difficulty of the travel. Once they reached the top of the mountain, night had covered most of the sky, but the planets themselves were still visible. All four were aligned, and the planet behind the star was blocked by the star's light. But Valefor could feel the presence of Omega inside that planet. Valkyrie reached to the sky and, using her Elderly powers, she attempted to quell the machine. Over and over, she did everything she could from the outside, but Valefor knew with Valkyrie's power alone he couldn't destroy Omega. Even with the machine down, Omega would find some way of rebuilding it and destroying the universe further into the future.

Decimus stepped out of the forest and saw the mountains ahead. Valkyrie was up there, he knew. From where he stood, he could pinpoint her exact location. He closed his eyes, and quietly meditated. His spine grew new bones as he concentrated. Between his shoulder-blades he could feel the new muscles and new structure growing into the wings of a mighty seraph. As the muscular masses stretched across his body, a wave of feathers fell along the muscles and in seconds he was in the air. His wings beat the air, lifting him up higher and soon over the tops of the mountains. As he soared, the wind knocked against him, and threw his body from side to side, but his wings stayed true to their course.

Then, he saw Valkyrie reaching towards the sky, her hair flew with the wind, and her heavenly gown flapped. Her fingers curled as if she were trying to gain control. Decimus swooped down and gracefully landed behind her.

"Valefor!" Decimus called.

Valkyrie dropped her arms and turned to Decimus, drawing her sword and shield. "Valkyrie is mine. I will do what I must to destroy Omega," she growled.

Decimus drew his sword, ready for the fight on the mountain tops. "Then we'll settle this with our swords!"

Decimus swung high and their swords met. Valkyrie swung low for his legs. He quickly brought his body up and caught a small current with his wings, floating slowly over Valkyrie. Valkyrie spun around and sliced for his feet, but Decimus closed his wings and flipped back to the ground. He blocked a blow to his face, then a blow to his abdomen. He dodged a lunge and blocked a swing. Decimus spun around and regained his composure. He aimed the tip of the sword at Valkyrie's face. Valkyrie knocked his sword away and sliced for his stomach. Decimus jumped back, swung low, then high, then low blocking every move.

"You will not keep me from my task!" she growled.

"No, I won't!" he called back. "I can help you. I can assist you in pulverizing this evil. Just tell me what I must do."

Valkyrie, looked at him shocked, then took a step back and sheathed her sword, standing up straight. "Omega is fighting against my hold.

You must take him inside of yourself and relinquish his hold on the machine. Then we can demolish it from both inside and out." Then Valkyrie's voice called inside of Decimus' head. "No!

You'll be Omega's vessel!"

Decimus knew that he only had few minutes to spare until the ignitor sparked the star with the electrical current, freeing Omega to conquer the universe. He calmly reassured her.

"Then we'll have to see what happens when he does."

Decimus slid his sword into its sheath, spread his wings and rushed off the mountain. Beating his wings in the air once again, he shot through the sky towards the igniter. As he reached the tip of the sky, his wings fell away and he beamed himself to the machine planet, fading inside of the very center. The dark cloud, Omega, surrounded him. He could feel the pressure of Omega constricting on him. Instead of fighting it, Decimus took control and forced Omega inside of his consciousness, giving Omega no choice but to accept Decimus as his host.

When Decimus felt the full strength of Omega inside of him, he took the planet, using his energy to empower his grip, and ripped the planet in from the inside as Valefor crushed it from the outside. When the igniter was completely demolished to a hunk of drifting scrap metal, he beamed back to Omega V and faded back behind Valkyrie. Omega was taking control. Valkyrie dropped her arms and leaned over, panting. Before Omega had total control, Decimus called out to Lara, giving her their position. She was close, and ready to do what she had to do, as was Decimus. He silently stepped closer to Valkyrie, drawing his sword. He came up right behind her, wrapping his arms around her, and pulling the sword in through the front of her stomach towards the spine. He locked her body in on the sword by running the blade through his own and holding them both in.

"I'm sorry, Valkyrie." Decimus whispered.

Valkyrie brought her hands up to Decimus' and took the hilt of the blade with him. Together, they fell to the ground, trembling as the cold blade shredded the skin when they jolted on the snow. Decimus held Valkyrie one more time as Omega took complete control. Valefor seeped away from Valkyrie's body, back into space as the dark cloud that he was. Omega knew that if he wanted to bring the universe to it's final end, as instructed, he would need to remove Valefor from the path of fate. Omega also knew, in order to strike at Valefor before he got away, he would have to leave the body behind. Following Valefor into space, the two mystical beings did their battle away from the planets.

And so it is as it was, Valefor and Omega are locked in a battle in time and space, and shall remain rivals in an endless war until the day of Ragnorak.

Lara faded onto Omega V, on the mountain top where Valkyrie and Decimus lay dying. She rushed to them and knelt next to them. Pulling the sword from their bodies, and throwing it to the ground, the two elders didn't make a sound. Lara touched them both, they were cold, more from the snow and winds from the mountain's heights, but it didn't help to stop the suffering.

Lara placed her hands tightly on each wound, concentrated, and used her power to heal them. The process was slow, but Lara could feel them beginning to heal.

Decimus turned to Valkyrie. "I'm sorry," he repeated.

Valkyrie couldn't stop shaking from the cold and the pain. She managed to take Decimus's hand. Her trembling lips moved but nothing came out. Decimus knew exactly what she was saying. He closed his eyes and thought to her, "I love you, too."

Lara couldn't heal them fast enough, and she felt their energy diminishing. She grunted, "You two are the most powerful beings in any universe. Surely you can heal yourselves! Or, at least heal each other. A mere stab to the stomach has you down? Get up! Use your energy! Use my energy! Heal yourselves!"

Decimus looked at Lara. "We need more power. Omega and Valefor drained us of ours when they left. If we use yours, you'll die. It's be too much for you."

Lara shook her head. "Then use mine. Use it all. Take it. You two can be the new Keeper's of the Souls. Fulfill the prophecy. Be the new order that you were meant to be."

Decimus didn't question her, knowing that this was what Lara wanted. He pulled Lara down, and Valkyrie closer, and held them both. Together, using Lara's energy, and adding it to their own, they healed each other. The energy forces passed between their own bodies of energy, and the overload quickened the pace. But, as they used more and more, both Valkyrie and Decimus could feel Lara becoming more transparent. Her energy dissipated until she was nothing more than a soul. Decimus and Valkyrie stood up and guided her to the afterlife at the end of the universe. They passed the stars and galaxies and entered the darkness at the edge of the universe. The portal opened and the three entities entered the afterlife. Standing on the great precipice, above the spiral of souls, below the twirl of the elders, Lara rose up and joined the other elders in their sleepy flight, forever resting in peace.

Decimus and Valkyrie left to build a new court, a new fantasy, a new age: The age of the New Order. Never again, will they commit the sins of the Father.

*****

On Hajun, a small boy sat alone at the end of a play table, outside in a meadow. A girl ran up for him, laughing and singing. She twirled and danced in the grass with the rest of the children of her class. The boy brought his wooden sword from the sash on his back, and placed it on the table. Quoting the stories his family and teacher told, Pargon boomed to his imaginary friends, "I make this case for speculation. If anyone of you holds a grudge against me personally, please do not fear to speak now. But if anyone can prove your cases against my blade and armor, let them speak and I will surrender all points and my campaign."

Book III

AS IT IS WRITTEN

CHAPTER 1

"Shall we begin again?"

Pargon awoke, screaming in pain. He wrestled against the straps of the torture bed with his teeth gnashing at the moonlight of the dungeon. Finally, he surrendered and rested to catch his breath.

"Where were you three nights ago?"

"I told you, already. I was in my bed."

"The evidence suggests otherwise," the masked torturer stretched Pargon's body on the rack. "You will tell us the truth, or you are going to die. The choice is yours."

Pargon gritted his teeth and groaned louder. When the rack loosened, he sobbed, but no tears fell. "I was home, sleeping. I don't know how my weapon got to that house. I've never been there." What Pargon was hiding was far more villainous for which the penalty was a fate worse than torture or death. "I swear, I was home," he lied.

"A man who swears on a lie is a dead man. Tell the truth and this torture will end. It is as simple as that."

Pargon slowly shook his head and balled his fists. He continued to fight back the tears and his heart beat like a drum. On the other end of the room, another member of the torture party brought a small table with a cloth covering it.

"I have never been a burglar. My accuser is lying."

"Your accuser is a trusted soldier in the ranks. He has no motive to create such a falsehood."

"Then, I have the right to face him directly as I am a former soldier."

"You waived those rights the moment you robbed his house," the torturer explained as he received a wrapped package from a messenger in a cloak. "However, you do have the right to receive letters from loved ones." The torturer opened the note and looked it over. "I'll have to read this to you, given the current circumstances, you understand.

'Dearest Odin, I will wait for you for as long as I can. Until my bones give way and my body quakes, I will not give up on you. I long for the nights that we can be together again. I yearn to be held in your arms again and feel your lips on mine. And until that day comes, my heart remains yours, as always. Forever and only your beloved Jade.'"

Pargon closed his eyes and let out what air was in his lungs. His pointed ears filed back against his head.

"What does it mean?" the torturer asked, presenting the letter as further evidence. "You have no mate to speak of. What does this mean?"

"Obviously, the messenger has the wrong package for the wrong receiver."

"Odin has been dead for almost two-hundred years. This is some kind of code and you know exactly what it means."

Of course, Pargon knew exactly who had sent it and what it meant. Mercy, the one Dryad who could get Pargon out of this burglary farce, had just sealed his doom with a love letter. And if word had reached ears of a prefect that Mercy had committed adultery with Pargon, then she would share in his fate.

The torturer sighed in aggravation, "tell me what the letter means, or we will have to begin the second course."

"I don't know what it means."

"Bring me the heart-stone," the torturer commanded.

The second member was quick to carry over the covered table. The torturer pulled off the cloth, revealing a hairy, glowing, red stone on a platter next to other torture tools. "These stones have many uses. They keep you from dying until I command otherwise. They force the truth from your lips. I've heard they can drive you mad with rage and augment your powers. Ultimately, they make you the perfect tool of destruction."

Pargon glared at the stone and turned his angry gaze on the torturer. "This sort of treatment cannot be ordained by the prophets."

"It is not," he said and took off his mask. It was Cain, Mercy's lifemate. "But, I reminded the council of a number of debts that they owed me. They are granting me some.. special permissions."

Pargon's eyes turned red with tears that were hard to fight.

"Tell me what the letter means, or this stone will kill you slowly and painfully."

"It means that Aries has found our home," Pargon blurted out, letting his mouth operate on it's own, "and it is up to me and my company to stop him. Had the letter been a death threat to Odin from Magnus, then the Ancient Ones would have succeeded and we wouldn't have to worry about another power occupying our grounds."

Cain smiled. "Your friends from Ferron are causing trouble again? Spreading rumors of rogue gods and a coming fire? I heard you talk of them in the ranks, but now I'm beginning to believe you really are insane."

It was all Pargon could do to keep the truth hidden. But, Cain picked up the knives and sharpened them on an iron.

"I told you what you wanted to know, what are you planning?"

"I am removing your heart and replacing it with the heart-stone. The prophets will want their weapon."

Pargon wrestled with the straps again. "I told you, I'm innocent!"

"I know," Cain replied with no emotion in his tone.

"Then, why-"

"I planted your weapon at the scene of the crime. I brought you here to torture you on my own terms and I alone will see the council's will be done."

"You? You did this-"

"You laid with my wife! You took her as your own. I was your friend and ally. I fought for you in the ranks; bled for you and killed beside you. And now, I am going to end you."

Pargon closed his eyes again and waited. "For Mercy's sake, don't let them-"

"There is a Dryad company already taking her into custody. She will die like the rest. You, however, are the right hand of the counsel. Whatever task they have for you, I was promised it will be your doom."

Without a second word or thought, Cain sliced Pargon's flesh from the navel to the sternum. The transplant had begun. Pargon fell unconscious as soon as his heart was removed.

*****

The angel fell from the skies above Ferron. He could see the tops of the trees through all the spinning. He spread his wings and tried to catch the up-drafts and wind currents. His wings stretched, and finally, he stopped spinning. He flapped hard trying not to fall any faster. Then a gust of wind picked him up and he soared over the tops of the trees, searching for the pool of fresh water. The open area in the woods, where trees surrounded it, was the meeting place, he knew. Finally, he saw where the trees parted and the water sank from clear to dark blue towards the center of the spring. He gracefully swooped in and landed at the edge of the pool.

The sky was dark, and the fairies and sprites lit the woods with their trails. The water glimmered with excitement and the fairies danced around happily. He tucked his wings back and stepped forward, towards the pool. He saw the patch of hair floating out on the water. Then the head came up, followed by small shoulders that the beautiful hair fell on. He smiled as the nymph stepped up to the surface. The flowers were braided into her hair and a small band of daisies were her crown. The nymph opened her eyes and looked on the angel with love. But, when she saw the ripped robes and tattered armor, she winced. She stepped up to him, with compassion and pity in her heart, and touched his face. As her fingertips met his cheek, he turned away.

"This is my doing." she whispered.

The angel softly touched the back of her hand and held it to his face. "Our doing. And I would gladly do it again."

"Why is this so hard?" the nymph asked.

"I don't know, Pandora. But, I'm not giving up. There's no turning back now," he replied.

She took his hand and led him into the deeper waters. As the small waves kissed their arms, he held her hand. She leaned back and they waded there in the pool. His magnificent wings flapped softly in the water, keeping him straight up. They closed their eyes and listened to the fairies dancing around the spring.

They woke the next morning on the side of the pool, wrapped in the feathery cocoon his wings provided. Pandora opened her eyes and heard giggling. She looked down and saw that the wings covered her whole body, except for her feet. She silently groaned, knowing full well that her sisters found out about her. She lifted his wing from her body and squinted her eyes at the sunlight.

"Pandora, you've been naughty," the first sister said, insinuating everything she could about the situation.

"You said he was an angel, but you didn't say he was an actual angel," the second nymph giggled jealously.

Pandora pointed her finger. "He is not for you two. This is the one that I'm not willing to share," she said sternly.

The other sisters giggled and stood up. "Come on. Frolic with us," one offered.

Pandora lay back down on her angelic lover's chest. "Oh, but I'm comfortable here."

The second sister cupped her hands together. "Please," she begged. "We have to frolic. I need to frolic."

Pandora groaned and got up with a smile. She touched his face and joined her sisters as they skipped merrily through the woods.

He opened his eyes and stretched his wings on the ground, welcoming the morning star on his chest. Suddenly, another figure appeared above him; a figure he knew he wouldn't like.

"You just had to take the bait, didn't you? You sacrificed your life's work for this nymph. One that would giggle at your affection for her and just as quickly move on to the next," the figure taunted.

The angel got up. "You shouldn't be here, Fang. With the dragons and minotaurs on the loose in these woods, you're only one Centurion. Searching me out isn't worth it."

Fang laughed. "Of course, you're right. But what about you, Eon? Your weapons have been taken, your status shot by your own arrows of love. It seems that you are nothing more than a bird of prey in the woods. Can you handle the woods of Ferron?"

Eon's wings curled back around his shoulders. "I have more than you think I do," he replied confidently.

Fang stamped his hooves. "I hope so, for your sake. The masters of darkness are not as merciful as the evils that have been seen here before. The Ancient Ones won't help you here now. The elders have all disappeared, and the only protector we have is Odin's spirit. Sometimes even that isn't enough." He galloped away.

Eon looked up to the sky. "Odin's coming back. I know that much," he whispered.

*****

Concealed in the shadows of the mountains of ages, what was once a sacred fortress of safety for the great beings of old, now holds a new terror within the caverns. From the depths of the caves, far below the very surface of Gorin, nine dark witches leapt from the ground. Taking refuge in a dead dragons lair, they plotted their next move on the planet.

Suddenly, one of these witches shrieked in pain. Covering her eyes and adapting to her vision, she described to the others what she saw, "I see light. It comes on wings from the heavens. The relentless young fool will be our undoing. He strikes in anger against us all, in retribution of a sin against him." She turned to the others who were staring at her. "He will make us all wish for the Niki Tiki."

When the witches heard of their coming demise, they all joined in moaning and groaning, shouting at each other, "For the sake of all unspeakable death! To save us all from weeping and gnashing of teeth! Find him and destroy him!" They dashed from the caves at lightning speed, using dark magic to strengthen their search.

CHAPTER 2

When he awoke this last time, Pargon lay before the council, maimed and dazed. Cain gripped his arm and hoisted him up to present him to the prophets.

"Pargon," the verdict was read from a script, "we sentence you to five years aboard the floating prison off the coast of Ferron. By the power and authority of this great hall, we banish you from our village as a dangerous being. Word will be sent to our neighboring villages that you and your company of misfits are not to be trusted. No doubt, your friends will be hunted down and destroyed in the time you spend in prison." A messenger handed the lead council member a letter from behind him. As he read, he passed it to the members on the right, and then the left. "We have just received word that Aries has returned and is plaguing the land. You will go to destroy him. The woman, Mercy, will take your sentence in your place. Should you have anything to say, now is the time."

Pargon could do little more than hunch over in pain from the heartstone in his chest. He strained to look up at the council as he spoke. "I will defeat Aries, and I'll take her sentence for myself, as if she were not a willing party. It means nothing to you who the debt is paid by as long as it is paid. Allow me to pay this debt to society."

"If she did not want to be a guilty party, then she should not have been a guilty party. That aside, this task is folly by nature. You only need to go and die. That is all."

Cain finally spoke. "Nobel council members, Mercy is my life-mate. If it pleases the council, I will punish her as the teachings conduct, as long as this wretch serves the sentence he has volunteered for."

The prophets glanced and nodded at each other to confirm a consensus and the sentence was changed. "The council agrees. Take him away."

Cain took Pargon from the great hall and marched him away from the village. Once outside the boundaries, Cain unshackled Pargon.

"Your arms and armor are in a hole near the mountains of the Pegasus' with a banner marking the stash. Go, and do not return."

Pargon, still, could only hunch over as he walked. Of all the emotional outbursts that were on his mind, he could only bring himself to thank Cain for keeping Mercy out of prison.

"The next time you choose to take a mans life-mate as your own, rethink your decision," Cain replied with his sword drawn.

*****

Atop the mountains, at the highest point, overlooking the village and the dune sea, just barely seeing the rest of the ruins of Magnus' realm decompose, Eon glided over the tree tops, watching and waiting for the ambassador of the Vamps to appear. Then Eon stopped and floated just above the drop of the mountain ranges. The black figure with scaly, bat-like wings came down from the skies. Every feature about this figure was dark. Not a single shade of any color other than black or brown. His eyes were night, and his hair was black wool. Only his teeth of red and yellow gave this figure color. His wings were covered in cloth, and the dark robe concealed his skin from the light. Eon gulped hard at facing the Vamp.

The Vamp hissed, "You called?"

Eon shuddered at the Vamp's voice. "Yes. I am now the leader of of my own army of Angels. I take orders from no one. Do with the Ancient ones as you wish, and never show your faces in the galaxy again."

The Vamp growled, "You know that we cannot travel among the stars as the Ancient Ones do. We only declare war on intruders such as yourselves."

Eon wouldn't let him finish. "And we declare war on all evil, such as yourselves. You have no right to take the good captive to your liking. There are so many other options for you to choose from. Leave innocents out of your conquest."

"Why do you think we sought out the Ancient Ones? If we win, we're fed forever. If we lose, our hunger is stopped by our death. We have nothing to lose," the Vamp replied.

Eon frowned. "That's a very victimizing way to go. Are all demons of your realm so quick to give up?"

The Vamp smirked. "We cannot be good, we will not be evil. What other options are there than death?"

"It's a wonder you haven't tried feeding off of each other," Eon commented.

The Vamp wasn't impressed. "Unless you've come to discuss a treaty and possibly a surrender, I'm through with hearing your slander."

Eon saw that the Vamp was waiting for a reply and shoved the last words out. "The people of this planet are good. They are innocent and know nothing of absolute corruption. Propriety is the style of living. Lust has no meaning. This world can do very little against dangers like your kind. I and my armies have taken this planet under our protection until Odin and the elders return. Unless you want an all out attack on your kind here, you will search elsewhere for feeding grounds."

The Vamp tilted its head. "Surely there has to be one lost soul on this planet that causes nothing but pain and suffering to the village. An outcast or criminal that we can put out of misery," his raspy voice suggested.

Eon closed his eyes. "If you find joy in feeding on Minotaurs or Dragons, I suggest you leave this world before either you die of starvation or I kill you myself."

The Vamp felt nothing but apathy. "Setting aside the fact that I have a job to do, I want you to know, we don't only take the good. We take whomever we can in the moment of absolute brink. No one person or thing is special."

The Vamp pounded its wings in the air and lifted back to the skies. Eon thought about how the Vamp could travel in daylight without dying, and he wondered if more would come out and face the ultraviolet beams. If that could happen, then a new breed of killers had already been born. If not now, then they were soon to come.

Eon glanced out across the tree tops. The winds brushed the trees back and revealed a purple and blue figure rushing through the trees in his direction. The object was inaudible, and no specific feature could be determined because of its speed. Eon didn't know what it was, but he knew he didn't like it. Closing his wings, he darted to the bottom of the mountain and glided back to Ferron. The evening star was setting, and Pandora would be waiting for him.

*****

Sashi lay on his bed wheezing through his beard. Fang trotted in and bowed.

"My lord," Fang began, "there's something you should know."

Sashi laughed weakly. "I know that I'm dying. That's enough for me."

"Sire, your sons were murdered … All of them," Fang explained.

Sashi let his breath go. "I no longer have an heir?"

"That is correct. Your highness, you must select someone to succeed you before you pass."

Sashi turned his head with a tear rolling down his beard. "Fang. The throne is yours. You know what to do. Unite the under powers. Bring them together." Sashi placed his hand on Fang's shoulder. "Shine the light for the New Kingdom."

Fang gripped Sashi's hand and held it. "I promise, my king; your vision will not die with you. I will press it on into the future."

On that day, Sashi died grieving the deaths of his three sons. In his dying breath, he asked the elders to avenge his sons and to help the New Kingdom to prosper. Sashi's name was written in history and will be remembered until the end of time as the peacemaker.

*****

Eon watched the Vampires surrounding him and Pandora. They swirled in and perched on the trees around the pools. Their wings were all bat-like and their mouths were foaming in hunger. Eon hadn't realized that all of the Vamps had grown wings of their own.

An angel and a nymph would be extremely satisfying after so long without food. The Vamps growled as Eon and Pandora waded back to the deeper ends of the pool. Terrified, Pandora held close to Eon, while Eon thought of a way out.

With no other alternative, Eon spread his wings and shouted, "Legion!" his voice echoed through the woods and thunder clapped at his spirit. In the sky, the army of angels that came in loyalty to Eon fell on the army of the Vamps and began their massacre. Eon stared into the eyes of the ambassador that he spoke with before. "I told you, I would wipe you all out in one clean move," he growled.

Pandora held her face down to Eon's shoulder and wouldn't look at the monsters. The leader of the mass swooped down and hovered over the angel and the nymph. His eyes were devilish and he leveled his arms and legs for a pounce.

The ambassador of the group stood at the edge and hissed, "we are not the executioners today, mighty angel. Our leader will take you for himself."

Suddenly, Aries closed his wings and fell on them both.

Eon opened his eyes and saw that the vampires and angels had completely disappeared. But the threat that took their place stood in nine positions around the pool. Each ugly being was chanting in a foreign tongue. With each passing second, the water began to boil hotter; the wind blew harder on the trees, and every creature seemed to wake in torment through the forest, wailing in pain.

Eon held Pandora close to him and placed his hand on the back of her head. "Pandora, I need you to hold your breath," he whispered.

Pandora looked up and saw the creatures surrounding them. She gasped and clung to Eon.

"What are they?" she asked.

"Evil," he replied.

Then the witches brought their hands up and fireballs erupted in their hands. They drew their arms back ready to throw them in unison. Their chanting grew louder and stronger as they continued. Suddenly, a giant reptilian head shot up from the water and splashed a witch.

Pandora wouldn't open her eyes. She wasn't at all curious to see the source of the giant splash or the roaring of the great monster. She kept her eyes shut.

Then, eleven more dragon heads sprang from the deep and splashed the other witches. The fins on their heads flapped and they surrounded the nymph and the angel with a wall of water. Eon brought his wings around him and Pandora, covering them both as the water fell hard on them. The heads of the great dragon joined together at one end of the pool and spat plasmic fluids at the group of witches, who in turn blocked the attack with a colliding force of fire and highly charged telekinetic energy.

When the collision dissipated, the group of witches fled.

The body of a dragon came up under the two victims and waded in the pool. Eon then noticed that the body connected all of the heads. As kept his hold on Pandora, he wondered out loud, "You're Hydra."

The heads turned to him and all of them bowed. "We are," they all replied together.

Eon stood on their back and Pandora stayed curled up, shivering in the cold of the night.

"Why did you save us? Dragons don't usually take notice to lowly subjects enough to engage in battle for them," Eon asked.

One of the heads answered, "Would you consider yourself a lowly being, triumphant one?"

Eon shook his head. "I am no hero. I have no sword, no armor, not even a place to call home. Just an army of outcasts on the move."

The many heads moved in thought. "You have led your army to victory on more than one occasion, have you not?" two heads asked overlapping each other.

Eon lifted his head. "I have. But I've also betrayed the forces that I serve in those battles," he explained.

Another head spoke. "Aries has brought his devils to this place in hopes of corrupting the lands and bringing about universal destruction. Would you bring your armies against his as a force of your own, and make this planet your home in return?"

Eon smiled. "My army isn't infinite, but I will join you in this cause, if I can help."

Pandora looked up and wondered what Eon had just gotten himself into.

All of the heads ducked under the water, but one remained. "Hold on, tight," it said and joined the others.

Eon and Pandora held on to the neck closest to the spine and took a deep breath as they submerged through the spring.

Twisting and winding through the caverns of the spring, Pandora and Eon were dragged along the current that the dragons swam through. Darkness swallowed them, then was briefly broken by the light shining through other springs.

Suddenly, they lifted from the water and were in the air, falling back to the ground. Landing on the back of the dragon, they waded in the water of a massive cave where all other dragons dwelt. Eon stood with Pandora and the multitude of dragons looked up.

A gold dragon stood and stared down the two outsiders. "Hydra! What have you done?" he shouted.

"Calm yourself, Nabob. Your new army has come," Hydra called.

Nabob stood his ground, but accepted Hydra's new thought. "Who are they?" he asked directly.

"The general of his own army of celestial hosts, and his nymph," Hydra replied.

Nabob tilted his head. "Acceptable numbers, but the characters are questionable in my mind."

Eon spread his wings and lifted into the air. "It is my understanding that you need us to conquer Aries. But, if you think we should turn back and let you fight your fight, then I can save my army for another day."

The other dragons instantly stood in alert, arguing on behalf of their leader, to stay. Even Hydra was alarmed. Nabob silenced the cave of their hubbub.

"It seems you need me more than you let on. The shadow of doubt should be overshadowed by the seriousness of these kinds of situations; wouldn't you agree?" Eon suggested.

CHAPTER 3

Pargon stood at the tops of the mountains and watched the herd of flying horses dancing in the skies. Pargon searched the manner of their flying. Whether they were flying for fun or in distress was crucial in his moment of purpose and design. When one horse nicked the other on the neck, Pargon knew it was friendly play.

He took a breath and touched his chest. The pain was incredible. He longed for a way to quiet it, but he had to stay on task.

"My name is Pargon, and I've come to bring the forces against Aries and his evil. I humbly ask you for your help."

When he was done with his speech, the herd of pegasus fell into formation and were joined by thousands more that were scattered in the mountains and forests of the boundaries beyond Hajun. All of them fell into lines along the skies, waiting as an army ready to depart for battle. Pargon knew they wouldn't know what he was saying, but somehow he knew they would understand.

"I believe that the elders have brought me here to your council in search of your help, as an Elder did centuries ago. If you still believe the forces of good will conquer all, then I ask you to join me in my struggle with the evil on this land," Pargon explained.

A voice whispered into his ear. "They understand, and are willing to help you."

Pargon glanced over and saw a fairy hovering over his shoulder. "Are you with me?" he asked.

The fairy giggled and shrugged, as if agreeing to fight, but not really minding. Pargon grinned and looked at the flying horses.

"Now, I need to get to the Ralligins," he thought aloud.

*****

Aries stood atop his tower, watching the mobs of Vamps and ogres clamoring over each other to get to their awaiting of food.

Aries turned to the assassin at his left and growled. "Your family is large enough to feed my horde. If you'll only tell me how I can defeat the Ancient Ones and take control of Hajun, I'll set them free" Aries said.

The assassin looked down and answered. "The Uniroth joined with the Aniroth. It's the only source of power that could break the will of the Ancient Ones. You'll have to find it first," she muttered.

Her thin skin-tight suit shivered on her, and her golden hair was a mess from the interrogation. When she saw Aries smiling at her faithfulness, a chill swept up her spine.

"Now, let them go! Free them!" she shouted.

Aries turned to the guards at the machine. "Set them free!" he commanded.

The guards nodded and a huge catapult rose up through the tower to the very top. Just at the roof where the assassin was, she saw her family in cages, one on top of the other. She ran up to them and touched their hands.

"It's going to be okay," she said to her family, who cried in terror and called out her name.

Suddenly, the hook of the catapult swung down, picking up the cage on top, and flinging it out to the horde. The family screamed as they flew through the air and the cage crashed on the horde. A group of Vamps and ogres ripped the victims to shreds, eating and drinking their fill. The catapult turned and flung another cage of her family to another portion of the horde.

Over and over, another cage would come up to be thrown to the savages. The assassin wept as her family was brutally fed to the horde.

Aries shouted, "Eat up! We have work to do!"

The assassin stepped up to Aries angrily, "You cold, heartless, wretch!" she shouted.

Aries leaned into her face. "You tried to kill me. Should I show you any mercy for that? I think not! But, I've never seen anyone find a way that close to me before. So, I'll give you another chance to do it right. Consider this incentive." He turned to the guards as the last cage was brought up. "Take her," he ordered coldly.

The assassin fought against the guards hold on her. "I swear to you, Aries: when I find you again, you'll pay for what you've done to my family."

Aries laughed. "Drop her into the abyss. Make sure she has fun while she can."

The guards took the assassin and flew off to the outskirts of the village. Over the horde, across the barren lands on the southern pole of Hajun, to the dark of the seas, they flew the long trip to the great abyss. The magnificent whirlpool funneled down the bottomless pit to the abyss' stomach. The assassin looked down to her death and had to guess if she would be able to make it out alive.

The guard to her left chuckled, "Hope you're as good at swimming as your people suggest."

And with that, they dropped her into the depths of the whirlpool.

Back at the tower, Aries grinned. "Women ..." he thought as the horde piled over itself to feed on the victims.

*****

The night was coming to an end. Fang and his troops were scattered through the forests of Ferron. They had been searching for days for any hidden forces that could be of some use to them. The forest was empty of all large animals. The Vamps had fed on most of the minotaurs. One by one, each species of creature was going extinct in the forests of Ferron. Suddenly, Fang heard rustling in the bushes. He sniffed the air, but all he could smell was the other centaurs. It had to be one of them. But, when he sniffed again, he could smell blood. It was strong in that direction. He drew his swords and trotted over to the bushes.

He saw two other centaurs guarding themselves, ready to strike at whatever was in the bushes. They surrounded the creature, and the morning star shown on them through the trees.

They couldn't see much of the creature, but they could tell it was big. The creature jolted its wings up and rose from the bushes with a screech. A mutated, tortured centaur. Part centaur, part pegasus, and vampiric, the winged centaur came out and its skin seemed to glare in the sunlight. He stayed in the shadows though to keep from harm. Its long fangs flashed at the attackers, and its arms spread, showing the full form of the corrupted centaur.

Fang looked into the creatures eyes and recognized him immediately. Flapping its wings above them, Kronos, the son of Sashi, started to fly away.

Fang gave the order, "Dispatch him!"

Without question, the centaurs shot him down. Prince Justicar fell to the ground, wallowing in misery, trying to remove the painful arrows from his body. The surrounding centaurs drove more arrows into his body, through to the ground so that there was no escaping. As the morning star rose, and shown through the trees on the prince, he screamed in the agony of his skin melting off.

The centaurs around Fang looked up at him. "We just killed the Prince of Centurion," one said.

Fang sheathed his swords. "The Prince of Centurion was already dead. I will not have a Vamp sitting on the throne of the Centurian kingdom. Sashi, of all centaurs, would understand this."

"But, sir," another protested.

Fang snapped at him. "Do not forget who you are, lieutenant! We are Centurions, born to serve under our ancestors, not the evil that aims to enslave us! We will not relent!"

Then a few of Fang's troops came galloping through the forest. "Sire! We're receiving opposition! In abundance!" the squad leader shouted.

Behind the squad, a multitude of minotaurs came storming up behind them. The squad grouped up with the rest of Fang's army, and the charging minotaurs stopped just meters away from the centaurs front line. The biggest minotaur stepped out in front of the line of minotaurs and met Fang in the middle of the two opposing forces.

The minotaur rested its ax on its shoulder. "You're army is trespassing on our mating grounds, your highness," he boomed.

Fang uncrossed his arms. "We're on a search for any forces that could possibly join our army against Aries. Your kind dwells in the kingdom of Centurion, so we have come to you, asking for your help. Will you join us?"

The minotaur searched Fang's expression, and saw that he was desperate. The centaurs waited anxiously for Fang to give the order to strike. The minotaur saw that most of his group were against the idea of siding with centaurs, so he went against his instincts.

"What is left of my army has led itself to its own demise. It is only under the leadership of my alpha-males that they became such a small number. Perhaps, if I made the decision for the lot of them, we may yet prosper. We owe you homage, my army is yours," the leader declared.

The rest of his army rose up disgusted with his decision, shouting their retorts.

"You can't do that!"

"You don't have the power to speak for us all!"

"We will surely die on their side!"

"They cannot be trusted!"

The leader held up his hairy hand. "The decision is mine, and it has been made!" he boomed silencing the group.

Fang held out his hand. "Then, let our alliance be against Aries. We for you, and you for us."

The minotaur took Fang's hand. "We will join you in hopes that you will continue to let us live in peace, here, in these woods."

Fang smiled. "If there is a forest left, then you may have it," he proclaimed.

CHAPTER 4

Pargon laid down to rest on the side of the mountain in Ferron. He prayed to the elders that his quest would go well and thought about his heritage as he slept. The moment he closed his eyes, he saw the heavens where the elders resided.

Pargon acknowledged the absence of the other elders. "Where have the original protectors of Hajun gone?" Pargon asked.

The elders that replaced the Father in the front of the courts answered. "The elders of old have begun their stages of ascension."

Decimus brought a hand to his chest. "I am Decimus."

Valkyrie continued. "And I am Valkyrie. We are the beginning of the New Order."

Pargon's expression never changed. "But who am I?"

Decimus and Valkyrie knew it was Odin. But when he introduced himself this way, they glanced at each other, unsure of how to respond.

"You are Odin," Decimus said. "All of the stories of Jade and Magnus and the elders; you are the hero of those tales."

"So it's true? These memories I have of someone else's life?"

"They're yours. From your previous life," Valkyrie answered.

"The Ancient Ones have called for our aid, and you have already begun the task of helping. The threat of Aries is not only to the planet Hajun, but also to the higher power of the Ancient Ones."

Valkyrie went on. "To prevent Aries from obtaining the Uniroth, you need to inform the Ralligins of the coming attacks and they will keep it safe."

"Should you fail, a battle of epic proportions will be inescapable to ensure the Ancient Ones survival," Decimus explained.

Pargon winced. "And if the battle should fail?"

"Then for an age, evil will rule all life in the universe," both elders answered.

Pargon sensed something else was emerging from wherever Aries came from. "What other threats to our survival could be brought from the land of Exile?" Pargon asked thoughtfully.

Decimus and Valkyrie glanced at each other again, then back to Pargon. "The land of Exile has many creatures; from giant insects to assassins being punished," Valkyrie answered.

"But only the Vamp lord has escaped from that world with his army," Decimus stated.

"If the Vamp lord could break free, then others could follow his lead," Valkyrie reasoned.

Decimus waved his hand. The Chevron replaced Pargon's sword. "If you can wound Aries with the sword of Orion, I will make sure Exile is secure, and Valkyrie will keep you safe. Your next mission is to bring the Ralligins to your cause."

Pargon drew his old blade and remembered his battles. "I won't fail," he proclaimed.

When Pargon awoke, the Chevron shown near his armor. The pain of the heart stone had completely gone. There wasn't a doubt in his mind that he was becoming the Eldest of Elders.

*****

Eon held Pandora in his arms as he flew her to the pool, where they met the night before. Eon swooped in and set her on the ground next to the pool. He hugged her and kissed her and got ready to go back into flight.

Pandora stopped him. "Aren't you going to stay with me?"

Eon looked back and saw the loneliness in her eyes. "I'll be back soon. I promise," he whispered.

And as quickly as he came, he left to gather his army. Pandora closed her eyes and sighed. She felt a harsh chill on the small of her back. When she turned around, she found Aries behind her, grinning devilishly.

Pandora swallowed hard. "Aries,"

Aries closed his wings and his eyes glowed in the reflection of the moonlight. "Yes, Pandora. I've just come to inform you that my plan was successful. So long as you're ready to do your part."

Pandora shifted her expression. "I have done my part. I've taken more than two thirds of the Ancient Ones' army from them, giving you the perfect strike. My end of the bargain is done."

Aries didn't stop grinning. "I'm altering the bargain. You're going to kill the angel yourself."

Pandora stood enraged. "You promised that he would be my prize!"

Aries stood over her. "And you have him, do you not? Now you will kill him!" he demanded, shouting.

Pandora shook her head. "I love him! You cannot force me to kill the one I love," she pleaded.

"You will kill him or pay the price for your insolence," Aries warned.

Pandora wanted to argue, but knew exactly what Aries would do if she further opposed. She stopped herself from continuing the fight.

Aries smirked at his own evil nature rubbing off to the lesser being. "Now, I must be off. I have a war to win, and a universe to rule. I'm going to be very busy for a few years," and he flew away.

Pandora fell to her knees crying, knowing that she was slowly siding with evil.

Aries flew to the southern side of Hajun, over the seas to the shores of unknown territories to the window of his room in his tower. He ordered the guards to leave and the evening lamb was brought in. Taking a moment, Aries stared at his vampiric form, looking up and down his own body. He stretched his wings and clawed his fingers. He loved the names that had been given him; Camazotz, Abigor, Balthazar, Mephistopheles, Nocturna, the first horseman. None matched up to Aries though. It felt as strong as it sounded.

The lamb in the room bleated and drew his attention from his narcissistic mood. He darted around, closing his wings around his shoulders. His eyes burned at his prey. He leapt at it as it bleated again, and snapped its neck with his teeth. He teased himself by breathing in the smell of the warm blood.

"Ah, tease me sweet victim. Make me want you more and more," he slowly growled into the dead lamb's ear.

He loved the blood of lamb, almost as much as the blood of the virgin women the Claptons would give. They both had the cleanliness he so desired in his meals. None of the blood was wasted or spilled on the floor. Not a drop missed his tongue. His lust for the blood was beyond his control. No matter how much more advanced he was to his horde, or wise from his age, he could not resist the taste of this blood. Finer than any wine, more delicate than honey, richer than any herb or bean, nothing could replace the taste of the blood of the lamb. He could bathe in it and be eternally happy, but he dare not waste a drop.

Huddling over the neck of the lamb, shielding it from anyone or anything that may enter his room. His breathing grew heavier, his heart pounded, he drained its blood, tasting and savoring the taste of every drop that exited the veins of this sacrifice. His heart continued to throb as he ingested the liquid, so bitter and so sweet. So evil and yet so pure. The satisfaction was abundant, and his desires were fulfilled. His breathing slowed as he finished his meal. With all the sincerity he could bring up, he wanted to thank the lamb for the gift of its blood.

He stood up and looked at his hands. He was full, and loved the way he felt when his body was at a healthy physical peak. Of all the names he had earned, he never once heard Narcissus being one of them, yet he knew it fit him so well. If only the witch that sent him into exile had not cursed him with the lack of a reflection, he would sit happily in front of his mirror for hours or even days. He could feel the new life making him stronger; the blood of the lamb giving him new strength. He loved it.

*****

The assassin washed up on the shore of Carnal beach. Her black suit washed up next to her, and her hair seemed to search out the individual grains of sand. The morning star woke her from her dreamless sleep.

Opening her eyes, and seeing her suit next to her reminded her that she took it off as soon as she hit the water.

The water touching her skin would have been dreadful in the suit when her fin stretched. She had to carry it all the way as the power in her fin kept her from dying in the abyss.

She remembered her family screaming as they were fed to those ruthless killers. How Aries smiled at her pain, and the army was fed with the bodies of the innocent. Her family, helpless and paralyzed, had no choice but to let it happen. She looked down at the fin that joined her legs together, and the scales that ran all the way down from her hips. She was her family's only legacy.

"Tetra, the time has come," her father's voice echoed in her mind. "You must search out the cerberus army. They will be the main source of help against Aries and his army."

Tetra fell back on the sand and fought the idea. "How will they help? They've been notorious through the ages for killing along side of evil."

Her father's voice silenced her. "Have faith in me, Tetra. You will avenge us, and with haste. Search out the cerberus army."

Tetra shivered thinking of the nasty three-headed dogs and their lust for meat. Now she would consider herself as their next meal. Why the cerberus army? Why not the Lamia's or the Chimera, or the dead army of Daboo? Why not something tangible, like the rogue sailors, or the tyroses, or the blinkers?

Why the most foul beast that would eat a dragon if it ever felt so daring? And why did she have to face them?

Still, it was her father's will. She would obey, no matter the cost. The cerberus army was underground, under the dune sea. She had to go there, where all elements would be against her, and where her worst fears would surely come true. She turned over and crawled away from the water and let the morning star dry her body. As it did, her fin slowly split into two legs, and the strength of her fishy ancestors left her body. She immediately brought up the suit and washed out the sand. She then dressed herself and on more agile legs. No longer feeling vulnerable, she set out to the dune sea. If the cerberus army would help her avenger her family, then she would gladly bring them to her cause.

*****

Valkyrie concentrated, meditating on the past. With Decimus gone, it was hard to conjure up events prior to their reign. Only with the connection between them could she see the previous elders and their actions. She could remember their talk of armies; armies of angels. When Odin left, he had his own army divided among them all. Would they all be inherited with the powers stolen by Valefor a generation back? If so, then why did he need an army of demons when he could just as easily, if not better, have succeeded with his plan? No, the angels had to be given away if not used in battle.

Where would they be? On another plane of dimension? In another time all together? Some place in another galaxy? Or here, in these walls; the walls of the New Courts. Each elder had their own army hidden in different locations, she knew. But where, or how, or when would each one be? Time was running out fast, and she had to find her army before the hour was too late in the night.

*****

Decimus fought his own battle. In space, past all manner of life, on the other edge of the universe, the portal was completely open for all to escape. One being after another had found some way out of Exile. As he advanced closer on the portal to the Plains of Exile, he drew his crystal sword and held it out to the portal. As he brought his blade to front, a cone of energy extended from the crystal and captivated every being that escaped, and forced them back into the portal, as if a black hole sucked them back inside. Each being fought to break free, but their efforts to resist were futile. His struggle worsened as the endless beings through the portal broke through, but he gained control and shoved them all back to force the ones on the outside back through.

The portal had to be closed when Aries went back. Until then, Decimus would have to stand guard and fight any other beings back in. He guessed that Valefor had killed off the elder that held guard here when other beings were sent to this prison.

Just one more minor responsibility he would have to take on as the new elder.

*****

Fang stood at the battle table looking over the estimated figures. The captain stood with him looking over the plans, nervously watching Fang move one piece after another.

Fang sighed. "Saffron, you've been acting strange ever since we took the minotaurs under our wings. Our army is coming together, what's wrong with you?"

Captain Saffron chuckled. "It's an odd thing when we are forced to take sides with an enemy."

Fang glanced at him, then back at the table. "Enemies with a common foe are only friends until that foe is killed, be it as relentless as the underworld," he replied.

"What if our friends have different ideals as we. What then, sir?" Saffron asked.

Fang stopped and looked up, agitated. "Captain, if you have something to say, speak plainly."

Saffron chose his words carefully. "What if they did not have in mind to bring birth to the New Kingdom, or even to help it along? What if segregation rules over the dream of our king?"

Fang sighed again, lowering his head to the thought of failure. "I had come to the conclusion years ago that the future Sashi had in mind would only be a dream. But, he believed in it so much that he was willing to go to the mountains himself and ask the elders for help. I don't know if he received any answer from them, but he had it in mind that they would. I believe, no matter who opposes this dream, it's coming true with each passing second," he pointed outside his tent.

"Look out there. Good and evil have joined as one to fight alongside each,other and rid us of the ultimate threat. What say you to that?"

Saffron's heart sank. "And if Prince Baal, or Incubus were still alive? Would his majesty's dream come true then?" he asked.

Fang closed his eyes, knowing that they were nowhere near as passionate about Sashi's dream as most of Sashi's soldiers were. He lowered his head again. "There are some things that will not change the course of the future. If they were alive or dead, it does not matter. They would know that Aries was our threat, and either one of them would search for help in any place they could. Without thinking, they would have united with the minotaurs in an attack against him. Does that answer your question, captain?"

Saffron lowered his head and placed his sword on the battle table. "I killed them," he whispered.

Fang opened his eyes and looked up. "If you said what I just heard you say, then say it like a soldier! Repeat that, Captain!" Fang shouted.

Saffron raised his head high and shouted, "I murdered Prince Baal and Prince Incubus to fulfill the dream of our king. I knew that they wouldn't even attempt to bring the New Kingdom into power, so I took those matters into,my own hands, knowing full well that Sashi would hand over the throne to you. Kronos died by Aries hand, but the other two were my kills."

Fang trotted around the battle table and faced Saffron. "I trusted you. Sashi trusted you. We all put our faith in you, and you would betray that?" Fang gripped Saffron's sword and touched the tip to Saffron's stomach. "Will you accept your death on this charge?"

Saffron never let his stance drop as he boldly replied, "If I die, it will be for the New Kingdom in all its glory. That, I will accept."

Fang narrowed his eyes and dropped the sword back on the table. "You're a coward, Saffron. But in all my years as a Centurion, I've never seen someone with enough passion over a cause that he would kill the last of the royal family over it. You should have let the Fates dictate Sashi's dream, and you've committed treason. For that, you will be put to death after the war."

Saffron nodded. "I understand."

Another Centurion stepped into the tent. "Sire, we have received word from the scouts. A multitude of Pegasus' were flying to the desert. They were surrounded by Fairies and led by a Dryad. We think someone else is constructing an army of their own," he explained.

Fang looked back at the battle table. "It could be a trap. An enemy looking to stop us early."

"Or, a useful ally," Saffron suggested.

Fang turned angrily toward Saffron, but did not voice his position against him with another Centurion present. He turned to the messenger. "Thank you. Make sure the company gets a good night's sleep tonight, and departs at dawn. We make for the desert tomorrow with all haste. We must meet with the Ralligins," he ordered.

The messenger nodded and left. Under his breath, he sighed and muttered, "That'll go well with the minotaurs."

Fang went to his box of battle pieces and carefully picked out the Pegasus' pieces, and placed them all on the table. The figures surrounded the desert, and intersected in the middle of it.

He looked up at Saffron. "This isn't going to be the greatest battle ever. Sand and blood are all that will come of this."

*****

Tetra was already in the middle of the rocky desert when noon struck, although she wished she that was not so. She hated the sand and any being that had command over it, or created it. She hated the heat and how it made this place the exact opposite and utter nightmare compared to her home in the ocean. She hated the struggle against the sands on her feet, and how it only slowed her down. Water would do nothing but quicken her pace to her destination.

She was relieved to find the sudden drop in the sand dunes, leading to great shade. There was no telling what would be in the underground rock, but she was eager to find out. If the cerberus army lived down here, they'd have to be either thriving in the thousands, or a dying race. Either way, she was desperate for shade and jumped in the cave, not caring how deep it was.

Darkness swallowed her. Her eyes quickly adjusted through the cave, but she never landed. The ground was further down than she thought. She could see the water-flow through the cave. The underground spring drove through the rock under her. She knew that as soon as she touched the water, her fin would spread and shred her suit. She quickly unzipped the suit and ripped it off, wrapping it around her arm. She bent her body into a dive and dropped through a hole in the rock that bled to the water-flow. The current took her through the cave, with the light of the lamps blinking as she passed by each valve in the rock of the water.

The fact that the water-flow had valves suggested a species thrived here that either used to need, or still used an irrigation system. In any case, the plumbing would only leave room for one species that lived on Hajun: Skord. She thought long and hard on what Skord used to do here that needed water systems such as these. If each valve fed to another flow, then this one would lead to the main water-hole, but Skord wouldn't drink from a trough.

Then the thought crossed her mind: the cerberus. The Skord bred, fed, and mutated the cerberus. If these beasts could keep up the training that their masters were driving into them, they could very well be the army she needed to wipe out the horde. However, they may react aggressively to her intrusion.

She could feel the presence of something else, though. She knew she was not alone in these caves. Something was following her. Immediately, she leapt from the next valve in the water-flow and landed on her side. She rolled around on the floor, searching for any source of heat. When she looked up, she found a crack in the ceiling, setting a large beam of light along the ground next to her. She rolled in and let the outside heat dry her off. With only seconds to spare, her fin slowly shrunk back to her legs, and she could get back into her suit.

She stood up, ready to search the caves on foot, when she suddenly realized she was surrounded by the cerberus army. The dark coated three-headed canines growled at her. When she looked at the way they glanced at the one behind her, then back to her, she realized the leader was behind her. She lowered her stance, bending her knees, looking to the ground. In that moment, she suddenly realized it was the Stone

Beings that were following her. It was that moment that she wanted nothing but to get out of there. She turned to the leader and entered its mind, using her ability of persuasion.

Through thought, she hypnotized the leader and made her think that it was a good idea to go along with Tetra. The leader lowered its heads, and allowed Tetra to climb on. She mounted her neck and had the leader take Tetra through the caves, and out into the desert. When the alpha female left, the armada of cerberus' followed her, each head barking and howling as they raced through the caves.

CHAPTER 5

Pargon rode through the air on the Pegasus leader. He felt his task was already succeeding. His own army began from sheer luck. With the elders on his side, who would oppose him? Suddenly, when he glanced at the ground, he saw a burst from the sand between the rocks, which blew with the wind and settled elsewhere. Another bit of sand shot up followed by others, leading him to the middle of the rock desert.

He got the attention of the Pegasus leader and had him follow the sand jumps. Following the leader, the entire flock turned and aimed for the sand-jumps. Then a huge sphere of sand revolved in front of them, causing the Pegasus' to dodge and take evasive action. Pargon stared at the sphere.

"So it is true. The stories, the rumors, it's all true," he thought. Yet, somehow, he felt as if he remembered this happening earlier on in his life, as if he were having deja-vu. "We are the Ralligins," the voices said in his head.

Pargon smiled excitedly as the Pegasus he rode flew around the sphere. "I am Pargon. I have come to bring warning. An evil creature called Aries has escaped from Exile and seeks to steal the Uniroth. You must beware and take heed that he wants to destroy a race known as the Ancient Ones. I am on a mission to assist the Ancient Ones, but I was also sent to keep you from being enslaved once again. If Aries takes hold of the Uniroth, then you will all perish to his will."

The Ralligins acknowledged his intentions with respect. "We give you our thanks, and take heed to your warning. If what you say is true, then Aries has escaped with his own army behind him. To show our gratitude, we will help you in bringing down this foe."

The Pegasus armada landed on the desert sand and waited for the next move. The sphere of sand died down and three Ralligins were left floating above the ground. Pargon smiled, now seeing what they really looked like, he still felt as if he had seen them before.

Suddenly, a scouting party of Centaurs came storming up behind the Ralligins on the slope of a nearby canyon. Fang drew his sword, glanced at Pargon, then back to the Ralligins.

"We are the Centurions. We seek out the Ralligins for assistance against the siege of Aries," Fang proclaimed.

A Ralligin turned to him. "We are the Ralligins," the voices said in Fang's mind. "We have already joined the cause against Aries with this one before you," they told him.

Almost spontaneously, a herd of almost a hundred dragons surrounded by legions of angels circled the two armies, covering the sky and completely shadowing the evening star from the armies on the land. The dragons bellowed and screeched at the sight of the massive scene with the two armies facing each other and landed on the north side, next to both armies. Eon landed in front of the group of dragons and the angels flew above the giant beings. With the inside of the desert almost completely covered, Eon glanced at Fang, then at Pargon, and back to the Ralligins.

"I am Eon. These dragons are my army. We wish to take a battle of epic proportions to, Aries and his horde of vampires that plague these lands."

Pargon tilted his head. "How many enemies does Aries have?" he wondered out loud.

A low long howl echoed from the south. Giant dark figures were racing up to the forces in the center of the desert. Pargon drew his sword as the horizon, blurred by the heat, was filled with these dark figures, that never seemed to stop growing. They were fast, and blanketed over the hills of sand.

Saffron whispered, "now, there's something you don't see every day."

When the beasts came close enough to see clearly, they slowed down and approached the huge mass of militants in an easy manner. Eon, Pargon, and Fang all noticed a smaller figure on the top of the leader of the large pack. Clearly, these beings were cerberus', but they were somehow being led.

Tetra saw the leaders in the middle, being surrounded by the soldiers and dragons. She called to them from a distance of about twenty paces. "I am Tetra, from the sea. I have brought these beings from the underground to the surface, to avenge my family in death. At the hand of the evil known as Aries, they were slaughtered. I wish to bring justice and ask you to stand by me in this cause. Will you help?"

Eon, Fang, and Pargon glanced at each other, then back to her, replying in unison, "Yes."

Tetra dropped from the cerberus and left them to join the apparent leaders of the great armies. The five leaders formed a circle and began discussing the terms of alliance. Tetra was only interested in infiltrating Aries tower and spilling his blood by her own hands. No one was to assist her or stop her. For this, she would give the basic layout of the base Aries had set up at the southern pole.

Fang was to secure Sashi's dream, and claimed the throne through this action. For this, he would expand territories to each who requested such needs.

Pargon only sought freedom for Hajun, and brought the elders blessing on their campaign. And Eon, too, only wanted freedom from his bonds to the Ancient Ones. For this, he would see to the endless security and join the elders in eternal protection of Hajun. The Ralligins remained sovereignly silent as to their own terms. They were simply pleased to keep their loyalty and fight for Hajun in the name of the elders.

They set camp on the forests beyond the south side of the desert, and with the combined forces, the Powers were united, as Sashi had always envisioned.

*****

The masters of darkness stood around the stone table in the cave. One sister looked at the others and screamed obnoxiously.

"The light grows brighter! With more numbers of wings! The annoying little sniggle-sniggle will have more on his side, and not even need the assistance to bring our downfall." she screeched.

The others groaned. "In the name of Aboogie moogie, find some way to destroy him!"

Then one sister silenced the rest with a solution of her own. "A way be shown," she whispered, "a path be seen. Secrets be spoken in one's sleep. What secrets be used against one another that can befall such a unity? In their sleep we spread such secrets, and in their sleep they turn against each other. When one becomes vulnerable, all become vulnerable. Where one secret is kept to keep from harming others, all other secrets can harm our targeted one. Whose side is whose, and who's who be on what side? I see a secret inside our who's who on the side against him in secret."

The other sisters nodded in agreement and chanted, "Then, the secrets being kept are the secrets we use. Trust is the game they are all bound to lose. What truths be told, what prices be paid? A death wish of love from the promise 'twas made."

They dashed from the caves of Gorin and used their dark magic to quicken their speed. Through the forests of Ferron, passing by Centurion, straight across the deserts, no opposition broke their speed. With the shadows on their side, they could see the newly assembled army's camp in the forests beyond the desert, and were ready to attack. As the army slept, they would use their thought waves against their now vulnerable consciousness and bring about the secrets kept from each other by their allies.

Each witch took a position at nine of the furthest points along the camp. One witch whispered to Fang in his sleep about how Saffron brought Prince Incubus, Prince Kronos and Prince Baal into an ambush by the minotaurs. The minotaurs roasted the two sons of Sashi, but Kronos had escaped, only to be captured alone by the Vamps.

A witch cloaked herself with the shadows and twirled her way around the fire where Tetra sharpened the end of the wooden steak that she would drive through Aries' chest. As the witch approached the huge winged beasts, she whispered to the dragons that their once allied Elves were run off by the Dryads ranks, their lands taken and their homes remade to keep the Dryads safe. The dragons now knew why their ancestors scoured the lands of the Dryads and kept a constant war with them.

Another witch whispered to Eon about Pandora befriending Evil to show him love. As the witch whispered, he saw the truth in her words. Pandora used his freedom against him. She was, as nymphs often are, nothing more than a siren: taking him off task and disarming the Ancient Ones.

One witch found a small group that was still awake, excited about the battle. A green dragon called Quiver, and a bronze dragon called Roffle chatted with a centaur called Spader and a few dryads that had stumbled into the camp.

"I'd wager two trolls that this whole thing is going to end up the way the Goliathans settled their dispute," Roffle bet.

Quiver twitched and nervously replied, "you mean killing each other until nothing is left?"

"Exactly," Roffle replied. "In any case, time share or Rock, Paper, Scissors is no longer an option."

He saw Quiver's attention dart to a flock of birds. Roffle jumped to stop Quiver from the inevitable, but it was too late.

Quiver couldn't stop himself; in a second, the flock of birds was falling to the ground as flaming balls of death. When they splashed into a puddle, Roffle shook his head in embarrassment. Spader and the nymphs just stared with blank expressions on their faces.

Quiver twitched again and curled his arms to his chest. "Sorry," he blurted out.

Roffle sighed and looked at the nymphs. "He can't help it. He's a little skittish," he warned.

Quiver caught a scent and moved towards the woods. "Bunny!" he shouted now on the hunt.

Spader ducked down to dodge any attention. "Are you two going to wake up the entire camp?" he hissed.

The nymphs curled up to Spader, both to be seductive, and to share in his body-heat. He didn't argue with their flirtatious motions, as it was tradition for nymphs to show affection to Centurion soldiers in times of battle. Whatever they offered, he would gladly accept.

Quiver slowly moved into the forest to where the witch was hiding. As she dashed from place to place in the forest, Quiver would stay on her trail, searching for the bunny. No questions entered his mind when the supposed bunny shot into a tree. All senses were on the hunt.

"Here, bunny, bunny, bunny," he whispered.

The clouds dwindled away from the moon, shining on the figure in the tree that Quiver was tracking.

He tilted his head. "You're no bunny."

The witch gulped hard when the notion hit her that Quiver could roast her at any moment. But when he turned around and complained to Roffle that there was no bunny, she dropped from the tree and followed Quiver to the group.

Suddenly, a figure unlike any other appeared in a flash of light with a family of Geonites.

"And here, we have an army of under powers. They're here to really stick it to Aries and his cronies," the odd looking reptilian explained to the family.

The group looked the family over and inwardly decided they weren't a threat.

The reptilian held out a hand. "My name's Dreadnought. The Dreadnought, with Dreadnought industries, and real-estate."

He spoke in a rapid-fire Palidonian accent. "I'm here to show this family the real-estate value of your planet, Hajun, in Sector Four." He glanced around the group and spotted the witch in the woods. "You're all aware of a presence of evil here, right?"

Quiver jumped. "Bunny?"

Dreadnought gave him a look and continued. "No, witch. If you want, I can take care of her for you … and the others, as well."

Roffle tilted his head. "Proceed," he said, going along with the stranger.

Before another word was spoken, Quiver struck his head forward and snapped his jaws shut on Dreadnought's head. Unfazed, Dreadnought felt his neck was only in between the dragon's teeth, and not one had punctured him. The Geonite father covered his daughter's eyes, as Dreadnought gripped the dragon's teeth with his four hands, and opened the dragon's mouth, relinquishing the dragon's grip on his neck. Quiver slowly pulled away and twitched ravenously apologizing.

Dreadnought smiled pleasantly and brought his hand up. As his hand rose, the witches were thrown in the air above the tops of the trees, stunned and shocked from the energy pulses that carried them. Then Dreadnought closed his hand into a fist, and the witches shouted as they were suddenly obliterated.

Spader looked up at the skies and raised up an eyebrow as he glanced back at Dreadnought. "You know, this planet isn't meant barter. You're thinking of Straptra, in the system above us."

Dreadnought looked confused. "You sure? I thought for certain I was selling Hajun today. Besides, the system above you is being demolished to make way for a new ultra mini-golf expanse. But I'll double check, just to make sure." With that, Dreadnought and the family disappeared.

Roffle looked at Quiver. "What's a mini-golf?" he asked.

Quiver glared at Roffle. "There was no bunny, was there?"

*****

Eon woke from the dream. He didn't want to believe it, but he knew it was more than just a dream. While everyone else was sleeping discontentedly, he silently spread his wings and flew around the trees. He darted over the desert on a wind current that gave him much higher speeds. He found his way back to the pool where Pandora sat waiting for him. She wasn't as seductive as before, but she gave away no hints to her true intentions. Eon landed by the pool, his robe wrapped around his waist. When he saw Pandora there, wading in the pool, a smile came to his face. He'd forgotten what he saw in his dream and gave in to her will.

When she stepped slowly out of the pool with the flowers getting caught in her hair, she gazed into his eyes and smiled at his naivety. She remembered how that was the first thing that drove her to him. He was so trusting and believed that she was worth giving up his military stature for. She thought about the poison herb in the flowers that she wore, how they would kill slowly and agonizing, and unrelenting, just like the evil she sided with. The dagger along her arm, hidden from her love, would only start the bloody ending to this entanglement.

As she wrapped her arms around Eon's neck and kissed him, reflecting on what she was about to do, believing wholeheartedly that Aries had turned her completely, she brought the dagger up behind Eon's neck. Eon held her close and saw something in her eyes, like she was going to reveal some dark secret. Before she could do or say anything, he wanted to break her thought and keep this moment in his heart.

As she smiled, he whispered, "I love you, Pandora."

She suddenly stopped, with a question written on her face. She wanted to ask what he meant by that, but all that came out was, "I love you, too."

He smiled at her shaking his head, not knowing that the blade that would end his life was inches away from his skin. "What's wrong? You look distressed."

"Did you mean it?" she asked.

As he kissed her, she knew he did. Satisfied, she took the dagger and slid the blade down her arm. She gasped and dropped the dagger on the ground. When Eon felt her body jerk, he pulled away from the kiss and looked all over her to see what had happened. She shivered and stared at him.

"I'm sorry," she whispered.

Eon saw the pain and shook his head frantically. "Pandora?" he asked.

Pandora pulled the flowers from her hair and the necklace from round her neck. "Place this on the cut, please," she begged.

Eon held the flowers in his hand and stared them down. They didn't look as enchanting when he held them, nor did they look like they were meant to heal. But he trusted her and did as she said. He pressed the flower pedals into the cut and lay her down on the shore in his arms.

Eon shook his head. "What happened? What did this to you?"

Pandora didn't speak, but touched Eon's face and waited for the poison to enter her blood stream. Questions flooded into his mind and nothing seemed to stop her from dying, as if she had lost the will to live. He wondered what had driven her to such depression.

Her lip shook as she muttered, "I love you, Eon. I won't let him use me to hurt you, anymore."

Eon glared at her wound. "Pandora, tell me you're not his tool. Tell me you're not dying because of it."

Pandora couldn't help letting the tears fall. With the chills shooting through her body, it didn't seem to matter that she was crying. The pain was too great.

Her whole body was shaking now, and the words were forced from her mouth.

"I'm sorry Eon."

Her lurching slowed, and her breathing calmed. She was near the end. Eon discovered that the herbs were what was killing her, so he scraped them out of her wound. Kissing her one last time, she died in his arms as she had dreamed she would. When he pulled away from the kiss, he closed her eyes as her breathing had stopped. With tears flowing, he brought her body up and listened for her heart. He remembered how she had promised him each heartbeat, and now they were gone. He grit his teeth and lay her completely down on the shore of the pool.

Letting his love go and leaving her body where he had first found it, his wings shot up and he lifted into the sky heading back to the camp to avenge the death of his love. He wanted nothing more than to watch Aries wallow in pain.

CHAPTER 6

The morning star shown through the southern forest trees. The leaders were in the battle tent arguing with each other. Fang felt betrayed by the minotaurs for participating in the demise of Sashi's sons. The dragons were almost insulted for the Elves that the Dryads were their purgers.

Pargon was caught on the defense in the argument, saying on behalf of his ancestors, the Elves were already taken as vampires by the time the Dryads had gotten there. Tetra was absolutely appalled that the leaders had lost their focus.

But when Eon swooped in, slammed his hands on the table and shouted, "Aries is going to die!" Focus was suddenly brought back to the war.

Tetra stood next to Eon knowing exactly how he felt and believing she had found someone now with the same passion as hers.

Eon glared at all of the leaders. "The time for quarreling with each other has past! Today, we fight!" he shouted.

Fang was the most furious out of all of them, but he was strong enough to put off his feeling for another day. The dragons, however, were prone to acting on their emotions. When the thought of the dragons allying with Aries enter Eon's mind, Eon slowly looked Nabob in the eyes, which was not something anyone was used to doing. This course of action only enraged the sovereign dragon further.

Then Eon said what Nabob needed to hear. "You may feel wronged by the Dryads for banishing your fallen allies. Aries, now, has your friends. His will has overpowered them which makes them the enemy.

Choose, here and now, who you will fight for. As for me and my armies, our fight is with Aries."

Nabob knew about the prophecy, and what Hajun meant to it. Even being enraged, huffing and puffing in anger, he was wise enough to calm himself and side with reason on the matter. The dragon nodded, and silenced his army from further opposition to the argument.

Eon turned to the Ralligins. "Is the Uniroth well protected?"

The Ralligins uncloaked themselves to everyone else and their voices entered everyone's mind. "The Uniroth is under our surveillance and protection. Aries will never acquire it."

Eon turned his head to Tetra. "You are prepared to dispatch Aries back to exile?"

Tetra placed the steak on the table and kept hold on it as she stared at Eon. The fire in her eyes was all an answer he needed.

*****

Aries found his way to the six century old temple in the desert. Only the tip could be seen from the surface of the sand. It was enough for him to reach the world of the Ralligins. He stood atop the replica temple from the Ralligins home and held the Aniroth in his hand. He remembered destroying the mer-people at the temple to acquire this power. How he'd trapped them all in cages and left Tetra to watch him carry the Aniroth away with her family.

Now his plan was the closest it had ever been to being complete. With the power to corrupt, to thrive on anger, to avenge the unjust, in his hand, the portal accepted his power, the Aniroth slowly pulsed to black, then to red, and brought him to the heavenly realm of the Ralligins. The hallowed figures danced in their formations in the heavens, but in the presence of the Aniroth, they shied away and lowered their guard at the Uniroth. Aries smiled at his corruption and slowly paced up the red carpet to the pillow where the Uniroth sat.

He spread his wings in excitement when he reached the pillow on the pedestal. In his left hand, he held the Aniroth, and with his right, he slowly gripped the Uniroth. The creatures around him watched in despair as he turned around and joined the two forces together. He absorbed the intensity, with the powers repelling against each other, but forcing them into submission. As the orbs of energy merged, flares seemed to ring around his wrists and spurt as if a star flare erupting from the two orbs.

With the power of invincibility, immortality, and the unification of the minds of the Ralligins, joined with the power to corrupt, thrive, and access to all supernatural powers, Aries held in his hand the power to rule life itself: the Voloroth. With so much energy, it attached itself to the life force that possessed it, bending itself to the will of its keeper. In turn, Aries' form began to alter as the energy immersed itself with its hosts soul and mind.

Aries felt the power of the Voloroth changing his form, and expanding his power. It overwhelmed him. His ears grew taller, and tipped at the ends. Through the dark head of hair, horns rose and curled. His pigment grew brighter to a shade of scarlet, and the shadows that were his eyes turned yellow. His muscles grew, his fingernails extended, and his robe ripped from the torso up. When he smiled, his fangs touched his lips. The power had made him almighty.

Through thought, he commanded the Voloroth to reveal the location of the power of the universe. He would search out the Vim. Only with the Vim could he possible destroy the Ancient Ones. The Vim was the only power stronger than the Voloroth, and the final step to complete his plan. But when the Voloroth complied with his command, it showed him only a vision of Hajun rotating around their star. Aries frowned at the error, but patiently repeated the command. The vision of Hajun was all he saw. He did his best to reason what the error meant, and after much thought, he understood. The Vim was hidden in Hajun.

He smiled at how clever the elders were with their distribution of universal power. But this was too obvious. So obvious that even Aries would overlook it. The power that gave birth to everything, spread the stars and planets and everything into space and time; the power that connected it all, that sustained it; the Vim was Hajun.

But how would Aries acquire the power that, apparently, was already inhabited by a planet? It didn't matter. If the Voloroth said the power of the universe resided in Hajun, then Hajun would be where he would search it out. It was an odd feeling, being so close to an evil purity. Almost perfect.

*****

The Ralligins surrounded the army of dragons, angels, centaurs, cerberus, winged horses, fairies, and minotaurs and teleported them straight to the boundaries of Aries' base on the southern pole. The snow and winds had ceased and all of the natural occurrences stopped. Aries had taken control over the elements with the powerful force of energy. But when the Ralligins disappeared, the leaders of the armies realized that Aries had become powerful enough to control the most abundant species on Hajun.

The dragons rose up and circled the tower, spitting flame, acid and ice shards through the army of Vamps and ogres. The centaurs rode into the army and began slashing the front line of the unsuspecting army. The minotaurs plowed their way through the army and slammed their foes to the ground with their axes and mallets. All of the Vamps on the ground were foot soldiers.

Eon ordered in the angelic strike. "Legion!" he shouted. As the army of celestial hosts came from the twirls of the clouds, they obliterated great portions of the army. But the Vamps never seemed to die. With the numbers being as great as they were, the dead only seemed to come back to life. Eon ascended over the battle while Pargon and Tetra jumped onto Fang and they all made way to the tower. Fang followed behind the minotaur that ripped through the army and slashed the incoming opposition with his swords. They all met at the entrance of the tower as the dragons destroyed destroyed their portions of the enemy's army.

As the leaders entered the tower, the Pegasus army came down and trampled on the ogres heads, knocking them to the ground. One of the minotaurs was knocked in the head by a club. When he fell, he looked back up and saw that he had received a personal challenge from an ogre. The minotaur gladly rose to the occasion, lifting his ax to meet the ogre's club. When the ogre pushed the minotaur back down and broke his club on one of the minotaur's horns, the minotaur realized that the ogres were not to be underestimated.

The cerberus' ran through, trampling on the Vamps and eating the ogres. The malicious attack was enough to feed the monsters for a few months. The low barks that were meant to scare away opposition only attracted it all and drew more food in.

Soon, the Vamps and ogres gave up and only attacked centaurs, but the cerberus' hunger would not be sated ao easily. Saffron slammed his hilt into the head of a Vamp, looked up, and saw Aries at the top of the tower, flapping his wings and letting the evening star shine behind him. With the Voloroth in his hands, it seemed both he and his army were impervious to the evening star's ultraviolet rays. The sunbeams shown around Aries and the glowing aura gave him the image of a god.

Saffron called the archers to him and gave the order to shoot Aries down. The archers lined up behind Saffron and fired the swarm of arrows at Aries. The cracks in the wood of the arrows whistled loudly as they approached their target. But when they touched Aries, they were all devoured by the energy shield provided by the Voloroth. Aries smirked at their valorous attempts to take him down.

The minotaur found a hard ordeal in this challenge by the ogre. It had been a long time since he'd had a fight he couldn't win, but an ogre should be simpler than this. The ogre had found another club. He spun around with his club over the ground and knocked his weapon into the minotaur's hooves. The minotaur fell to the ground as the ogre swung the club over his shoulder and struck the club down on the minotaur. The minotaur had enough of the annoyance that the ogre brought. The minotaur frowned and brought his hand up catching the club before it crashed down on his chest. He pulled the club from the ogres hands and stood up, now with two weapons to use against the ogre. With his left hand holding the club, he struck for the ogre's head. When the ogre mimicked the minotaur and caught the club, the minotaur struck with his ax, severing the ogre's arm. The minotaur pulled the club away and swung off the ogre's dead arm. With the ogre wailing in pain, the minotaur dropped the club and sliced off the other limbs of the ogre. Caught in the bloody mess, the minotaur wiped the fluid from his face and left the stub of the ogre to join the rest of the battle.

CHAPTER 7

Both Pargon and Tetra rode on Fang as Eon led the way up the tower. The stairway was majestic, with tapestries on the walls and murals of Aries everywhere, the candles lit the way to Aries' private quarters. The stairs spiraled up the walls, and the inside of the stairs were fenced off by a net, so the machine that was built in the center of the tower could be visible. The stilts of the machine had boulders stacked on top of each other.

Tetra knew exactly what it was. "That's the catapult," she explained. "Aries is going to throw these stones at our army, no matter who's in the way. He'll destroy his own army if it means laying siege on ours. I don't know if anyone will survive that."

Fang drew his swords and kept his eye on Eon. "The battle between Magnus and Odin was mere horse-play among brothers with toys compared to this. Slaughter will not go unpunished."

Pargon gripped the Chevron and looked it over, saying a prayer to the elders to keep him and those he was fighting with safe. When he saw the crack in the breastplate, the memory of the spear piercing his chest blocked out all thought. He saw the giants impaling his chest as he was tied up for torture. He remembered fighting Magnus. Pargon saw him with Jade, or the bride he had come to know as Mercy. He remembered each of the titans, vividly, and how he destroyed each one. With all the memory of the Elder himself, Pargon looked at his sword again through new eyes.

With the gloves on his hands gripping his sword, the breastplate on his chest, and the boots fitted on his feet, he could feel the power of the elders overwhelming his body; it felt good. He sheathed his sword and opened himself to the new power he barely remembered that he possessed. His birthright had returned to him. Riding on Fang in Sashi's stead, with an angel lighting the way and a mermaid at his back, Pargon knew already he would triumph this day.

Eon stopped at the door of Aries' chambers so the other leaders could catch up. Pargon and Tetra hopped off of Fang, and Fang kicked the door down. Out the window, Aries hovered off the rail, watching the armies collide and destroy each other. The clouded sky was trying to bring back the cold to the south pole, and the evening star was slowly starting to set again. Tetra hardly recognized Aries; if it weren't for the fact that he was the only one not fighting, but only observing from a high distance, she wouldn't have been able to tell him apart from his horde.

Pargon handed Eon his daggers from his boots and Eon ran up to Aries, spread his wings and gliding in for a kill. Eon grit his teeth and wrapped his arms around Aries' neck, stabbing the blades through Aries' throat. Aries ignored the fallen angel climbing on his back, and turned to the other leaders in his room. Fang, Pargon, and Tetra all stood ready for a fight as Aries stared them down.

"Now, you die," Eon growled into Aries' ear.

Aries tossed the Voloroth aside and gripped Eon's arm, flinging him back to the line of soldiers in his room. Eon caught himself and joined the other three, holding the daggers in his hands.

Aries simpered at them all. "So, this is what I am to face? A band of misfits? How quaint."

Tetra's eyes burned against him. "I swore to you, Aries, you will pay for what you've done to my family. And now that I've found you, I will kill you."

Aries threw his hands to the sides, and the swords on the walls in his armories drew to his call. They hovered around him and waited for the invaders to move. Pargon felt the power of the elders heightening his senses, bringing his instincts into a manic drive. He jumped in front of his friends and guarded them. The swords pointed at him and dove in, striking at him. But all that Pargon could see was a group of slowly moving blades, all of them easily deflected. He could count them as he threw them aside with his sword. The last one made fifty, but instead of deflecting it, he dodged the tip of the blade and caught the hilt, turning to Aries with both blades pointed at him.

Aries tilted his head. "So you have a little skill," he said arrogantly.

Pargon stood straight up and tossed Aries' blade back at him. "Perhaps you'd like to play fairly?" he asked as Aries caught the blade.

Aries twirled his blade. "You four actually think you're a match for the mighty Aries, the god of war? I brought all of this to pass! This is all my doing! I am the very spirit of this fight!" Aries spread his wings and lifted off just above the ground, shouting, "I am the fight!"

Then, Tetra, Eon and Fang circled Aries in all directions. Pargon watched Aries turn to find the perfect first strike, but when Aries came back to him, Pargon could see a transparent figure surrounding his friends. To Pargon, it looked like three Valkyrie entities were holding their weapons with them, as if a trainer showing a student the movements of sword fighting.

Aries struck at Tetra, and when Tetra guarded, everyone else struck. Aries kicked Pargon away, punched Eon down and switched his attack from Tetra to Fang. Tetra leapt over Aries as he fought Fang off, and landed on Fang's back. Together, Fang attacked low as Tetra attacked high. Pargon recovered and Eon took Tetra's previous place. Aries dodged the blows that both Tetra and Fang attacked with and glanced at Eon to see him swinging for his upper leg and only noticed Pargon was on his left side. In the instant Aries jumped up to dodge Eon's slice to his leg, Pargon dropped to the ground and rolled under Aries to his right, as Aries deflected the high blows from Tetra.

Now, completely open on his right side, Pargon stuck his sword through Aries side. Aries lurched in pain from the unsuspected blow, and slapped at Pargon while trying to fend off the other attacks. Pargon dodged Aries' hand and pulled his sword away from Aries' body. Aries grunted in pain, but knew nothing could kill him. He was invincible. Aries swung his blade in for Fang's head. Fang ducked under it and Tetra flipped in the air over it, completely surrounding Aries once again. Pargon stopped the blade with his, and Eon lunged in for Aries back.

*****

All of the ogres lay dead on the battle field, but the Vamps still kept coming. The cerberus' kept eating their fill and the minotaurs were having a much easier fight riding on the three-headed dogs. The fairies came in for the dead centaurs and dead minotaurs and healed their wounds, bringing them all back to life as the Vamps would do. The battle seemed endless, but when the evening star went completely down, only those that could see in the dark, or see heat, like the cerberus', centaurs and the Vamps would have the advantage. Angels and minotaurs picked out their targets when the dragons sent fire bombs crashing near them.

Quiver and the other green dragons had a frenzy with the ground targets. They completely enjoyed themselves slashing and slicing the Vamps that would die and come back to life. Their only thought was to get everyone down and keep them down. For years, the had all been holding in their urges to attack without reason, and now their day of glory had come.

The centaurs found the Vamps to be easy targets. They were even more fragile beings than the Dryads were. But it was the numbers that overwhelmed them. They would knock the Vamps out of the fight, only to have to come back and fight the same ones down again. The centaurs rounded groups of Vamps and surrounded them. With the isolated groups cornered, it made it harder for the Vamps in the middle to fight. Soon, only two centaurs were all that was needed to control a group of twenty Vamps with their weapons.

The evening star fell, and darkness swallowed the horizon. The cerberus' howled and barked at the noise of the Vamps trying to break free, and the dragons searched for a way to destroy the tower that Aries resided in. With the tower gone, there would be very little chance of Aries coming back.

*****

Aries had knocked Eon and Tetra unconscious, but took a more difficult challenge from the other two. He twirled his sword around at

198

Pargon, and kicked Fang away. Pargon blocked the blow, but Aries was too fast. Spiraling Pargon's sword in his hands, the hilt twisted through Pargon's fingers and flew in the air. The instant his sword left his hand, Pargon spread his hands out at Aries and an energy pulse blasted Aries against the wall in his room. Pargon reached up and caught the sword as it fell. Surprised, Aries pushed himself away from the cracking wall and unleashed a flurry of attacks at Pargon, who blocked them all at lightning speed. His heart was pounding as Aries kept attacking, but when Fang came up behind Aries and stabbed both blades through his back, Aries stopped and knocked Fang back against the wall, then turned back to Pargon.

It was clear that Aries wanted a straight fight with Pargon before moving on to any other targets. Fang wasn't going to be ignored, though. He eagerly got back into the fight. Annoyed, Aries turned to Fang and clubbed him in the head with the hilt of his sword, knocking Fang unconscious as well. Pargon had a clean shot at Aries, and took it. He brought his sword up and sent it crashing down on his foe. Suddenly, Aries reached up and caught Pargon's arms in one hand and glared at him. Pargon was shocked and couldn't think of a fast retreat in time. With Aries now in control, he brought his sword to Pargon's side and dragged the blade, cutting through the break in the armor and slicing the skin.

Suddenly, Eon woke and jumped back into the fight. Eon pushed Pargon to the side and faced Aries alone. Eon never let the image of Pandora's death leave his mind. He would avenge his love here and now. Aries grinned, knowing exactly what was running through Eon's head.

"So, if you're still alive, then that means Pandora missed the mark somehow. I wonder, did you dispatch her before she finished you, or did she even come close?" Aries sneered.

Eon twirled the daggers with his fingers and brought them back, ready to fight, "she died because she thought she had no other choice, in order to keep you from hurting me through her. She died at your hand. And now, you will join her in death."

The angel spread his wings and lifted into the air, weaving his blades in the air, blocking and attacking at incredible speed, as Aries' sword moved with him like a dance between metal. In the air, they moved over the furniture and bodies, until Aries brought his blade down on Eon. Eon crossed his blades and caught Aries' sword closer to his face than he was comfortable with.

Then Aries pushed Pargon to the wall, keeping his hold on Eon's blade. Eon smiled at Aries attempt to corner him, but Aries' move only empowered Eon's comeback. Eon stretched his wings and lifted his feet in the air to the level of his head, caught the wall with his feet and shoved Aries back and down to the floor.

As they fell, Aries' sword got caught in the wood floor. Eon crossed his blades at Aries' throat.

"Any last words?" Eon asked.

Aries had a sinister smile. "That won't work," his voice rumbled.

Eon shook his head with the deepest satisfaction and slid the blades into his throat. But where there was supposed to be a huge gash, the cut glued back together, completely restored. Aries laughed and disappeared. Eon couldn't feel anything under him. Aries was gone. Pargon, Tetra and Fang stood up feeling the pain on their heads.

Pargon darted his eyes everywhere at something he saw out of the corner of his eye, but never came quite clear. "Where is he?" he asked.

Eon held the daggers in his hands and watched carefully for Aries. "He's still here," he warned.

Tetra took her sword and, swinging it to her side, it transformed into a powerful triton, the weapon of her people. "He's here. I can sense him," she thought.

Fang took his sword and watched for Aries, backing himself against the wall. If Aries chose him as a target, he would pin the devil to the wall and dispatch him that way, rather than fight the air.

Pargon found a strip of cloth on the ground next to his foot. He smiled and picked it up. Pacing to the middle of the room, he wrapped the cloth around his eyes and brought his sword to guard.

"No one move or say a word," Pargon ordered. "Make no noise." He moved around, listening for the flapping of wings and the possible land on the ground or furniture. "I'm here, Aries. If this is what you want, then this is what I'll give. Fight me."

Aries silently dashed in and swung, but the gust of his current gave his position away. Pargon guarded his head, and felt the invisible blade roll on his sword to his front. Aries may not have landed, but he was definitely in front of Pargon. If Pargon was going to have any chance of survival, he would need to be on the offensive. Pargon immediately struck and felt Aries deflect each attack as if it were a petty attempt on his person.

No matter what, Pargon didn't let up and never held back. Soon, Aries began to give in as Pargon sped up the pace. He grunted at the pain welling up in his arms and stinging on his wound, but Pargon kept going, the heart stone giving him an overdrive. With each hit, Aries was guarding later and later, giving Pargon the idea that Aries was searching for the right opening and wanting badly to strike abruptly.

Suddenly, Aries caught Pargon and pinned him down. Aries held Pargon down as long as he could, but Pargon could feel Valkyrie giving him more power and strength. He pushed Aries back, jumped straight up and drove his foot into Aries' neck, knocking him back and flipping in the air.

CHAPTER 8

When all of the Vamps were taken captive, the centaurs suddenly had a new enemy to worry about. The Ralligins had fought off the corruption of Aries as long as they could. They could no longer fight the power of the Voloroth. They spiraled through the sand and picked up every centaur around them, and dropped them from the highest point they could. If the centaurs got up, the Ralligins would attack them again. The minotaurs wouldn't sit back and lose the army with the loss of their allies, so they dashed in wherever the Ralligins would spring up and knock their weapons through the sand. A Ralligin or two would be smote, but the rest would only continue their quest at total destruction.

When all of the centaurs were down, the Ralligins would turn to the minotaurs and cerberus' as targets. Then, the clouds twirled again and another armada of angels fell from the heavens, led by Valkyrie and Decimus. One of the minotaurs pointed at the Ralligins' defeat and smiled that the elders had joined them in the battle. The angels could see through the cloak of invisibility that each Ralligin seemed to have. They came in with no weapons or armor, but still grabbed hard structures of the Ralligins and held them down to the sand. Millions of angels flooded the area, their very glow replacing the evening star and illuminating the entire southern pole of the world. Eon's angelic army was fighting out the battle with the rogue Vamps, but soon joined the battle with the Ralligins.

But with the centaurs down, the Vamps suddenly realized they were free to wreck havoc of their own. They ran in on the angels, trying to free the Ralligins. The twelve minotaurs grouped together and spotted the thickest group of Vamps attacking the angels. The leader pointed his ax at the group and his voice boomed "To the death!" The minotaurs charged down the hills and pulverized as many of the Vamps as they could, but the Vamps retaliated by biting them or scratching them. Decimus backed them up, swinging his sword and throwing six Vamps into the air at a time. The small group of angels were free of opposition, so Decimus and the minotaurs moved on to another herd of Vamps attacking other angels.

Valkyrie threw her shield into the neck of another Vamp, only to watch it be replaced by another. She twirled her sword in front of her and severed their heads, almost flying from group to group, destroying as many as she could. She knew that her efforts wouldn't last for long, but they would give the fairies enough time to resurrect the centaurs. This battle would last all through the night and into the morning until they were escorted back to Exile. Valkyrie felt Pargon's presence, and could feel he was winning.

*****

Pargon's arms were almost a blur from moving so fast, but the pain was immense from the never ending attacks. He gritted his teeth, trying to hide the pain, but he couldn't stand it anymore.

"Eon! Fang! I need help!" Pargon called.

They stepped in, but when Pargon slowly turned his body, they were confused as to where he meant for them to attack.

"Where is he?" Fang asked.

Pargon grunted in aggravation and swung his sword to the side and drove the Chevron into Aries' stomach. Aries lurched forward and screamed in pain, becoming visible again.

"Right there." Pargon replied.

Eon knew Aries wouldn't be held against that sword for long. If given the chance, Aries would pull himself off, quickly heal himself and fight even harder. He dashed over the furniture and stabbed Aries in the lower back, holding him in position for Fang to thrust his sword into Aries' side. Aries dropped his sword and stretched his wings, wailing in pain. Tetra gripped the wooden stake in her hand, her knuckles turning white. She rushed in to Aries and drove the stake through his heart.

"Now, you will pay," Tetra growled.

Eon, Pargon and Fang pulled their swords from Aries sides and watched Tetra slowly dig the stake deeper into his heart.

Aries clutched Tetra's arms and gasped, "You have beaten me. What is it you want? Name it, and it is yours if you set me free."

Tetra's body shook with the fire in her burning for revenge. "Die!"

And with that, she twisted the stake all the way through his chest. He staggered away and fell on his back, realizing that of all things he was prepared for, a wooden stick would be his undoing. He closed his eyes and waited to be taken back to exile.

Eon smiled on Aries' death, and with this devil gone, all of Hajun would finally be at peace. The Ancient Ones were saved. Decimus rose up through the window and met Aries' soul in the room. He pointed his sword at Aries' soul and pulled him out of the tower, with the thousands of Vamps following after them. Decimus locked them all back in Exile where they stayed until the dawn of the Ragnarok.

Valkyrie, too, entered the room where Aries' dead body lay. She took the Voloroth in her hand and let it bind itself to her. As it did, the two forces of power repelled each other and fell apart. The Uniroth glowed yellow like the morning star, and the Aniroth glowed red. With this, Valkyrie could feel the liberation of the Ralligins, and felt them all leave the southern pole.

The building rumbled and shook. The minotaurs rounded the tower, knocking out the stilts that held it up. The five leaders in the tower leapt from the balcony, and fell. Valkyrie was the last to leave. She reached out and caught them all with her energy shields. Landing safely on the ground, they watched the tower tip with the winds and fall on its side. Now, they could be certain, Aries would never return again.

Valkyrie glanced at Eon, hovering over the ground and watching the dust under the tower lift.

"So, you're the commander of this angelic army?" Valkyrie asked him.

Eon smiled at his army's final victory. "Yes. Although, instead of losing numbers, it seems I've somehow gained a few," he said rubbing the back of his head.

Valkyrie laughed hooking her shield to the hook on the strap on her back. "Does your army have a place to call home?" she asked knowing the answer already.

Eon shook his head. "No, we don't. For now, we're a wondering group of outcasts."

Valkyrie nodded at his remorse. "You would make a fine commander of our ranks."

Eon's heart lifted. "You want me in command of your army, after my misconduct with my previous masters?"

Valkyrie tilted her head. "Seasons change all things. You've demonstrated your level of responsibility. If you're interested, then the position is open."

Eon nodded. "We would gladly join you," he replied.

Tetra stood next to Eon. "First, I believe you've left someone behind. She can be resurrected with the power of the elders. I've seen it happen," she said.

Eon closed his eyes, knowing that even if she could be brought back, she may not want to be. Then Valkyrie touched his arm and faded away from the battle field.

*****

Eon and Valkyrie faded next to the pool and saw the dead nymph lying motionlessly on the shore. Nothing had changed here. Valkyrie looked around in the trees for Pandora's wandering soul, and found her drifting in the woods, alone. Valkyrie called for the soul to come to her voice. Pandora sadly drifted back to the pool as Valkyrie healed the wound on the dead body and cleansed it of impurities. She instructed Pandora to enter her body again.

"Aries has me. I cannot go back," Pandora lamented.

Valkyrie shook her head and communicated on that dimensional plane to her. "Aries thought he had you, too. But all that held your heart was love, not him."

Pandora's soul lay down in her body and closed her eyes. She gasped for air and coughed through the pain of coming back to life. She was lifted into Eon's arms, receiving his complete forgiveness. Valkyrie smiled on them and looked Eon in the eyes.

"Whenever you want to join us, we'll be waiting. In the meantime, I'll be negotiating with the Ancient Ones and preparing you dwelling places."

Pandora looked up at Eon. "This means …"

Eon touched a finger to her lips and waited for Valkyrie to finish.

"See you in heaven," Valkyrie said with a wink and faded off of Hajun.

Eon couldn't stop grinning and gazed into Pandora's eyes. "We'll be together, forever. I promise."

*****

The Centurions came home to a loud welcoming party waiting for them. Each soldier that had a family fell out of line with the King's permission and waited in the crowd with them. The crowd cheered and threw palm branches into the path of the king and his victors as they entered the kingdom. Then the army aligned itself at the entrance of the palace, and the king stood at the top of the palace stairs, under the arch of the castle walls. Fang turned to his people and raised his arms to silence the crowds. As the roar died, Fang let his words cry out to his new nation.

"Centurions! Today dawns the era of peace throughout all of Hajun!"

The crowds cheered and Fang dwelt in the magnitude of respect his leadership brought to his army.

*****

Pargon returned to the borders of his home village almost a year from the time he left. He had thought about running. Every step he took was a step closer to prison. But the heart-stone forced him to think again. If he deviated from his orders, even to lay down and die, the stone would fill his body with a searing poison, and Mercy would die alone.

A patrolling Dryad met him before he could go any further.

"Do you have papers of passage?" the guard asked.

Pargon shook his head. "My name is Pargon, Odin's reincarnate. I have done as the prophets asked. I have defeated the god of war as promised and I have returned to serve my sentence as they see fit."

The guard motioned for Pargon to lead the way back to the prophets. When Pargon was processed and sent to the boat for the floating prison, he turned back and looked, waiting for Jade's reincarnate to say goodbye. The boat cast off and Pargon watched for her until the shore was out of sight.

For ten long years, he wrote her letters and waited for his freedom. For ten long years, Mercy cried at night for the elders to bring back her lover. For ten long years, they couldn't reach each other, even by thought as they had the first time.

*****

"Almost a hundred years ago, Pargon served his time, and came home to find his lover dead," the oracle told the child in her arms, "but this time, things will be different. This time, the pendulum of good and evil will swing so quickly that the gods will not be allowed to intervene."

Odin looked up at her as she bounced baby Jade to sleep. He loved this centaur as his new mother.

"This time, you'll know how to fight with all you are. You'll kill without thought and succeed in all you do. You'll be stronger, faster and far more fierce than any of your past lives." The oracle laid Jade down in her basket. "We shall not fail this time."

Book IV

IN THE END

CHAPTER 1

Decimus was held down by the god-chains and brought to his knees before the Sovereigns. He looked up and fought against the heavy hold on him. The five beings above him sat on their thrones, looking down on him as a lower being and a culprit.

Kronos, the Sovereign in the center spoke first. "You have violated your agreement and sacred vow to neutrality. Such a charge is punishable by death. Have you anything to say in your defense?"

Decimus stayed low, giving reverence to the god of time, and replied, "I was not aware of this treaty. But, I assure you, I have made no such violation."

Kronos waved his hand and motioned someone from the back of the court to come forth. When Decimus saw the figure, he recognized it as an Ancient One and smiled at the friend he had saved so many ages ago. Then he realized his crime was saving them and locking Aries away in Exile. He looked down at the ground and thought of the defense the Ancient One would have for him.

Lavish, on the right of Kronos, spoke next. "Did this entity lock Aries into exile?"

The Ancient One replied, "He did."

Decimus shouted at the Ancient One. "To save you from his coming attacks!"

"Did this action bring the imbalance of Good and Evil in the universe?" Lavish asked.

"It did," The Ancient One answered.

"What I did is the reason you're alive right now!" Decimus shouted again.

"One more outburst from you and you'll be held in contempt. Is that understood?" Kronos said calmly to Decimus.

· Decimus glared at the Ancient One and nodded to Kronos, respectfully.

Kronos nodded to Rhea, to his left. Rhea stood and read the penalties. "Decimus, for violating your agreement as a neutral being, you have been sentenced to death. You are forthwith stripped of your power and status and will be given the abilities of a Walking Dead member and held for three days imprisoned while in that time someone may come to your defense. You will then be executed through feohtan eower, the death of a traitor. Once you have died, your energy will be contributed to the collective of higher powers, and your soul will be held in torment until Ragnarok."

Decimus grit his teeth, knowing feohtan eower was better than anything else the Sovereigns could have dealt him. Even in his moment of rage against them, they still had mercy on him. A Hunter gripped the god-chains and took him away from the court and led him to his cell. The walls of his cell were covered in soul energy, strong enough to keep him from escaping. His escape attempts failed each time he tried.

*****

Odin and Sashi approached the shack where Dauntless had Jade captive. Odin jumped off of Sashi and drew his sword from his back sheath.

Sashi stood, not really knowing what to do from here.

"Ok, you go have fun and I'll just wait here," he called.

But Odin was already inside and the door had just closed. Odin scowled at the captor holding a knife up to Jade's neck. Jade, however, had an impatient look on her face, as if Odin was late for a deadline. Odin twirled his sword as he tread up to Dauntless.

"Take one more step, and I'll slit her throat," Dauntless warned.

Odin flipped his sword in his hand and threw it across the shack, pinning Dauntless against the wall, silent and lifeless.

"What took you so long?" Jade groaned as Odin untied her.

"Traffic," he replied sarcastically. "Did you get it?"

Jade stood and rubbed the circulation of blood back into her wrists. "His name is Aquarius. He has the Chevron," she answered.

Odin took a short look around the shack and Jade stopped and looked Dauntless over with a sigh to his lifeless body.

"I'm going to miss those days of long walks on the beach; sleeping under the stars. Cuddling all night ..."

Odin stepped over the chair and yanked his sword from Dauntless' neck. The dead body dropped to the floor before Jade could finish the tale of her memory. She smiled sarcastically as Sashi tilted his head. "You made it a quick death? I thought you were going to have your fun with him."

Odin and Jade jumped on his back. "I'll save the fun for later. Aquarius has my sword, and I owe him a missing finger."

Jade giggled at Odin's determination. "Looks like we're in for a ... what's that thing called again?"

"Coup de tat?" Sashi answered.

"No, the other thing," Jade replied.

"Mass genocide," Sashi suggested, galloping off to see the oracle.

*****

Valkyrie appeared before the Ancient Ones and demanded an audience with them. Millions of them surrounded her as an answer to her call. For once in her Elderly life, she felt threatened.

"Decimus has been taken to the Sovereigns, and something told me you would know more about it than anyone else would," Valkyrie began. "I want him back."

The pure white cloaks of the Ancient Ones seemed to light this realm of space with a golden aura. Valkyrie looked around at all of them, never hearing even a whisper. It was becoming clearer with every second that they were behind Decimus' disappearing.

"What have you done?" she shouted.

The Ancient Ones remained still and silent, but she wouldn't allow their silence for much longer. She was about to bring their realm down on top of them all when Rhea, the accomplice of the Ancient Ones, stepped forward.

"What would you do if you knew that your beloved was put to death?" Rhea asked.

Valkyrie turned to her and reached for her sword. In an instant, every Ancient One held a fully developed energy ball in their hands, ready to obliterate her if she moved again. Valkyrie backed down, but let her anger show.

"Where is he?" she demanded.

Rhea answered, "with the Sovereigns, where he can no longer make a mess of things. He's facing foehtan eower. It's a pity he's not in for more." She laughed again.

The tingle in Valkyrie's ears only concurred with Rhea's claim.

"He will not die in three days. Not for saving your race." Valkyrie said to the Ancient Ones. Then she saw the truth, the sadness stirring in Rhea's soul.

Valkyrie tilted her head. "You loved him, didn't you."

Rhea looked up, hiding the truth with confusion, giving no quarter to her feelings. "Justice must be served," Rhea growled.

Valkyrie repeated louder, her voice echoing. "You loved Aries, didn't you? That's why you had Decimus condemned to damnation!"

Rhea turned away. "Aries has been punished for two lifetimes of a god. He has paid the price and redeemed himself. If he is not set free, then justice is flawed and the universe is thrown out of balance. You and Decimus have tipped the scale, and none of us will be spared from that shift. Nothing will stop this now. That is why I'm doing this."

Valkyrie dared not move, but pleaded where she stood. "Rhea, please, see reason. Please understand that you can't change Aries."

Another voice called from the side, "She doesn't want to change me." The crowd of Ancient Ones parted revealing Aries coming in with a smile. "She wants to join me."

Rhea and Aries met and kissed their hellos.

Valkyrie clenched her fists, making the realm shake under the pressure of her power. Rhea and Aries smiled at her sudden shock of seeing her foe joined with her enemy.

"Back down, Valkyrie, or I'll have you destroyed," Rhea replied.

"This is madness!" Valkyrie shouted.

Aries chuckled. "This is justice." He whispered touching Rhea's hair.

Valkyrie disappeared and fled as fast as she could to the afterlife. Someone there would help her.

CHAPTER 2

Sashi sliced down the hob goblins in his way and Odin and Jade took on the Son of Scorpio. The giant scorpion alternated between stinging at them, stepping on them and squishing them with its claws. Odin rolled under its claw and dodged its foot coming down to crush his head. Jade was on its back, stabbing it with her daggers. Every move the scorpion made was almost a pleasurable experience for Jade. Odin stood in front of its face and lowered his sword.

"I really don't have time for this," Odin growled.

All of the scorpion's black eyes blinked once. Howling through the air, the stinger came crashing down. Odin jumped high rolling backwards in the air. He took his sword and severed the sting from the scorpion's tail. Black blood spewed everywhere, and the scorpion recoiled back into its hole in the mountain, screeching in pain.

Jade gripped her daggers and jumped off the front of the scorpion spreading her body into the wind and rolling on the ground in front of Odin. Jade looked up into Odin's eyes with a cheeky smile.

"That was exciting," she said.

Odin's expression was agitated and hollow. They glanced back at Sashi, who was also enjoying his killing spree. Slitting throats, severing limbs, vanquishing this new found evil, he loved what he was doing and knew it wasn't the most wonderful thing in the world.

Now, down to his last kill, he wondered how he should spend this last thrill. He could squish the green, scaly creature with his hooves, cut off every limb, with its head being the last. Other ideas flooded his thoughts. He decided to pick the rapidly squirming creature up. Its wings fluttered fast, its arms and legs punched and kicked Sashi's arm. Sashi looked up at the strangling creature, watching the blood leak from its mouth.

Unexpectedly, a throwing knife severed the poor creature's brain stem, lodged inside its head. Sashi groaned at the buzz kill and watched Jade softly clap at Odin's murder.

"Do you have to squeeze the joy out of everything?" Sashi whined dropping the hob goblin to the ground.

Odin handed Sashi the sting and jerked the dagger out of the goblin's head. He wiped off the blood and gave Jade back her knife.

"Now, to find our way out of this canyon," Odin said, mounting on Sashi.

Sashi jerked in surprise. "This is the sting?" he asked, as if touched by a leper.

Odin took it from him. "Yes, it is, and I'd like you to not drop all of the venom, please." He tipped the sting downward so the glands would point up near the cut.

Jade was squeamish. "You're not really going to drink that, are you?"

Odin held tight to it. "When the time comes, this venom will make my powers supreme," he said.

Sashi galloped on. "Where to next, sir?" he asked.

Odin placed the sting in the pouch on his hip. "We have to get Vampire blood in the goblet of a troll."

"Where are we going to find that?" Jade asked.

Sashi frowned. "Ferron," he answered.

All three of them cringed at the thought. Ferron was not a friendly place anymore.

*****

Decimus sat in his chamber. He had only been there a few hours, but it felt like a lifetime. The Chamber door opened, and in walked a Hunter with god-chains and the Sovereign, Alpha. The Hunter placed the god-chains on Decimus' shoulders and stood him up, holding him in place. Alpha stood facing Decimus.

"You saved my life, too. I was Omega's primary target before the war between Lucifer and Orion. You kept me from that demise, so I'm here to help you," Alpha explained, closing the chamber door.

Decimus glared at him. "Can you keep me from my fate?"

Alpha shook his head. "That isn't going to change. You did violate the treaty."

"I don't even know what treaty we're talking about," Decimus replied rather annoyed.

Alpha bobbed his head once. "You took the place of Odin and the elders, correct?"

"And Orion, yes."

Alpha held his hands behind his back. "There are three levels of Higher Powers. There's the Creator which creates planets and beings to dwell on them. The Watcher keeps order among all beings. The Trader takes the remains of a fallen Higher Power and oversees the distribution of any exchanges made between Higher Powers. Most of the elders were watchers. One had to be a Trader, and another had to be a Creator. One could have been all three, but that wouldn't be a very wise idea. None of them wanted that kind of attention from the Universe."

"I'm not seeing where you're going with this," Decimus said.

"Decimus, this is the contract of a Higher Power. The elders should have mentioned it to you before they helped you ascend, but they didn't. I guess they didn't figure on you taking command of Exile."

"There were dark beings leaking out of that place. I locked it up. Is that so horrible?" Decimus asked.

"Those were beings that were supposed to get out. They had served their time, and they were being set free. A lot of them change after spending a millennium in there. Then, you closed those doors, which offset the balance of Good and Evil," Alpha answered.

"They were dark beings. I saw their intentions. They hadn't changed. None of them had."

"Then, they would have been brought before us and sentenced to banishment again. You can't make those decisions for us. You have your work, and we have ours."

Decimus' head dropped. "Aries is freed, then."

Alpha nodded. "I'm afraid that's out of anyone's control. His next move will determine if he goes back to Exile or not."

Decimus shook in rage. "His next move will destroy an entire system of innocents. He's pure evil. What more do you need for proof?"

"He's a Higher Power. He deserves as much a chance to redeem himself as any," Alpha said.

"And what chance have I? How can I get out of here and fight my fight; defend my responsibility to the elders?"

Alpha closed his eyes. "The treaty of remaining neutral has been broken by you. Aries was never neutral. He was destructive by nature and has selected worlds that he conquers. Until he lays destruction on another system, I'm sorry, but he's in no violation."

"And why was he sent to Exile in the first place? Why not sentenced to death, like me? Why can't you destroy him?" Decimus asked.

"Because of his dark nature, it throws off the balance of the universe. Good and Evil must remain level on the universal scale."

"Then to the Underworld with him! Let him be evil there!" Decimus shouted.

"He in no violation. And he's already been punished for whatever wrongs he has committed."

"Let me save my people before I die! Let me save my world!" Decimus cried.

"If I let you go, then a war will start between you and Aries. Millions will die."

"Let them!"

"You're better than that."

"You lie! I would sacrifice all to stop him!"

Alpha sighed. "And that's why we have to keep you here. I'm sorry."

The god-chain shook on Decimus' shoulders. Decimus only stared at Alpha with his fists clinched. The cell they were in started to shake and the soul energy began to part.

"What are you doing?" Alpha said, almost terrified that Decimus had this much power.

The god-chain shocked him, draining him of his energy. When Decimus stood unfazed, it shocked him again. He grunted once, but the cell was coming apart. Decimus was breaking free. The god-chain began electrocuting him, but Decimus only grunted from pain. Finally, the cell was gone, and the three stood in space along the side of the temple.

"Decimus, you fool. You'll only bring yourself to the attention of Death on hastier wings. You must not leave!" Alpha shouted.

"I will defend my world. I will fight to the death as a god of love would. And I will succeed." He grunted barbarically under the shocks of the god-chain.

Finally, the god-chain arched to his head, and electrocuted him there. Decimus fell as the soul energy reconstructed the cell.

Alpha knelt down to check Decimus. "You killed him ... for now," he whispered to the Universe. "I must report this to the council." Alpha sighed, shaking his head, "As soon as they hear that Decimus has this much power, they'll take better precautions." He turned Decimus' head, "I'm sorry," he whispered and left.

CHAPTER 3

Odin tied the vampire down into his trap. The vampire tore through most of the ropes, but it was overwhelmed and just stopped fighting it all. Sashi held it by the neck, facing it toward Odin, who had the knife.

"Jade, have the goblet ready. This sucker's going to bleed for us now," Odin said.

Jade held the cup next to the vampire's neck, ready for Odin to make the slit.

Odin held the knife up and smiled. "Enjoying the irony?" he asked the vampire. "Don't worry. I hear your kind can't die from what we're about to do to you. So the worst that'll happen is you'll feel a little sting."

He slid the blade along the vampire's neck and blood squirted from its veins. Jade caught as much as she could in the cup, but she still couldn't avoid getting it on her. The vampire's wound healed almost instantly.

Odin changed his expression. "Interesting. Let's try again," he said slitting the vampire's throat again.

Jade caught the blood in the goblet, but the flow stopped within seconds.

"Maybe you should stab it in the throat. That might keep the wound from healing," Sashi explained.

Odin curled his lips. "Well, I don't want to hurt it," he replied.

Jade smiled softly at Odin. "I think half a cup should do it, don't you?"

Odin frowned, "Fine, I guess that will be enough."

And with that, Odin stuck the blade all the way through the vampire's neck. The blood flowed like a pitcher pouring wine into a glass. When the goblet was full, Odin yanked the knife away from the vampire's throat. The cut closed again and the vampire started shrieking in pain.

Sashi rolled his eyes. "Now, it starts to cry?"

Jade stood up concentrating on the goblet. "Should we let it go?" she asked.

Odin shrugged. "It's been good for us so far. It hasn't tried to bite Sashi or anything. I guess we can trust it."

Sashi struggled to keep it settled. "You just stabbed its neck so you could take its blood. I highly doubt it likes you right now."

Odin took the goblet from Jade. "You want to kill it?" he offered.

Sashi walked over to the light beyond the shade of the surrounding trees and held the vampire down, feeling it boil in his hands. Its cries echoed through the forest, but it died quickly under Sashi's grip.

Jade jumped on the front of Sashi's back and Odin held on behind her.

"Sashi, your ruth has just left." Jade said. "You have no ruth. You are completely ruthless."

Sashi nodded. "Thank you," he said and galloped away, traveling through the forest to the outskirts of Centurion. Sashi leapt over a log and entered daylight. The oracle's small dome sat lonely, outside of Centurion. They reached her home and Odin entered in. The old Centaur was lying on her belly with her legs curled in. Her arms were stirring the ingredients,inside the boiling cauldron.

"Pour in the blood," the oracle said hoarsely.

Odin lifted the glass and let the blood splash into the potion.

"And the venom," she said.

He placed the goblet to the side and held the sting over the cauldron, squeezing out every drop of venom that was left. The oracle held a knife in her hand and with her other hand, she motioned for Odin to hold his over the cauldron.

Odin groaned. "I've already lost a finger to this madness."

The oracle nodded. "I understand, and you're allowed to be upset. But I still need your hand."

Odin scoffed and held her hand. The oracle spread his fingers out and his hand caught the steam from the cauldron. In one move, she brought the knife up and stabbed his hand between the tendons, dripping blood down the blade, into the cauldron.

Odin's cheek twitched, but he looked at the oracle rather confused. "That was it? You're not going to cut it off?"

The oracle glanced up at him and back down at the brew. "This is the Dark Craft, not the cheap tricks from the underworld. This is a method as old as time." She brought the cup and pushed Odin's hand away, letting him take the knife out himself.

"The eyes of the seers, blood of the dead, venom of a monster, and blood of a purebred, light of day, cold of night, weapon of the enemy and death in flight all come together to bring you power. Power of old and new, power of the world caged in you." The oracle finished and dipped the goblet into the brew and handing Odin a small portion to drink.

Odin took the steaming cup and drank it all. The taste was disgusting, and he didn't even want to finish what little bit he had. But he instantly felt the power enveloping inside him. He dropped the goblet to the ground and lurched forward, wanting to regurgitate whatever he had inside him. His heart was pounding; he could feel the energies being pumped through his body. It rushed to his head, heavily buzzing inside.

"Breathe, Odin. Just breathe," the oracle said.

Odin took deep breaths, and let the fluids run through his body. When the power started to die down, he recovered the goblet, dipped it into the brew and drank some more, gulping down this time. He ground his teeth together, loving the new power he was drinking into himself.

He looked at his hand and the finger that Aquarius had cut off had grown back. As he stared at his finger, his focus was lost in a spontaneous vision. He saw Aquarius on his knees in front of Odin, begging for mercy. Odin took his father's sword in his hands and raised it high. Then he brought it down on Aquarius' head, crushing his skull, killing him instantly. Odin smiled, feeling the bone cave in under his force. Rocking the blade back and forth, digging it into his father's enemy. He closed his eyes, relishing every sensation until finally, the body fell to the ground, sliding down the blade. Odin bit his bottom lip and took a sharp breath, falling unconditionally in love with this fantasy.

He opened his eyes, dipped the cup in for more of the concoction. He drank the rest, thanked the oracle and stepped outside the dome and joined Jade and Sashi. Jade naturally enjoyed seeing Odin's change. She fell on his shoulder, hanging on his body, wanting him right then and there. Odin gladly teased her, but when Sashi suggested they leave, Odin agreed and only heated Jade up more.

*****

Valkyrie looked up at the dead elders and called to Lara. Lara came down from the other souls and stood before her.

"My allies have befriended my foes and I stand alone against them all, and on top of all this, Decimus is now a prisoner of the Sovereigns. What can I do? Hajun will be destroyed if I let fate take its course."

Lara shook her head, "Fate will not allow Hajun to fall. You will succeed. You must consult with your Elder companion. Your link will help you to communicate. You need to re-link with him so clarity can be restored."

Valkyrie sighed in agony. "I know that one of the Sovereigns has chosen a side. Rhea, I believe, has become emotionally involved with Aries. Ancient Ones and Vamps, once mortal enemies, are now combative brothers. Does this not sound like elements of the prophecy? Does this not remind you of what the prophets were told by the Sovereigns; about peace where there would be war and battle where there should be harmony?"

Valkyrie asked hoping to find some answer in the old ways. Lara closed her eyes. "If these are the signs you're referring to, then I'll have to awaken the elders and let them know their time has come."

Valkyrie knew what this meant and shook her head. "No. You still have an age yet. Your hundred years is the last to be accomplished and I've disturbed that enough already. I'll find some way to give you more time."

Lara smiled. "I hope this helps you in some way."

Valkyrie admired the colors that rippled across Lara's transparent form. "Thank you. This does help."

Lara nodded once and rose back to the swirl of the elders waiting souls.

*****

Decimus sat in his cell feeling the vertigo from the god-chain swim in his head. He leaned against the cell wall and dared not try to stand. He even had to close his eyes to contain the dizziness. He'd gone through his abilities, but at the slightest use of energy, his head would pull itself back and to every angle it could from the dizziness of the helmet. He couldn't feel any pulls of gravity; for all he knew, he was sitting on the ceiling of the cell.

He turned his head to the right and saw feet walking sideways towards him. "The spinning sensation you're feeling comes from the chains draining you of your energy," Alpha explained. "Although, I can't see why you've chosen to sit on the wall to soothe your pains. Sitting sideways only makes things that much worse."

Decimus could barely lift his head to look at Alpha. It bobbed whenever he turned, but finally his eyes met Alpha's.

"Actually, it's quite pleasing. You should try it," Decimus said, not realizing what he had done in the disorientation.

Alpha leaned on the wall next to Decimus' feet and looked him over. "I hate seeing you like this. But there isn't much choice in the matter. All I can really tell you from this point is what you face in feohtan eower, as I assume you've never been through it before."

Decimus closed his eyes again, trying to stay stable enough to think. "Does it help me get out of here?"

"No, but it could help you find a way of winning. No one ever has though," Alpha replied.

Decimus bobbed his head again, trying to straighten up. "How, in the name of Odin, am I any different from any other higher power that has been set up in these courts? How can I defeat the undefeatable?"

Alpha raised an eyebrow. "You've done it before, haven't you?"

Decimus closed his eyes and sighed. "I didn't defeat Omega. I and my Elder companion who happened to be possessed by an even higher power called Valefor defeated the Omega System. Then Valefor and Omega began their battle as they drifted off into space. They are still very much alive."

"But you're the only Dryads to have ascended to a higher power. None of your peers have achieved such a goal."

Decimus scratched his nose and decided to move on. "Why don't you tell me what I face?"

Alpha bobbed his head in agreement. "You'll do battle in the Sovereign court. We will observe as you engage yourself in hand to hand combat."

Decimus felt his brain swim in his head and it pained him to think curiously. "How, exactly, am I going to engage myself in hand to hand combat?" he asked.

Alpha's lips stiffened. "It's not important how you see what you see. What is important is when you step into that ring, you will see yourself walk out of the door opposite you, and he will be ready to fight you. All of your strengths, all of your weaknesses, all of your skills will be manifested in this body. You both have the powers of the Walking Dead."

"Why is that, may I ask? I'm not exactly infected with anything, or dying, as I have no body to decay. How am I a dead man?" Decimus asked.

Alpha closed his eyes. "The reason nobody has ever won is because if you kill him, you die. Before you enter the court, you will be embodied into a shape shifter. If you stab your opponent in the spleen, a cut will open on your belly and you will fall. If you cut off his head, the skin on your neck will split up and the vertebrae in your neck will fall apart. It's the link between you two that makes the fight dangerous, not so much that you're fighting yourself."

Decimus was tired from the helmet, but just aware enough to grasp the concepts that Alpha was throwing at him. "So, if he kills me, I die. If I kill him, I die. I guess I am a dead man." He sighed. "What were you saying about a way of winning?"

Alpha shook his head. "I don't know how, but I figured you could figure out some sort of plan."

Decimus tried to stand on the wall, but fell at the slightest exertion of energy.

Alpha walked back to the chamber door and turned to face Decimus. "If Valkyrie gets inside of the Sovereign zone, you'll be able to communicate to her through your link. That's all I can tell you."

And with that, Alpha disappeared.

CHAPTER 4

Sashi leaned forward on a rock and fell sound asleep in seconds. Jade snuggled up to Odin and fell asleep on his shoulder. Odin was the only one left staring up at the night sky, letting the anger rush through his veins. He knew for a fact that without the Oracle's help, he wouldn't even have these memories. These cursed thoughts of his father's death at his brother's hand. The Father promised Valefor would never break free. The Father promised. Odin had been forsaken by one or all of the elders, and the Father let it happen. Their ascension was, of course, always the goal, even if it meant sacrificing their beloved brother.

He closed his eyes and drifted into space, asking anyone, anywhere for answers. Lying there in the sand, the voices echoed in his ears. He asked all of his questions and all of them had garbled answers.

"Even after he ascended in the Underworld, he shouldn't have gotten free. Who set him free?" he asked.

"Solaris, Aquarius, Aries, Erebus," a whisper answered.

"Why did the Father allow such an action?"

"The prophecy," echoed an answer.

"And that was worth abandoning me? Why have I been forsaken?"

"The prophecy," the echo repeated.

"Which one?" Odin shouted.

A beam of light blinded him for a moment and one of the Sovereigns came forward from the light. He didn't recognize which one it was, but it was definitely male.

"Your kinsmen have not abandoned you," he boomed. "They have ascended to bring forth the sovereign vision. All of the promises that have been made have been kept. And you will be the first to enter that vision with us."

"My father broke a promise and allowed Valefor to be set free. Even now Valefor is at large. He could destroy the visions of the future, and my father would be to blame for every attempt Valefor makes."

"Your father saw what was coming and knew he could not prevent it. He accepted his defeat honorably and boldly. Valefor has been dealt with. He has been destroyed, as has Omega, and they will join the other dark energies in the far reaches of the universe for the Ragnarok. You, however, have diverted from your path in life in a massive way. You have almost ascended to a higher power, but if you go through with what you are about to do, you will sway greatly from Good to Evil. The chosen one must be pure at heart and must remain neutral. You have fallen short of that quota, and that alone will destroy the great vision."

"The New Kingdom failed. What makes this vision of yours any different? Why must I be the chosen one? Who chose me to be the key to the locked door? Why can't I take my bow out of this story and move off of the ever turning wheel of reincarnation?" Odin pleaded.

"You chose your path. You will be what you agreed you would be. Your fate was not predetermined. It is being made with everything you do. Every step you take will be a step closer to your place in the universe. Believe me when I say, you will save us all, and you will rule us all," the Sovereign replied.

"I don't want to rule you. I want to see my brother's end. I want my father to be the one to do it. I want my father's sword to have the stain of my brother's blood for the rest of time," Odin sneered.

"Odin, you were brought up in a dark time for Hajun. Being abandoned and raised by the oracle from birth has poisoned your purpose. You must overcome this. In all of the eternities you've lived, your hardest test would be to resist all that you know and to have mercy on a victim you would gladly execute. In one season, we will come for you. Make your soul ready by then," the Sovereign commanded.

Odin glared at the thought of not exacting his vengeance, but accepted the magnitude of the situation of a Sovereign making a request. The light closed behind the Sovereign figure and Odin awoke panting from the intensity of this vision. Jade opened her eyes and gave him a frisky look.

"How was it?" she inquired.

He turned his gaze to her and stroked her cheek. "It's time," he whispered.

She jumped up, leaning on her hands. "He's here?" she replied excitedly.

Odin's lips curled into an evil smile. "Wake Sashi. We're going now," he said.

Jade rushed to Sashi and massaged his waist. "Sashi, I know this tickles, so get up. Aquarius is trapped."

Sashi stood and lifted Jade with him. "Where is he?" he yawned.

Odin saw the morning star making its entrance. Time was running short. He drew his sword and stepped into the water on the beach. He dipped the tip of the sword into the water in front of him and waited for just a little more color to fill the clouds. Jade started to shiver in the morning chill.

"What are you waiting for?" Jade whispered, lying on Sashi's back.

Odin could feel the water succumbing to his control. The water remembered him and never failed to obey. Color reflected off of the waves and Odin closed his eyes, softly beginning the chant.

"I am Odin; the overwhelming force upon the sea. The body in motion that cannot be stopped. My will and command are to be obeyed. No peace, no stillness, no silence will break my voice from your every wave. Rise up and give me life!" he shouted jerking his sword from the waves of the ocean to the morning star.

Instantly, the waters rose in front of him, leaving his feat and forming a wall in front of him, which parted down the middle, splashing away a dry path for the three to tread. The water roared at first when it rose, but its roar dulled in respect to its master. The very thickness of the water formed a shadow over Sashi and Jade, who were absolutely awe-stricken by this. Finally, the path ended at the stairway of Aquarius' castle.

Odin brought his sword down and turned to Sashi. "Let's go!" he roared with a smile.

Sashi galloped up to him and he swung up and sat behind Jade, and they rode the whole way to Aquarius' castle.

*****

"Decimus," a whisper echoed in Decimus' mind. He awoke on the ground, feeling incredibly weak. The whisper echoed again with more intensity, but never growing louder. He sat up on the floor, feeling the headache the helmet left.

"At least it's off," he sighed in relief.

"Decimus!" the whisper shouted. But this time, he recognized it.

"Valkyrie?" he thought.

"I'm in the Sovereign zone. Are you okay?" she replied.

Decimus felt so much better hearing her voice in his head.

"I've certainly been better, but I'm glad you're here. You know I'm about to die, right?"

"I know. It's Rhea. She's involved with Aries. That's why you've been sentenced to death," Valkyrie informed him.

"Rhea? Is emotionally involved? That would make her a force of Evil. She wouldn't risk that," he reasoned.

"I don't understand it either. But I know what I saw. They're in love. You need to let one of the Sovereigns know, quickly."

"Thank you, Valkyrie. Don't give up on me, yet."

"I'm here, aren't I? I'll have my eyes open for some way out of this. Don't you give up on me," she replied.

He smiled and sent her his love and let her get on her way.

Alpha appeared in his chamber. "You requested me?"

"You knew about Rhea falling in love with Aries, didn't you?" Decimus said softly.

"The Ancient One's were adamant about keeping their independence. But, I knew Rhea was up to something. I didn't know it went as far as Aries, though. I suppose Valkyrie gave you this information," Alpha replied.

"Rhea has the army of the Ancient Ones at her fingertips and you're allowing her to reach into dark realms. Celestials and Vampires should never mix, and yet their unity was made right under your watchful eyes. How can the Sovereigns get away with this course of action?" Decimus cried out.

Alpha took a deep breath. "Neither I, nor the other Sovereigns saw this coming. We will look into the matter. In the meantime, your penance is hours away. I suggest you ready yourself."

Alpha disappeared, once again.

"Valkyrie, are you there?" Decimus thought.

"I'm here, Decimus. I heard it all. I'm going to find Eon. If he knows anything, he'll tell me. Beyond that, I don't know what else to do, or who else to consult. I'll be back before the night is over," she said giving him her affections.

Decimus was once again alone, wondering how he would ever escape this fate. It seemed he was destined to die from the beginning.

*****

On another plane in the universe, the Hunters, the new army of the Sovereigns, were laying siege in an unknown realm against dark forces never seen before. The glass of their blades was stained with the blood of these dark powers. The Iron Flies were bug-like in form, but they were more of a corrupting race rather than a threatening race. The realm they fought in was a massive temple structure, but not on a planet or moon. The battle in this temple threw fluids everywhere, destroyed everything inside, and waged in every angle of the temple.

With a shimmer of light, an Ancient One appeared and looked up to the Hunters and Iron Flies fighting on the ceiling.

The Ancient One pulled his hood back revealing his curled blond hair and distinguished masculine face.

"Artemis!" the Ancient One called.

In the midst of raining Iron Fly corpses, a Hunter sprang down from the ceiling and landed on his feet in front of the Ancient One.

The Ancient One gave an impressed gaze. "Artemis, I presume?"

Artemis gave a small bow, and replied, "Normally, I'd be at your service, but if it's not obvious enough, I and my team are a little preoccupied."

"I do apologize, but I must inform you that the Sovereign, Rhea, has betrayed her oath to the Sovereigns. The other Sovereigns have no knowledge of this that I am aware of, but it does pose a threat to the great vision. Will you act?" the Ancient One finished.

Artemis glanced around at the battle around him and waved a hand towards one of the Iron Flies threatening to sever a Hunters head. The Iron Fly fell to the ground and he looked back at the Ancient One. "I will return shortly. Rhea will be dealt with," he answered.

The Ancient One bowed and disappeared. Artemis quickly returned to the fight.

CHAPTER 5

Sashi raised his hooves up and crashed the massive doors down. Odin drew his sword and leapt to the middle of the court room. The morning star shown through the windows and reflected off of his sword when he drew it. Aquarius stood from his throne and gripped his triton.

Odin glared in rage and twirled his sword, waiting for the fight to begin.

Aquarius stretched his triton toward Odin. "I am the god of the water. I am merciless and unforgiving. Your disrespect will earn you pain beyond measure," Aquarius growled. A swirl of water shot from his triton, and was deflected by the side of Odin's blade. Odin held fast to his stance and fought the current against him. Once he gained control, he could push his blade into the current and fight back with telekinetic powers.

Aquarius gave in and both of them recoiled. "No doubt, you have come for revenge. But I haven't even begun to torment you yet. Survivor tales say that the sea ensnares you, like the walls of a room are closing around you with no way out. Let's make your vengeance worth it, shall we?" he said, pointing two fingers at the doors.

Odin glanced back where Sashi and Jade no longer were. The doors had disappeared as well. Then, the courts shook and, as certain as it was spoken, the walls began to close in on them both. Odin gave a slight smile at the challenge and jumped into combat with Aquarius. Aquarius lunged for him with the barbed spikes of the triton. Odin knocked the triton away with his blade and twirled it above him, striking for his neck. Aquarius blocked with one end of the triton, and slapped Odin away with the other end. Odin nearly lost control of his small flight, but landed on his feet and hand, holding his sword above him.

Aquarius brought up his triton and pulled it down on Odin's blade, fighting to shove him to the ground. Finally, Odin fell back, losing his only advantage, but held up against Aquarius' weight on his blade. Odin waited for the next unknown move. Of course, the move presented itself when Aquarius tilted the barbed end of the triton toward Odin's neck. Odin diverted his energy from holding off the triton to a sudden blast of energy from his head. Throwing Aquarius off-balance, Odin pushed his body up, his feet back and his stance held for any attack.

Aquarius laughed at himself for not anticipating such an attack, and rushed for Odin with his triton stretched out in front. Odin dodged the triton but was knocked by Aquarius' shoulder to the wall. Odin could feel the wall moving in to crush him into the wall opposite him. Aquarius saw his chance to steak Odin to the wall and took it immediately. Odin planted both feet on the moving wall and stepped up looking down at Aquarius. Annoyed that he missed another attack, Aquarius followed after him up the wall, slashing at Odin and moving further up.

Soon, they reached the ceiling and jumped upside-down to move across it. Odin blocked every move and found it getting easier to fight this foe. But as soon as he blocked for the move he expected, Aquarius slammed the hilt of the triton into Odin's chest and flung his sword out and away from any guard. Odin regained his bearings and jumped, flipping backwards and landing on the ground. Aquarius dropped down to join him once again. Odin held his stance, waiting for the attack. Aquarius twirled the triton in his hand to jolt into Odin's chest. Odin smirked, counting every molecule in his body, on his armor, in his hand, and all around him, commanding each individual one to obey his every thought. Aquarius hurdled the triton into Odin, and it drifted straight through him, without so much as a reaction by the impact. Odin held his stance, unfazed throughout.

"Now, you have no weapon." Odin growled.

"And, thanks to me, you have no father. Is this to be my fate, then? Destroyed by a menacing, unstoppable force?" Aquarius retorted.

Odin disappeared and instantly reappeared in front of his adversary, kicking him to the ground. "Your transgressions will be atoned for," he said holding the tip of his sword to Aquarius' face.

"Even I know that you can't do this. The Ragnarok is as merciless and swift as a strike of lightning. Without you, nobody will be spared and the universe will remain dark and dormant for the rest of time," Aquarius reminded him.

Odin shook his head. "I can be replaced. These Sovereign beings always have a back up somewhere. They'll get through it with or without me. And it would be so easy to take your life right now."

Aquarius lowered an eyebrow. "This is anger against your brother that you're putting on me. Why loose your venom on me, when you could have the real thing?" he said raising his hand to where the door would be.

When Odin saw his older brother there, smirking at him, the raging fire inside him spread throughout his entire body.

"Good morning, brother," the eldest said.

Odin glared, his breathing intensified, and he couldn't control himself any longer. He dashed for an attack.

"This should be fun," the eldest thought blocking the first multiple attacks with ease.

Odin threw his attacks at him with so much magnitude that the power discharged with each blow electrified the sword. His body turned, his arms flew, his blade sang, and every angry blow was blocked. He quickly jumped up and over the eldest, blocking a move and going in for a kill. He thrust his blade in for the eldest's chest, but the eldest slid his blade in, and griped Odin's wrist, holding this position.

"Didn't we do this a couple hundred years ago?" he said with a smile.

Odin knew what he was talking about. "Your soul had merged with dark energy, so much to the point that it made a new entity out of you. It was more the dark energy that defeated me than you," he replied with a sarcastic smile. "Don't flatter yourself too much."

They broke away and the eldest started swinging his sword in the air. With every swing an energy blast would discharge from the blade and ricochet off Odin's sword. Odin stepped forward, realizing what Aquarius was doing. The walls had stopped closing in, but the eldest was on the attack now.

Aquarius, however, had gotten up, completely rejuvenated. Odin got as close as he could to the eldest, bouncing every energy ball away. Finally, Odin reached out and caught an energy ball. Both Aquarius and the eldest stopped and stared in awe as Odin dissipated the energy ball and created his own energy field inside of the eldest' body.

"You aren't real," Odin whispered in disappointment.

The eldest' body completely locked up with the energy field inside of him. Unable to move, speak or even breathe. The eldest dropped his weapon and his body exploded with the expanding energy field. But in the midst of the explosion, no parts were left. It was as if Odin had destroyed a figment or a mirage. Like the visions sailors used to be distracted by on the sea. Aquarius gripped his triton, ready for another fight.

Odin regained his breath and paced the courts, staring at Aquarius. He was tired of fighting, and wanted to end it all. Aquarius saw the desperation in his eyes and took his chance to gain Odin's trust. "What is it you really want? Killing me won't satisfy you. You want some sort of answer." he suggested.

Odin glared, knowing he was right, but unsure if he wanted to reply. So he kept pacing, letting Aquarius say his fill.

"Why do you persist, Odin? What is it that drives you?" Aquarius asked. "Is it some form of pride? A need to avenge your father? Or even your whole family? Is it for these people? Your creation of the Dryads? Is it for some sort of greater good; for peace; for tranquility, or something personal? Maybe love?"

Odin never stopped pacing, but considered what he was suggesting.

"Could it be your obsession with battling against the odds? Do you have something to prove to yourself? To the elders? Or even to the Sovereigns? What is it you want to achieve?" Aquarius finished.

Odin disappeared again and reappeared with both of his feet on Aquarius' shoulders, pushing him back to the ground. Aquarius tried to attack with his triton, but Odin locked his sword in the prongs of the triton and threw it to the side.

Odin leaned into Aquarius face, with the fire raging in his eyes. "I want my Chevron!"

Odin got up, and raised Aquarius up with his power. Unable to fight back, Aquarius hovered over the ground.

"Where is my father's sword?" Odin asked.

Aquarius almost laughed. "In the same place where I put Sashi and Jade," he replied

Without hesitation or warning, Odin swung his sword and shoved the blade all the way through Aquarius' arm. Aquarius cried out in agony, trying to stop Odin from taking his powers one by one. He could feel the regenerative ability being the first to be taken. Then the immortality left.

"Where have you put them?" Odin asked.

"In a place where nobody will ever find them," Aquarius replied pridefully.

Odin ripped the blade from his arm and shoved it into his thigh. Once again, Aquarius cried out.

"Where are they?" Odin roared.

Once Aquarius got through the pain, he weakly chuckled, "you have nothing without my knowledge. You really can't kill me, can you? You are completely at my mercy."

Odin didn't wait for him to finish this time. In one swift twirl, Odin severed both arms from Aquarius' body. Aquarius was losing more power with every swing of Odin's sword and could feel the moment coming on him where he would be nothing more than a pile of flesh. When he smiled again, Odin skipped asking anything and sliced through the middle of Aquarius' thighs. Fluids squirted from Aquarius body, and the energies he had used to sustain himself had vanished from his command. Odin lowered Aquarius by a foot so they could see each other's eyes.

"Where are they?" Odin growled.

Panting through the immense pain, trying to keep Odin from seeing how much damage he was actually doing, Aquarius replied, "You can't beat me. You can't kill water with a sword."

Odin dropped his sword, breathing his anger in deep, furious breaths. He clawed his hands and gripped the sides of Aquarius' head, entering his thoughts. Thoughts of death in every form were passed between them, but soon, the electrocuting thought entered Aquarius' head, and locked him up into shock. Odin probed Aquarius' mind for the location and found it.

An entirely other life was all Aquarius would give. A life where Jade and Sashi and Orion's sword dwelt. They were there in the castle, standing next to him. Then, Aquarius stood, completely regenerated. Confused but ready, Odin dropped the dead body, opened his eyes, and picked up the sword.

Odin, Aquarius, Sashi, Jade, and a dead corpse were all in the throne room.

"How!" Odin shouted. "You died in my hands!"

The new Aquarius smirked, "You cannot kill water with a sword."

"Yes, I can," Odin growled, thrashing at Aquarius' neck. Aquarius' head rolled on the ground and another Aquarius appeared in front of Odin, kicking him to the ground. Odin shouted, startled from the sudden jolt to his chest.

"I like that move." Aquarius said. "Thank you for showing me."

Instantly, two blades punctured out of Aquarius' chest, and he fell to the ground from Sashi's blow. Odin got up, and thrust his sword into the air. Another Aquarius appeared, but Odin's sword was directly through his heart.

He slid down looking at the sword in his chest. "Oh," he whispered as he died.

"Is that all?" Jade asked.

"How is he doing this?" Sashi yelled.

"These are other lives. One of his powers was jumping from one universe to another," Odin explained.

Sashi shook his head. "That's a myth. If he's doing that, then there's an infinite number of him. We can't kill them all and live long enough to tell about it."

Suddenly, another one appeared attacking Sashi with his triton.

Odin ran for his father's sword, gripped it and held it to Aquarius' neck.

Aquarius raised his hands. "Wait!" he shouted. "Not that! Don't touch me with that!"

"The god of the sea is afraid? Tell me what happens when I touch you with this sword," Odin said.

"I'll evaporate, and of the waters will no longer be tamed by my power. They'll rise up against you," Aquarius answered.

Odin shook his head. "Now the waters will be tamed by me," he said raising the sword above his head. "Get on your knees, Aquarius, and beg me not to bring this down on your head."

Aquarius got on his knees. "You, who live by the sword, shall die by the sword. You cannot destroy the sea with a mere blade," he replied.

Odin's glare burned through him. "With the power of this weapon, I smite you," he said, watching his actions match the vision he had earlier.

Then the Sovereign's voice echoed in his mind, telling him of the path he would take if he went through with his revenge. This blade in his hand would destroy not only the Aquarius before him, but every one in each parallel universe.

Odin closed his eyes, wanting more than anything to bring the blade down on Aquarius' skull. It would be so easy to do. Getting rid of this villain would even be a favor to the elders. But the sacrifice would be the unsteady balance in his own soul. Aquarius recognized the mercy Odin had on him and smiled at his opportunity to make one last distraction. "You weren't destined to destroy me. But Aries has returned to this planet to once again claim universal power. He has his army joined with the Ancient Ones. If you hurry to Ferron, you'll catch him and his army before they take their claim on the land," he warned.

Odin slowly brought the sword down and looked at him. "I can't promise I'll let you live the next time I see you. But I can promise if you ever find yourself dealing with these dark powers again, there won't be a single body of water that can save you from this sword digging deep into your heart."

This was the first time they had let a mark live to tell his tale of survival. They left for Ferron with mixed emotions.

CHAPTER 6

Valkyrie returned to the Sovereign zone with less information than she needed. She entered the Sovereign realm and confronted the five in their courts.

With reverence and sorrow in her heart, she pleaded, "why has my planet fallen under attack? Why is Aries tormenting us again?"

Alpha turned his gaze to Kronos, who shook his head, disgusted, but unsurprised.

Rhea broke the silence. "He will be dealt with. Return to your world and let him know the Sovereigns are recalling him."

Kronos raised a hand to silence her. "No. He has been warned. The Dryad world is under our protection, and he would respect that, or be face our wrath. The Hunters will send him with the other dark forces to wait for the Ragnarok immediately."

Rhea lowered her head and continued. "Should the Hunters defect from their current mission? The Iron Flies are a priority task for the time-line to be rescued. Surely we can deal with him."

Kronos turned a patient, but firm eye to her. "What prompts such a suggestion?" he asked.

Valkyrie's heart pounded for what she was about to do, but she knew any other Elder would do the same in her place. She boldly responded, "Aries' army has more than doubled in numbers. His new army consists of Vamps and Ancient Ones. Once mortal enemies, now united together to destroy my home. I must ask the Sovereigns, why has this come to pass?"

All four Sovereigns turned to Rhea with deadly glares. "Is this true?" Kronos asked.

Rhea gave a distraught look to them all. "I was unaware of this! My days of inappropriate bargaining are behind me."

Valkyrie was going to speak out against her, but waited just a few more respectful seconds, holding her anger back. The doors to the courtroom opened and the Hunters piled in, with Artemis at the front.

"Don't be fooled, Sovereign ones. Rhea has been flirting with damnation since times unknown. I have a witness to this claim. He would be willing to testify to everything I claim, but for the sake of time, Majesty, I suggest you take it at my word. As a Hunter, it is my duty to strip Rhea of her status and powers as a Sovereign and take her place as god of life. I will continue negotiations with the Ancient Ones and the lead Hunters to further victories. This alliance between Good and Evil will be severed: never again to be forged."

Kronos turned his face away from his sister, and with bitterness on his heart, he ordered Artemis to go through with it. Rhea fought hard against this trial, but to no avail. The Hunters seized her and took her to their realm above Elder territories.

"Will Decimus be set free?" Valkyrie requested.

Kronos brought his curled index finger to his chin thoughtfully. "His punishment must be carried out for violating the contract of the Powers. The feohtan eower will be followed through. However, since it was an agent of Aries that pressed these charges, once finished, all of his acquired abilities will be returned to him and he will be set free. Is this arrangement fair?" he asked.

Artemis sat next to the god of time and looked Valkyrie over.

Valkyrie nodded in both joy and dismay.

Alpha turned to Kronos and Artemis. "Speaking of which, the time has come," he said.

Kronos nodded and they all watched as the floor to the lower courts slide to the walls, revealing an arena below them. The gates on each side of the field slid up and both figures stepped into the field.

Decimus circled the field forming a diameter with the figure across from him. The figure twirled his sword from side to side, and stared

Decimus down. Decimus kept his form solid and confident, unsure of what to say, or if he should say anything at this point. The figure bounced a few times, getting ready for an epic battle. He looked completely identical to Decimus, but his smile had a darker nature.

The figure darted up and held the sword pointed down for the first deadly blow. Decimus could feel the excessive rate of speed he could move becoming more apparent. The figure seemed to move slower with every second. The Walking Dead powers were taking their hold on him. The figure dropped just a little bit lower, and Decimus still hadn't moved. Now falling at the rate of unreasonably slow speeds, the figure was at a complete disadvantage to Decimus. Decimus knocked the sword away with this own, moved under and around to the figure's back and knocked the hilt of his blade against the figure's back. The figure tilted forward, falling out of balance, but Decimus felt the pain in his own back from his blow. He lurched forward and gnashed his teeth in pain, massaging his wound with his fist.

The figure stood up, recovering from Decimus' blow and turned to Decimus, vengefully. Decimus never took his eyes away from his target. The figure lunged for him, but Decimus dodged the blow and slit the figures arm. Immediately, both fighters were bleeding down the wrists. Decimus ignored it and turned to the figure, who had done the same. The figure swung for Decimus' head, then for his arm. Each move was easily blocked, but Decimus didn't like being defensive like this.

Decimus lined up his moves carefully and spun his blade against the figures sword, causing a tumbling swirl. If Decimus had his powers, he'd be fully able to magnetically attract the figures sword to his and yank it from his grip, but his limited abilities left him little choice but to continue this course of action.

The figure knew exactly what to expect, and fought back, hard. When Decimus jerked the sword up to throw the figure's grip off, the figure only gripped harder and twisted with him. Their blades parted and were joined again. When swords weren't clanking together, skin was severed, or punches and kicks were exchanged.

Finally, without thinking, Decimus slipped his foot around the figures leg and tripped him while deflecting a swing. Kicking the figures sword away, and throwing aside his own, he let the figure get back up and readied himself for the next stage of the fight.

An unsettling surge shot through Decimus and the speed his mind was running at slowed immensely. Less than a second after, Decimus was lifted into the air, then shoved to the ground. The figure stood over him and brought his foot up to smash his head.

Decimus brought his hands up and caught the figures foot as he brought it down above his face. His new power presented itself, and his hold on the figure was unbreakable. He twisted the figures ankle and threw him against the wall of the battlefield. Decimus jumped up and held his sword ready. The figure recovered from his sudden jolt across the field.

"What does this accomplish? You know all of my moves, and I can't defeat you willingly. We're locked in this battle until the Ragnarok," Decimus said.

The figure tilted his head. "This is justice being served. As you failed your creation, the elders, and everyone who believed in you, now you will fail to save yourself. Death is inevitable to all, Decimus," he answered.

Decimus regained his breath and their swords clanged together once again. As they fought, Decimus tried to reassure the figure that he hadn't failed at his responsibilities.

"It was Aries. He had to be dealt with, I had to stop him. I couldn't let my people die like that."

"You put away an innocent being; overstepped your bounds. Now your planet has no defender. You've left them with nothing."

Their swords struck together in front of them, and were followed by a series of masochistic blows.

"I did what I had to in order to keep my home safe."

"And you've condemned them," the figure replied. "You've failed them all."

"I'm no murderer. I defended my home. Even the Sovereigns know what I felt then."

With a mighty swing, the figure knocked Decimus' sword from his hands, and shoved his blade through Decimus' heart. When the pain entered his own chest, the figure clutched to the sword and took a sharp breath. "The Sovereigns are all-powerful. Even knowing what you were feeling, they still kept from making your mistakes. The pitiful excuse of a Power you are has just been wiped away from this universe."

Decimus couldn't stop hemorrhaging. Both parties fell to the ground slowly dying. With his last breath, Decimus looked up and found Valkyrie with a look of relief on her face. The figure, however took the last bit of energy he had and developed an energy ball in his hand and threw Decimus dead body against the wall of the battlefield with immense force.

Both fighters disappeared from the field; the figures energy joined the collective of universal powers, and Decimus appeared in his Elder form in front of the Sovereigns. The ground to the courts was restored, and Valkyrie with eager eyes stood behind Decimus. Decimus was amazed that he hadn't joined the collective, but waited without questioning the blessing of another moment.

Kronos spoke first. "Your prosecutor was a guilty party in the acts against the great vision. Therefore, the charges against you have been dropped. However, your charge as a vigilante was a mark against you. Because your actions did not lead to a destructive end, you have been spared. Do not tempt fate again."

Decimus humbled his gaze. "If I may be so bold, Sovereigns, the laws are still unclear."

Artemis gave a slight smile. "All powers agree, from ascension, to play their part in the universe. Deviate from your purpose as Good, Neutral or Evil, and you will be sent to Exile," he finished.

Lavish, god of Fate spoke next. "Procreation is strictly limited. You may not mate with any being lower than your status."

Alpha spoke. "With the growth of your abilities as a power, the responsibilities weigh heavier. The levels of creator beings are the example here."

Minerva, god of Wisdom spoke, "The vision is every higher power's priority. When called upon, you will defend it at any cost."

Kronos held out his hand to Decimus and an orb floated down and hovered in front of him. Showing images of everything comprehensible in the universe. "Time is as unlimited as the universe. The time-line to the great vision is not a dream, as some may see it. It is a destination. The events that come before this have systematically come to pass. We have less than one swing of the universal pendulum left until the last few events unfold," he explained.

Minerva spoke again. "So much depends on equilibrium in the universe. Every turn of the table, every tip of the scale, every win and loss of a battle can change our course to the great vision."

Alpha continued, "without your actions in locking Aries away into exile, we would never have seen the corruption in Rhea's soul and the contaminating force would have ruined everything."

Artemis' smile fell and shifted his gaze as if receiving a vision. "Your world is under attacked," he read his battle report. "Aries is there. Your protector is about to intercept them. You'll need to be there to escort the dark energies to the Hunters."

Both Valkyrie and Decimus faded away and hurried back to Hajun.

*****

Odin, Sashi, and Jade arrived back in Ferron, where the morning star had set, and a cloud was moving faster than everything in the night sky.

Sashi stopped and looked up. "One against a million isn't great odds," he said.

"Odds never mattered to me," Odin said jumping off of Sashi. Then he turned to his companion. "Don't you read your history?" he said with a smile.

Jade hopped down from Sashi's back and hung on Odin's shoulder. "Do you have a plan?" She asked.

Odin glanced back at her face and watched the shadows of the trees fall on her face. "Do I ever have plans?" he replied.

He gave Jade one final kiss, and using his new powers, he rose into the air, holding his sword to the army of vampires. They seemed to take no notice of him as he advanced on them, so he stretched his concentration out to the air around him and ignited the oxygen in the air, causing a massive blow-back around him.

The horde of vampires began to scatter as the explosion grew before them instead of dissipating like it should have. The fire that stretched through the sky made Odin seem like a small shadow. Lightning struck from his blade, fire engulfed the first wave of vampires and the crowd turned to ash. The vampires screeched in pain as the Ancient Ones abandoned the fight and fled the planet. The explosion engulfed Odin and rippled out along the sky.

Sashi and Jade stared in devastation while the growing flame overcast the night sky, lighting up the hemisphere. Fire rained down around them with flaming Vamps falling to their deaths across the land of Ferron. In the middle of the sky, Odin let go of his destruction on the sky. All that was left in the sky was Odin holding his glowing blade, and Aries flapping his wings.

Angrily, Aries shouted, "You have taken my armies from me! My chance for my own great vision is lost! You will pay for this!"

Odin pointed his sword to the stars. "Look there, to the Hunters! Someone is being sent to the Dark Powers. You will meet her soon."

Aries glanced up to the Sovereign courts and saw the Hunters degrading Rhea of her powers.

"No!" he shouted. "Not her!"

Then, two lights flashed in the sky as Odin struck for Aries' heart. Aries did not react to the blade Odin plunged into his body. Everything in him wanted to be slain, to die with his lover and join with her, even in an eternity of damnation. Aries' body fell from the sky, and Valkyrie and Decimus appeared next to Odin taking hold of Aries' soul.

"You have been banished to the dark energies on the other side of the universe," Valkyrie said to Aries. "The Hunters will take you to join the collective of dark energies, where you will wait for the Ragnarok."

Aries' soul didn't fight back. His dark energies succumbed to the hold of the elders and they waited for the Hunters to arrive. Hearing the call of the fugitives captors, the Hunters came with great haste and carried Aries away into the distance of the universe.

Odin returned to Jade and Sashi with the elders at his side. Both Sashi and Jade were grinning with excitement at Odin's victory. But Odin knew that they all had to purge their dark natures if they were to fulfill their rolls in the great vision. He held out his hand and his father's sword appeared. He dug the blade into the ground and looked at both Sashi and Jade, unsure if he wanted this or not.

"Touch the hilt," he told them, reassuring himself of his own convictions.

They did as he said and the elders held Odin's shoulders, helping the power surge of the blade.

Odin closed his eyes and thought, "With the purity of my father's sword, I purge the darkness of my soul and from my companions. Passions will no longer drive us. Cleanse us and make us whole."

The sword surged its energies through the three and the dark energies left their souls and joined with the Hunters to go to the far reaches of space. Breathing heavily from the change in character, they turned to the elders and listened.

"In one season, the great vision will come to an end," Decimus said. "Remain pure in heart, and prepare for the call. We will all be needed to save the rest of what is good in our quadraplex of the universe."

The elders left to their courts. Odin, Sashi, and Jade helped rebuild the Dryad village, and peace was restored for months. Ferron remained a vile place, and Centurion had been completely destroyed, but the Dryad village would thrive once again. All they had to worry about was whatever would come next.

CHAPTER 7

All that has come to pass has been for the benefit of the great vision of the Sovereigns. The Hunters had traveled through galaxies across the universe. Trillions upon trillions of legions of Hunters spread across space, taking their targets captive, and sending them to the end regions, where the dark forces dwell.

The dark energies want more than anything to indulge in their destructive natures. In the thousand years that this gathering took place, their minds had molded together. The dark energies became conscious, and waited until it had more than enough power to destroy all that stood in its path.

Omega, Valefor, Aries, the Iron Flies, and infinitely more contributed to this consciousness, creating an entity so enraged at nothing in particular, frustrated at its lack of movement, aggravating its need to destroy. The Sovereigns had created a being so powerful, that it could destroy even space itself in a whim, if it had only known its own power. All that blocked the enlightenment to its ultimate destruction was its focus on simply destroying something.

The barriers that the Hunters had made could hold the dark energies, but only for so long. When a Hunter brought another group of dark energies to the collective, the darkness struck. The barriers collapsed and the Hunter was swallowed up and added to the collective. It expanded from that point in space and overtook everything.

*****

Elsewhere in the universe, another dark force had submerged. Hiding in the black of space, Erebus wandered through realms and anomalies of unknown regions. The dark wisp of energy suddenly stopped and felt the disruption along the flow of space. Of every anomalous force he'd encountered, only something with extreme power could cause a quadraplex-wide tremor. In the middle of the black of space, he looked along the stars for any kind of shadow. He glanced everywhere for moments which only passed by too quickly and saw one star disappear.

He stopped, and shivered; not from the cold of space, nor the chill of his own empty soul, but in fear that the Ragnarok had come. Stars everywhere in that area disappeared, along with nebulae, and black-holes alike. An entire galaxy had been devoured by an unstoppable force.

His eyes aglow being the only animated feature, he spirited away, racing space-dwelling creatures to shelter. Erebus, once known and feared in thousands of cultures, was running for his life to search for a means to fight this impaling force. The thought had crossed his mind to seek out the Sovereigns and their great plan, but it was sure to be suicide just entering their realm. He had been a fugitive of the Hunters since the beginning of the Bright Sieges, as most dark fugitives had come to call it.

Unexpectedly, he was gripped by another dark figure. He fought hard against it to escape the coming doom. But when he realized it was an old companion of his, he felt another sudden urge to leave with great haste.

Dionysia gripped him harder and gave him a distressed look. "What are you doing here?" she asked.

"Escaping the Ragnarok. Why are you in this part of the universe?" Erebus replied.

Dionysia answered, "I've been looking for you. There's a gathering of dark forces in the underworld, and we need your help."

Erebus morphed from his shadow form to his Darkling form. "Where are Aries, Hades, or Balthazar?"

"Aries and Balthazar were taken in the Bright Sieges. Hades has been gathering us, but we need every great Darkling we can get. Perseus,

Phobos, and Rajani have been waiting for us, and Praxis has just recently joined us," she answered.

Erebus shook his head. "Rajani? We can't trust him. He's from a completely illogical tribe. All they want is power. We're nothing but sheep to him."

Dionysia answered, "Things have changed, Erebus. You must start living up to your name once again."

"How can I trust you? You've tried to destroy me on many accounts." Erebus replied.

They quickly noticed that the area of space they were in had gone completely silent. There were no thoughts, no concepts being passed between figures. No movement, but an expanse of shadow along the horizon of space.

"This may be your chance to find out. Let's go," Dionysia said, opening a doorway to the Underworld next to them. "Join me, or make your own way out of here. The choice is yours."

Without another thought for question, Erebus and Dionysia entered the Underworld before the Darkness could ever reach them. The door closed behind them, and the first thing Erebus noticed was a castle in the middle of the Underworld. Two black dragons circled the castle, blowing fire along the bridge to the entrance to keep the condemned spirits away.

The sky above had been filled with gray clouds and lightning struck the ground everywhere. The fire-pits of the Underworld only flickered against the canvas, but the Underworld was darker than normal, as if a final nightfall had come.

"A new décor for the Underworld?" Erebus asked.

"When Hades came home, he decided he wanted to make things more up to date. We've added a few things of our own," Dionysia answered.

"If I had to guess, I'd say the dragons were your idea."

Dionysia tilted her head. "I told you, things have changed. I wanted hell-hounds, but dragons took the vote."

Erebus lightly smiled. "I like it," he said.

They descended to the castle and appeared before the council of dark forces. Perseus, Phobos and Praxis stood around the table and Rajani stood at the head. They all turned to Erebus and Dionysia.

"Welcome to the Underworld," Perseus said. "We're many trillions of light-years away from the Ragnarok, for now. So we'll take this time to plan counteracting it."

"Where is Hades?" Dionysia gasped at the leaderless group.

"He left to search for you," Praxis replied. "He hasn't come back. We don't think he will be returning."

"You have a plan?" Dionysia asked.

"A plan, yes. Agreement, no." Rajani replied.

Phobos slammed his hand on the table. "I will not sacrifice my life for your awesome plan. I will seek help from the Sovereigns before I die for you," he shouted.

Dionysia gave a dumbfounded look. "What did I miss?" she asked.

Praxis answered, "Rajani suggests we all die and he take our energies so he can take on the Ragnarok."

Rajani saw the looks everyone gave him. "I think it's an excellent plan. We'd be invincible, and could wear it down for a generation until we finally crush it."

Erebus spoke. "Except for the part where we all die and you become the most powerful being in the Universe, it is an excellent plan. Unconventional, but it gets the job done."

"Do you have something better?" Rajani asked.

Dionysia looked up at him and waited. Erebus replied, "I'm a Darkling. I can revive anything I come across. I can't heal myself if I sustain damage, but I can heal others and bring them back from the afterlife. If I were the one that inherited your energies, I could promise that you would be brought back, and your energies returned."

Phobos protested, "What's to keep you from going back on your word? How can we trust you?"

Erebus answered, "when I promise death, no one receives mercy. When I promise chaos, destruction, plagues of a thousand forms across a thousand miles, I don't hold back. When I promise you that I don't want to keep your energies, and your deaths would cause an imbalance in the universe that I would like not to see through, you'll know I'm telling the truth."

Praxis nodded. "Sounds good enough to me," he replied.

Phobos shook his head. "Is there a successful idea that doesn't involve us dying?" he asked.

Dionysia shrugged. "I'm sure we're all open to suggestions."

Rajani was also displeased with the idea. "I have many armies of demons and beasts alike, and each representative here would contribute more than they're comfortable of dealing in. There is too much to lose if you turn on us at the last minute."

Erebus thought and replied, "the Ragnarok is a living, breathing organism now. It has a consciousness of its own and is completely aware of what it needs and wants. Its undying desire to destroy is all that drives it. We would be the same, but concentrated, focused. With our minds together, adding dark forces to us, we can match it and take it together. My Darkling powers make it so each one of you would have an effect on my decisions. If anyone is on the losing side, it would be me."

With this new reassurance, Phobos turned his look and thought. Then he answered, "I can agree to these terms."

Perseus nodded. "I'll join you, too."

Rajani stood silent, but turned to Erebus and gave him his sword. "Let it begin with me, then."

"Nobody asked you to go first, though I can hardly see them protesting."

Erebus raised the sword and plunged it into Rajani's chest. The energy surged through the blade and into his body. Rajani faded away until he completely disappeared.

Praxis stood and stepped up to be taken. "Your voice of reason is at your service," he said.

Without another word, Erebus struck for his chest and took the energies Praxis possessed.

Phobos was next followed by Perseus. Erebus marveled at his new powers and turned to Dionysia. "Was this what you wanted?" he asked.

Dionysia smiled. "I knew you would take the lead. I didn't think it would be like this. I'll bring you more Darklings and other forces. You'll need all the help you can get," she replied.

Erebus turned his head, noticing all of the new voices in his mind had many thoughts, but one thought was matched with every voice. "I must force the Sovereigns to stop the Ragnarok," he said.

"How?" Dionysia asked.

"Hajun. The answer is on Hajun." Then he searched the thoughts again, and grinned at an idea. "I'm going to unleash the Underworld unto Hajun. Open a doorway from this place to that planet, and allow the corrupt souls to run free. The dark creatures here can loose their venom on the inhabitants," he said.

Dionysia almost giggled in excitement. "That's the Erebus I know."

Erebus gave her a dark look. "The son of The Hunter is on that planet. He'll be my leverage."

"How will killing him turn the tables in our favor?" She asked.

"I won't kill him. I'll destroy him. His heart lies in his lovers hands. I'll bring her here, and hold her here under the terms that he stops the Ragnarok completely, or she dies. He will go to the elders and pray that they ask the Sovereigns for help. If they don't, he'll come after her here, where we will destroy him, taking away the key to the Sovereigns great vision. They will have no choice but to destroy the Ragnarok completely." Erebus explained.

Dionysia grimaced. "They don't plan on destroying it?"

"Not at the moment," he replied. "Open the doorway. We attack immediately."

CHAPTER 8

Odin had finished rebuilding his barn, completing the rebuilding of Hajun, brick for brick. The temple and order had been restored; the Appointed Ones and the prophets were reestablished, and all was once again as it should be.

In Odin's barn, Sashi had already laid down to rest. Odin and Jade were reunited as pure and whole beings, at last. It was their first intimate moment in almost five-hundred years, and it was a moment that would be cherished by both for years to come.

Odin had committed himself to study and practice the ways of the Appointed Ones, and the prophets, and had acquired all of his Elderly abilities. He could feel his family awakening from their sleep, one by one in the order they had left the universe. They too had new abilities through their ascensions. In this moment of intimacy with his lover, Odin felt everything come together so perfectly that he felt a peace that he hadn't felt in all of his lives. The end was near, and he relished every thought. Joining with Jade being the most potent of all. Being in love with her soul, and feeling the body he created for her, everything was, for a single moment, perfect. And then, as passionately as it approached, the moment they shared had finished. Holding each other, listening to their hearts race, they fell asleep in each other's arms.

Hours later, Odin awoke to the sound of a loud explosion in the village. He jumped to his feet, strapped his sword to his back and buckled his chest-piece. Fitting his boots into place, he suddenly stopped and realized Jade was missing. He stood, looking everywhere for her as the crowd outside grew into a screaming mob, running for their lives from another explosion. He called for her, and immediately left when she didn't answer.

Hobgoblins and hell-hounds rampaged through the village, destroying houses and killing the inhabitants. All of his efforts were destroyed. Months of preparations and rebuilding had been obliterated in a single devastating moment.

Without thinking, Odin raised his sword in the air, and brought the blade down driving it into the ground. He knelt down shoving his energies into his weapon. Sparks flew from the blade and a wave of energy pulsed from the sword, destroying every dark force in its path.

The village was silent. Odin pulled the sword from the ground, stood up and looked at the temple, up the street. Erebus was hovering over the top of the temple. His silhouette in the shining moon revealed he was holding an unconscious female Dryad. Her head hung over his arm, and her hair swayed with the wind. Her legs hung over the opposite arm. His eyes glowed bright yellow, and everything else was just a wisp of smoke.

Odin knew Erebus was waiting for him. He walked down the street to the shadow of the temple and looked up at his adversary.

"Name your terms, Darkling, and set her free." Odin demanded.

Erebus descended to the ground, holding Jade in his arms. "My terms," he replied, "are simple. Go to the elders and demand they put an end to their Ragnarok. Some of us are not ready to die."

Odin sheathed his sword and replied harshly, "The elders don't have that kind of power."

Erebus' faceless expressions didn't change. "They can go to the Sovereigns if they need. There are powers in the Universe that can put an end to this destruction. It can be done, and it will be done."

Odin held his hands behind his back to keep from lashing out. "And if I can't find a way to follow through with your terms; what then?"

"Then Jade dies," Erebus replied. "You may try and save her from the Underworld, if you wish, but it'll only prove folly. You'll never get passed the demons on the battlefield where my doorway is."

Odin brought his fists to his sides remembering the battle with Magnus: how far and wide the battlefield expanded. And now it was filled with demons, and whatever creatures were born in the Underworld.

"Leave my world, and take your beasts with you, and I'll make sure your demands are met. Let Jade go, and I won't come after you." Odin roared.

Erebus laughed at Odin's presumptions and a flame erupted through Jade's chest.

Odin threw his blade at Erebus. "No!" he shouted.

The blade drove straight through Erebus' face and clanged to the ground.

"Have the Sovereigns remedy their mistakes, and your lover's soul will rise from the Underworld and her body will be revived," Erebus ordered. And with that, Erebus disappeared, leaving a cloud of settling smoke.

Odin turned around, and found Sashi waiting to start his one last journey.

"Something about this seems familiar," Sashi said, knowing without a doubt that they'd get Jade back safely.

Odin jumped on his back and they headed back for the mountains. They left the destroyed village behind them and crossed the hills of grass and puddles. The mountains had changed enough in the last thousand years that climbing the mountain wasn't necessary. They simply rode the few hours uphill. The Treants had gone extinct, which allowed more natural trees to grow on the side of the mountain. Once they reached the top, they called to the elders. As promised, Valkyrie and Decimus descended to the mountain upon their call with lights shining around them.

Odin waited for them to meet him on the mountain and made his request. "Erebus has returned, and is laying waste on my toils. He has kidnapped Jade and demands we put an end to the Ragnarok or she'll die. What can we do?" he asked.

The elders glanced at each other with worry in their eyes. Then they turned back to Odin. "The Ragnarok cannot be held back, not even for a moment," Valkyrie replied. "However, now that the dark forces have come together to fight the Ragnarok, we know we're scaring them."

Decimus softly held his hand out so he could speak. "You've ascended to an Elder. You have your immortal abilities and so much more on your side. We will send a legion of Hunters to your aide, and you will submerge into the Underworld with their help. Does this satisfy you?" he asked with a very serious expression.

Odin nodded with disappointment that he'd have to wait for the Hunters to get there, but grateful that he wouldn't have to go through this ordeal alone. Without another word the elders rose to the skies and faded back to the new courts. Odin turned to Sashi who had a very displeased look.

"That was it?" Sashi asked. "That's how your conversations with the elders go?"

Odin, sighed and looked at sashi. "Pretty much," he replied and hopped back up on Sashi's back.

*****

Valkyrie and Decimus appeared in the Sovereign zone and entered their courts. Humbly, Decimus appealed to them. "Erebus has laid siege on Hajun. I have suspicions that he is not alone. All of the dark forces of the Underworld have been set loose on Hajun. I'm calling on the Hunters to take care of this threat. The Underworld is not a place that the elders are allowed to enter," Decimus finished.

Artemis stood. "We can't open a doorway to the Underworld. We don't know where it is. Are you absolutely certain all of the dark forces are being freed on this planet?"

Valkyrie answered, "We are certain. There may be a doorway open on Hajun. Will you answer our call?"

Artemis pointed to his messenger, who immediately disappeared. "We're on our way," He answered.

Alpha asked, "Why is Erebus taking his anger out on Hajun?"

"His terms state that we have to stop the Ragnarok, or he'll destroy Odin," Valkyrie answered.

Minerva turned to Kronos. "Then this is a reaction to our creation. No doubt, he's searching for other ways to counteract this threat."

"We must not hinder its course," Kronos answered. "The Ragnarok is the universal priority. It must not be stopped. The time for second guessing has passed us by."

Minerva sighed. "How many times are we going to do this, Kronos?" she asked, "How many time lapses will you ask of us? How much power, how many millions of years of waiting? How many times must we endure for you to get it right? We know that Odin is the key. We know that his soul is tied to his beloved. Rhea is gone. The time-line has been cleansed of her destruction, but it will still come to ruin if we do not follow through with his wishes."

Kronos gave her a deadly glare. "What would you have me do? Call another time lapse? Pause time so Odin can overcome his adversaries? What then? Wait for the next threat and do it again until we've hunted down every dark creature in the universe?"

Minerva answered, "Yes. Give Odin our powers this time. Give him a chance. He must be fully focused on his objective. If Jade dies, he'll only be distracted by her death when the universe shifts. If he dies, we'll have nothing to confuse the darkness. His heart is with her. Everything else is a warrior. His mind, his energies, everything else in him is a beast."

Kronos sat back in his chair, closed his eyes and thought. "You ask the impossible. The Darkling has other forces inside him. If we give Odin our power and if he were to fall, we won't have another chance to lapse time," he answered. "The time-line is fixed-"

He looked at her again and stopped her from speaking. "I know what you're thinking. You must not give Odin your power. It'll take all of us to bring the Great Vision to life. And if we fail, it'll take all of us to lapse time again."

Minerva sat in silence and waited for Kronos to make up his mind.

Minerva spoke. "You're dying, Kronos. Time is running out. When we succeed, this time, you won't live to see the Great Vision all the way through. All of these souls will be living in you and your energy. Give him your powers, and the Great Vision will thrive in the darkness of the universe."

Kronos had believed that he would see his vision to the end, but knew this new plan would ensure the safety of all he was responsible for. He closed his eyes again and with two words he brought upon his own doom, the thriving fate of the universe, and the future of every sentient soul in his quadraplex.

"Do it," Kronos said, tilting his head down.

Valkyrie and Decimus disappeared. The tension in the courts grew thicker with every second, to a degree that made the other three Sovereigns want to leave the room. Each one believed Kronos would slaughter them all for the position they had put him in.

Alpha leaned in to talk to Minerva. "We can't possibly collect all of the souls in the universe. We've tried before. We don't have the power for it. What will we do about the souls outside of our reach?" he asked.

Minerva looked at Kronos to see if he'd explain.

"The other Powers throughout the universe are spreading the word and making preparations. They've been notified of the Ragnarok's weakness and are on their own from there."

Lavish turned to Kronos. "It sounds like we've condemned those in the universe that can't match this threat, to death. Didn't you think of them before you set your great vision in motion?"

All of these questions only aggravated him more. "Of course I thought of them! The truly good souls will be tormented for an age by the destructive powers of the Ragnorak and the other powers will rescue them once the Ragnorak is through with them."

"So they all have to die?" Alpha asked.

"It's a great cost, but the outcome is greater," Kronos answered.

Alpha didn't say another word after that. He knew that Kronos could hear all of his questions, and would answer them if it was necessary.

"We should never have tested the powers of the Universe. If this is the cost of our actions, then we should give up our power."

Kronos stood, enraged. "Who would you give our power to! Aries? Praxis? Kamazots? A mortal like Odin or Orion before him! Power is the currency of the Universe and it exists to be tested! If we all hive our powers to Odin, then our mistakes will be made by someone else. Someone less skilled than we are."

The other sovereigns knew he was right. The god of time saw and knew all things. It was beyond his power to control the Universe any further. This final act of desperation, costly though it was, would cleanse the Universe of their actions.

*****

The elders gathered around the area of space known as Zion. It was the only place that Kronos had deemed worthy for this event. Orion had already opened another doorway to the Afterlife and began to fill the vast area with these souls. More came drifting in space, as if called to the light of the soul energy. The elders spread out, surrounding the souls, and keeping them safe there. They sheltered each one from the pending doom with their new powers.

Quadrillions of souls from all over the universe had split to the sides they were attracted to and raced to their destinations. They passed between the elders and swirled around with the other souls, and made their lighting brighter and more energetic. Soon, the line of elders was surrounding a massive ball of soul energy that was brighter than any star.

With each expansion of the soul sphere, there was another Elder that would join the circle. Finally, Magnus joined them, and glanced all around at the dark of space. Stars were disappearing everywhere. He hadn't expected to wake up to the Ragnarok, and was awe-stricken when he realized this time had come. A while later, Stratus appeared next to him and held his portion of the energy field. Lara was the last to join them.

*****

Erebus sat at the table in his new castle. He watched Jade's unconscious body hover horizontally over the table. Dinoysia massaged his arms and whispered in his ear. "Do you remember the job on

Carrilia? You destroyed an entire species so I could find the sixth chevron for Skarra."

Erebus answered, "you sold me out to Skarra that night for more dark powers. I had to destroy the high council of that planet to escape. I never saw you again."

Dionysia turned to him. "Are you upset with me over that?" she asked. "I knew you could do it."

Erebus looked her in the eye. "I was upset because you didn't get what you could have out of the deal. You could have been one of the most destructive forces of the universe if you'd thought of what the head of a Darkling is worth."

Dionysia shifted her gaze to look over his whole body. It was no secret that she wanted him, as always, but her cheeky natures overcame her lust. She wrapped her arms around his collar bones and held him there. Their dark cloaks joined together with their bodies moving in on each other. Erebus knew to be weary of her when she was like this. The voices inside his mind made him more than paranoid about her. He positioned himself so he could throw her to the table if she tried anything to ruin him again.

Her hands fell down his cloak and touched his chest. Her lips were too close for comfort though, and reaching for his flesh, though not surprising, it only made her seem more suspicious. All she had to do now was claw at his chest, dig her fingers a few inches in and begin sucking the dark forces out of him.

He reached up to touch her face. But when she didn't kiss his hand, he realized the ploy she was performing. He immediately morphed into his shadow form with his eyes growing bright red in rage. She caught herself from falling straight through him and stood up. He floated from the chair he sat in and faced her.

"What are you playing at?" he hissed.

Dionysia shook her head, "I have nothing to hide; nothing to try. I was just reminiscing the times that I enjoyed being with you."

The voices all shouted that she was lying, and to slay her now. He couldn't fight them off. In a second, he had his sword at the ready.

Dionysia shuddered, "What are you doing?"

"I can't control it," he replied. "You shouldn't have made that move."

Dionysia raised her hands as Erebus brought his sword down on her. Instantly, she repelled the blade with energy blasts, each one more concentrated and potent then the last one she threw. Finally, Erebus lost his grip and the sword flung away. Erebus morphed back into his Darkling form and rushed her. She dodged his attack and jumped on his back.

"I didn't know you liked having this kind of fun." Dionysia laughed, "you always seemed so serious."

As concentrated as he was on destroying her, her flirtations had lightened him up enough to want her back. He reached up to grab her, but she twirled around his neck and hung in front of him, almost throwing him off balance. She, then, dug her fingers in his chest and froze him in his place for a moment.

Finally, every force in his body gathered together and deflected her arms away, but her legs had latched to his waist. He grabbed her wrists and twisted her around so that he was behind her and had her arms, tying up her moves. She tried to fight his grip, but he now had the upper-hand.

She turned her head to him and pressed her lips to his, pulling his lust for her to the front of his mind. All of the voices screamed for him to stop, but now, he couldn't fight the force of her affections for him anymore. He let her go so she could turn to him and push him to the table and climb back on top of him.

Every voice in his mind shouted "Resist" and he obeyed.

He morphed into his shadow form once again, and stayed like this until she got off of him and agreed to stay away.

She breathed heavily, almost embarrassed that she had put herself in such a compromising position. "I could have taken your new abilities at any second if I wanted to. Why are you so worried now?" Dionysia asked.

Erebus' eyes blinked once. "I can't be too careful, can I?" the wisp of smoke replied.

Disappointed, Dionysia left to search out more Darklings for him. Erebus turned to Jade's body, wondering the same as Magnus did.

What made her so special? She was a Dryad, created by an elder, one of a million, and yet she held the key to his own great vision. She wasn't a warrior, nor a higher power, and yet this unconscious girl meant everything to his survival.

He stood over her and looked at every inch of her body. He questioned why Odin would stake everything on this girl, and deduced only one reason which was both plausible but irresistibly destructive: love. The disease that had torn its path through the entire universe. It had conquered gods, men, and everything in between, and had even ensnared Erebus at a point. What some had called a chemical imbalance, others called a possession, and others left out of the question. Those lucky enough to not have a physical embodiment bound to emotions had all but gone extinct.

As for Erebus, he had wished for Odin's honor that there was another reason for such a disappointing course of action. But as disappointing as it was, it worked to his advantage. And so, he waited for Odin to bring the powers of the elders that he had accumulated. And there, in Erebus' new castle, they would battle to the death and the victor would continue with his great vision. Erebus' powers were growing by the day, and Odin had peaked in his Elderly abilities. Erebus was confident he would triumph if they should meet, but he hoped that Odin would succeed in destroying the Ragnarok.

*****

Artemis fitted on his armor. His armies were well on their way to Hajun, but he, as was tradition, asked for blessings from his mentor. Kneeling in front of the great monument of his friend, Artemis remembered every victory he had shared with him.

"Someday," he said, "on some distant planet, your story will be known, written in the stars. Your conquests against the Taurans, the Lionians, and the witch, and the like will be remembered for the rest of time. Bless this fight, now, against the Underworld. Let your spirit guide these troops. This is sure to be the greatest victory ever known."

CHAPTER 9

Odin and Sashi fought their way through the forests with the help of the dragons. Demons, vampires, jackals, banshees, and the rest of the Underworld had covered more than half of the planet. With no way of destroying them all, Odin and Sashi could only hope to lay a path to the gates of the Underworld. They followed the clusters of dark figures through the planet to their destination.

Odin jumped off of Sashi and both fought gallantly. Swords swung, claws slashed, fire burned down the forests on Odin's orders. All of Hajun agreed that they'd rather see it all burn than paying homage to dark forces. Odin rolled on the ground and dodged a gust of fire. Branches fell to the ground all around him, taking down only a few enemies. The hungry dragons would eat the vampires, chewing them up, crunching their bones, slicing them into tiny pieces. No amount of regeneration would save them. Odin's powers kept the Banshees at bay. He had them all enchanted by the songs of sirens and attracted them all to the tree that played the song.

One Banshee had broken free of the trap, and found Odin fighting off the demons and jackals. Odin finished them off when the Banshee came up behind him, opened its mouth and overwhelmed him with fear with its screech. Being kin to Darklings, Banshees were cloud-like figures. They didn't morph like Darklings did, so they were always in shadow form, making themselves impervious to any physical attack. Sashi leapt through the banshee and grabbed Odin as another ball of fire engulfed the area.

"Odin!" Sashi shouted leaning him against a dead tree.

Odin was panting. "I can't do it, Sashi. I don't have the power," he said looking into Sashi's eyes.

Sashi slapped Odin in the face and stood him up. "Odin, I can't let you live if you're going to keep us from victory. Only you have the power to distract the Banshees. We need you to keep them occupied. Remember fighting the Skord? This is nothing like that."

They quickly realized they had fallen into a jackal pit. The dog-like monsters surrounded them with the overgrown fur on their necks stiffer than sticks. They growled and barked at the two seemingly helpless intruders. Sashi drew his swords and stood ready for their attack.

He hid Odin behind him and whispered, "Speaking of that power."

Odin was still stricken from the Banshee's attack, but walked around Sashi and drowsily raised his hands to the group of beasts. Instantly, all of the Jackals burst into flames and ran away yelping for death. The dragons gladly granted their requests.

Sashi turned Odin to the tree. "Odin, the banshees. We need you to take care of them."

Odin shook off the rest of the effects of the fear and jumped on Sashi's back. They rode for the group and Odin amplified the siren's song. All of the banshees were thoroughly distracted and led away from the battle. Every tree in the area had burned to the ground, and the stench of death and smoke filled the forest.

They pressed on through the forest, fighting, slashing, crushing, and dodging every blow of every creature in their path. They still hadn't found the house of the wizards, and Odin was becoming discouraged. The descendants of Throth had long been dead, but Odin was sure there would be some remnant that could help him see the exact location of the open doorway to the Underworld. He wasn't certain if he was frightened or bold, but he knew this journey would be the death of him, one way or another.

There was a small ridge in the forest where the ground dropped almost twice Odin's height. The trees and leaves had hidden it from him before he got there, but when they reached the ridge, they had no choice but to drop to the lower ground.

Sashi got a running start and leapt into another battle with more jackals and demons. Odin dropped from the ridge and noticed an overgrowth of moss and shrubs in a single area along the wall of the ridge. He ran straight for it, dodging dead jackals and doused demons that Sashi flung from the blades of his swords.

And like an overwhelming wave of pleasure and rage, Sashi's battle instincts took him over once again. He gripped the straps on his swords and twirled the swords at his sides, creating lethal fans. The jackals and demons willingly charged for him and were instantly decimated. Sashi leaned his head down while he concentrated on the balance of power he put into spinning his swords. Just one uncertain move could end his own life just as easily as he destroyed his foes.

Odin reached the buildup of vegetation on the ridge and uncovered the door he was looking for. He shoved it open and broke it out of place with the force of his body against the rotting wood. He dropped the pieces to the ground and raised his sword in front of him. He used his energy to shine light from the blade, illuminating the dying memories of the nine wizards. He shown the light on the wall next to him and the rail along the wall instantly burst into flame when the light touched it. The flame traveled around the room and up the corners of the walls, and crossed along the ceiling. The entire room was revealed in a flame that never heated nor burned. The fire simply lit the remnants and tools of the wizards.

Odin sheathed his sword and quickly searched the room for something he felt would call to him and tell him what he needed. He lifted papers and documents from a table and found nothing. He moved to a counter and found explosives and poisons, but nothing he could use to his advantage.

Finally, his hand touched a stone next to a pile of documents. In an instant, his mind traveled across the forest, down the road to the battlefield, passing millions upon millions of enemies, and finally, over the battlefield, where the griffin, phoenixes, trolls, giant serpents, and more were waiting for him. And there, replacing the doors of Magnus' courts, was the opened doorway to the underworld, rimmed with flame, leading to darkness. Odin wasn't sure how he could do it, but he knew he'd get there and take Jade back. The lights dimmed as he quickly left the house and joined Sashi and the dragons in battle.

*****

Dionysia brought another Darkling to Erebus with a very flustered look on her face. The Darkling had been rambling ever since his capture. Erebus waved his hand at the Darkling and everything was silent.

Dionysia let him go and sighed. "Finally. He's been going on for hours. I couldn't get a moment's peace."

Erebus stood still with a slight grin. "What's your name?" he asked.

The Darkling answered, "As I've been trying to explain to this friend of yours, I'm Dreadnought of Dreadnought Industries. I'm not a Darkling, or anything of the sort. I'm an entrepreneur. Speaking of which, I'd like to buy this castle from you. The Ragnarok has put a real damper in the real estate portion of my business and this place could definitely sell."

Erebus glanced at Dionysia, then back to Dreadnought. "How is it that you are not a Darkling, when clearly you have all of the abilities of a Darkling?"

Dreadnought thought, and replied, "I guess you could say I've acquired each individual ability I have through trade. One thing is worth more here and there than another. These abilities are merely payments someone has made on an intrinsic item I used to own. I fail to see what this has to do with our business, though. How much will you sell me this place for?"

Erebus looked back at Dionysia. "He wants me to sell him the Underworld."

Dreadnought wasn't amused. "A very peculiar play on words; this place looks nothing like the Underworld. That place would be much more … red … er. Wouldn't it?"

Erebus drew his sword and looked Dreadnought up and down. Dreadnought began to plea with offers of planets, universally illegal beverages, pardons from law for different sectors of space, safe passage through the Dead Zone, but one item finally caught Erebus' attention.

"A legion of Hunters!" Dreadnought called out.

"Stop!" Erebus shouted. He picked Dreadnought up and held him in the air. "Say that again," he ordered.

"A legion of Hunters. I can give you a legion of Hunters."

"Where do you get them?" Erebus asked.

Dreadnought's voice was shaking, but the reptilian finally answered, "I have a group of assassins that catch them. So far, we've captured about nine-hundred and eighty-four, but it's almost a legion. We've dosed them all with a serum to make them more organic, and another drug here and there to keep them under control, but it gets the job done, you know."

Erebus set him down on the ground and placed his hand on Dreadnought's shoulder. "Where is this group of assassins now?" Erebus asked.

"I haven't heard back from them in eighty-four cycles. Please don't kill me!"

Erebus shook his head. "You won't really die. You'll just shift from one mind to another."

Erebus quickly plunged his sword into Dreadnought's chest, and all of the abilities were melded together. Dreadnought's hyperactive mind began to overwhelm the voices in Erebus' head, but he soon commanded them to keep Dreadnought controlled. Dreadnought's voice dulled and the other voices unanimously agreed that they needed more energy to take on the Ragnarok. Without even looking at Dionysia, she knew what was needed, and had already left to accomplish the task.

Erebus rose above the castle and overlooked the empty Underworld. He relished in the devastation that the beasts he had unleashed were laying on Odin's home.

Hajun: the planet had such a humble name, and yet it was taking on such a magnitude of destruction. Such an unsuspecting race for an elder to dwell upon. And now that the elder had been drawn out of hiding, and everything he knew burned to the ground, Odin would become the monster that Erebus would either fall victim to, or triumph over. But to lay rest this unstoppable force, Erebus would have to put an immovable object in Odin's way. With all of his power and all of his strengths, Erebus knew he still wouldn't be able to defeat Odin in his full elder form. He left the Underworld and scoured space for his brother, Typhon. The beast would be his only chance at weakening Odin enough to fight him and destroy him.

CHAPTER 10

The evening star had set and Odin and Sashi had stopped to rest. They had cleared the area of all destructive beings and the dragons rested on the perimeters, making sure no surprise attacks would befall them. The fires in the trees were dimming. Odin and Sashi had gotten used to the sad smell of smoke and death.

"Remember the first time we saved Hajun?" Odin asked.

Sashi smiled at the memories of single-handedly descending on the Skord and Ogres. "We were a force to be reckoned with, as the prophets put it."

Odin almost laughed. "I remember your anger at the Skord when you met them again in the caves. You moved in ways that are unnatural for a centaur to move."

"You wouldn't remember the quarrel with the Skrulltan Jackals. The moves I pulled with the wizard's help were unlike anything I'd ever done before or after that."

At the mention of the wizards, Odin thought about being in their home, seeing the end of the road on Hajun and the monsters he would face on the battlefield. Sashi knew it was troubling him, and now he had the chance to ask.

"What did you see when you were there?"

Odin didn't look up. "The doorway to the Underworld is replacing the doors of Magnus' castle." He explained as he stared at the small fire and focused on the images that were seared into his head. "Remember the battle we fought when Magnus came the second time and we had to save Jade?"

Sashi nodded remembering the massive scale of that war and not wanting to go through the ordeal again; fearing that Odin was going to predict a repeat of that battle.

Odin shook his head. "We're not in for anything like that. Erebus has unleashed the Underworld on us and we may not get through the doorway alive."

Sashi looked at the fire and added everything together. "If we are killed, we'll be sent to the elders. The Underworld, Hajun, and everything will be destroyed in the Ragnarok."

Odin leaned back and closed his eyes. "Whatever the Sovereigns have planned, they had better hurry and make it happen."

*****

Artemis led the Hunters to Hajun. The little ball that blocked the light of the star seemed so peaceful. They could clearly see that the section of land that Odin resided on was the only amount of land on the planet. With white ice at the poles, and this large continent being all that had to be searched, they headed for the portion that had the most activity. The little light in the sky quickly grew, as if a star set on a collision course with the planet. The light quickly stretched across the sky and twinkled everywhere. Traveling at stellar speeds, the Hunters became more distinct with each passing second.

Finally, they smashed against the battlefield and laid their siege on the monsters. The battle cries of the Hunters shook the plain as they dodged the serpents, slaughtered the griffin, and giants, and obliterated the phoenixes. The trolls, however, burrowed their way into the ground and evaded the Hunters for what little time they could. Hunters and griffin rained to the scoured ground. The phoenixes were blasted into nothingness. Jackals and little dragons were run through and attacked at their flying adversaries. As for the trolls, the Hunters would only have to land and the ground under them would cave in and crush the trolls. The Hunters finally destroyed all of the flying creatures and could now engage in what they called "real combat".

They all landed lining the perimeter of the battlefield and stepped in, slicing everything in their path. They took wave after wave of different enemies. With every wave, they would take a step forward and close in on the source. The everlasting swarms of creatures flooded out of the gate; ravenous, enraged, merciless beings from the darkest points of the Underworld.

Odin and Sashi stood on the hills that lined the battlefield. Swords drawn and the morning star rising to their backs, they watched as the hand of the gods clutched the enemy and crushed it. Odin reached up and sheathed his sword on his back. The awesome sight that they beheld was a trumpet blast of the coming plans of the Sovereigns. Sashi knew as well as Odin that the end was near, simply by seeing the Hunters here on their small planet.

*****

Erebus hovered above the castle and lit up the entire realm of the Underworld with titanic flames from the rock pits of the Underworld.

"The time has come," he whispered to Dionysia. "He's almost here."

She turned to him, accepted her contribution and allowed him to run her through with his sword. All the energies that she had absorbed from her enemies flooded into him. All of the thoughts joined together.

"Summon the Typhon," they said in unison.

Erebus raised his hands to the sky and shouted, "Typhon! Mammon! Prince of Darkness! Come to your brother's aid! Make haste and destroy our enemies!"

The Typhon faded into the Underworld standing behind the endless army of Erebus. He stood taller than the mightiest of complexes known to any being in the universe. His hands were heads of dragons and his tale was a serpent. The entire creature was blacker than night and his eyes could not be seen. The inside of his mouth was made of flame, his ears were his crown. Erebus could only see the bulging spine and the serpent that slithered on the ground, rounding to the front.

Erebus smiled at the monster that came to his aid. Then, he noticed that the army wasn't flowing through the doorway to Hajun, but rather, it was regurgitating back into the Underworld. The trolls and jackals were screeching as they reentered the Underworld. Suddenly, the source of their fear entered the Underworld. Hunters came soaring in, destroying sections of the army and banding together to fight the Typhon. The Typhon reached up and the dragon-head of a claw snatched at the small Hunters. The Hunters would block with their shields and swords, and swirled around its arms stabbing anywhere they could; any weak spot they could find; but they found none. The Typhon's tail whipped around and the snake head struck at everything that passed it by.

The dragon heads roared at the passing Hunters. All of the Hunters had entered and Odin and Sashi followed. As soon as Odin entered, the Typhon roared in its intensely low and raspy voice. The voice echoed through the entire Underworld and the very ground trembled in fear. Odin and Sashi were distraught at the hectic state of the Underworld.

Clouds appeared out of nothingness and swirled above Erebus, with his hand clutched and held high. From the swirl of the clouds, the legion of Hunters flooded in, obeying Erebus' every whim. They distracted the Hunters that served Artemis and allowed the Underworld's creatures to regroup and advance once again towards the gate. Odin and Sashi were the only ones that stood in their way. The army quickly rushed for the two beings.

"I need to destroy the gate," Odin said. "They can't get back to Hajun."

Odin jumped from Sashi's back. "Take care of the souls," Odin told him and gathered enough energy to shove the entire wave of creatures away and throw Sashi back through the gate, as the pulse of energy crumbled the portal behind the centaur. Sashi looked at the doors of Magnus' castle and tried to get back through the portal before it was too late.

"Odin! No!" he shouted knocking the castle doors to the ground. He muttered his curses to Odin's mistake and knew he wasn't going to participate in the final battle for the Universe.

CHAPTER 11

Odin ran through the army of the Underworld and was picked up by a Hunter as he slashed at the goblin that caught onto his leg, chewing on his feet. Many of the Hunters were divided between fighting each other and destroying the horde of the Underworld. The others did their best to fight off the Typhon. The Typhon spat fire in the air at the Hunters. Many of the Hunters that were fighting each other were caught in the blaze, and fell to their graveless deaths.

"Don't you have a soul to save?" the Hunter asked.

Odin shook his head. "Not yet. Let me stand on the Typhon's head. You take care of the Underworld and the other Hunters."

"I exist to serve," the Hunter replied dodging the other Hunters in flight and gently placing Odin on the Typhon's head.

Without another word, Odin raised his sword and over a thousand bolts of lightning shocked from the skyless top of the Underworld, passing through the elder and obliterating the Typhon's skull. The great beast fell from the towering heights and landed on a great portion of the army. Odin had fallen off of the Typhon long before it landed and was caught by another Hunter.

"The time to save your beloved has come. Take her and go. Hurry!" the Hunter said throwing Odin through a window of the tower.

Odin rolled on the ground and found Jade's soul. She hovered motionless over a table. He was across the room from her and the wood paneling creaked with his every step. Suddenly, Erebus appeared in a cloud of smoke. No words were said. Odin simply twirled his sword and rushed to attack. Erebus defended himself with his fiery sword that appeared out of nothingness.

Odin fought hard, pushing and shoving into Erebus more than engaging his blade. He put all of his strength in every blow. He slammed his sword against his enemy, brought it crashing down on top, and swiped to the side. Erebus enjoyed defensive fighting. He could absorb all of Odin's rage, and build his powers on Odin's every thought. The elder's powers struck and Odin used them so his heavy moves would accelerate. The speed almost overwhelmed Erebus for a few heartbeats, but he soon adapted to the new pace. Swords spun and clanged, and bounced off each other.

*****

Kronos stood on the precipice of space where the gods were to ascend and join the Power. His time, like had come at last, and his power was waning. Below, he watched Odin in conflict with Erebus over his lover's soul. He shook his head thinking of Odin's foolish heart. Odin wasn't ready for such a power, and yet the entire Sovereign vision relied on him using it at full force. To his left, Kronos could just barely see all of the higher powers; the gods, the elders, the Forces, and the Seers gathering together and the Ragnarok drawing ever closer to their position. Odin was missing once again. And now, the god of time was absent.

He looked down again and watched through the roof of the castle in the Underworld. The god of time, looking like an orb of light, dropped from the precipice and traveled through the portals of space and time to the Underworld, where Odin fought.

*****

Odin blocked a low blow and spun into a high kick for Erebus' face. His boot was blocked by the butt of his enemy's weapon. Making a quick recovery, their blades clashed again. The sound of metal on metal, scraping, bashing and shoving resounded through the hall. Odin positioned himself to take a step onto the table and somersault over Erebus for an attack from above, but to no use. Erebus seemed to be saving his energy for an all-out attack.

In an attempt to cut him down, Odin struck for Erebus' feet, but he only morphed into his ethereal form to evade the attack. There was nothing for it. Odin stepped away from the black shadow and twirled his sword, waiting for an attack. Everything else was just a waste of energy.

"Why do you do this, Elder?" Erebus asked. "Why do you fight me? You and your kind could end the Ragnarok with ease. You have the resources. Why not do what we all need you to and save us?"

"I'm not here to debate with you. The sovereigns have made their decisions. All that matters is I have what's mine before the Ragnarok claims us all."

"Of course, if you die, their entire plan is mucked. Something tells me they won't allow that. You will live, you'll be whisked away to fulfill your destiny, and you will watch her obliterated soul become nothing but a resource to the Ragnarok."

For a second, Odin took his eyes off the target to glance at Jade's sleeping soul. She was peaceful, at rest, unaware of the coming doom. He twirled his sword once at the thought of losing her irrevocably. At this, Erebus charged with a fully concentrated position to run Odin through the gut, which was all Odin needed. As soon as Erebus fell in striking range, Odin dropped for a low center of gravity, swiping for Erebus' feet. Following a successful counter, he spun to bring his blade up the darkling's center, then down for Erebus' neck as he fell into the counter. The attack was too quick for Erebus to shift back into shadow form. His head fell to the ground and black smoke leaked from the slice. Seconds later, the body disappeared into nothing.

Odin took a breath and moved to Jade's soul. Time and time again, he had won her soul from villainous characters, but this had become a race against time. He slid his arms under Jade, cradling her into his arms. Everything he fought for, everything he lived for, was now safe in the strength of his embrace.

"I'm ready," he muttered with all the confidence the universe had to offer.

With a flash of white light, the power of Kronos crashed through the ceiling of Erebus' castle and fused itself with Odin's spirit. Odin's eyes went white with energy and black with power. His pupils shone like white novas in the night. The power of the time god took effect, granting Odin every ounce of power he needed to defend his family. Before another second passed, Odin traveled through the portals of space and time and circled the magnificent sphere of souls, ringed by the gods, elders, and other powers of that quadraplex of the universe. Odin saw the Ragnarok: a cloud of dark, malicious intent that was pressing for this construct of souls and energy; so small and trivial in comparison to the raging darkness. As he watched, the Ragnarok encountered the planet of the Restians, ten billion souls wrenched apart at a molecular level. Odin could hear their screams hear how the Ragnarok broke down the energy in their bodies until the entirety of the planet was nothing more than dust particles. It took mere moments for an entire race to be obliterated, completely consumed by the growing darkness. Odin darted through the souls of the sphere, placing Jade in the center of the mass. Everything surrounded her, shielding her from all harm, protecting her from the impending danger. Then he pivoted up through the mass and reached to the highest point of the souls.

The dark forces clawed for him and snatched for his soul, striking deep gashes throughout his ethereal body. As quickly as the wounds were inflicted, they were healed, though the pain of their infliction was longer lasting. As soon as the darkness would score his skin, Odin's power would mend the damage, but there was only so much an entity could take. Even a god had his limits. Odin stretched his arms out and faced his back to the Ragnarok, his eyes fixed on his people. His aura glowed bright gold, a beacon for hope and light in the face of the oncoming darkness. He stretched his power to the rest of the protectors and used their power to create a bubble of energy in constant temporal flux, to keep anything that manipulated time and space, out. The evil natures that dwelt inside him beckoned the Ragnarok to take hold of him. But as soon as they touched him, they recoiled in pain from the greatness of power that he held. The Ragnarok pounded on the bubble shield as it traveled around the large scale of souls that managed to escape their grasp.

All that Odin could think was that he was keeping the darkness away from Jade. She would never again be in danger and his power only grew with his will to keep her safe. The sound of shocks and cracks echoed along the mass of souls. The Ragnarok tried attacking the smaller targets of defenders, but failed at even touching them, for Odin's power was simply that great.

Finally, the Ragnarok passed completely over them, consuming them in darkness but unable to join such energy to their power. Faces and hands of the bodies the Ragnarok stole slid along the energy shield. Each character that could be seen in the distortion of darkness had an expression of pain. Every hand was a claw for the immortal souls inside this bubble. Odin's eyes flashed as he compressed his energy and blanketed it all along the bubble. The Ragnarok was repelled from the sphere and forced to continue on its way.

The never ending cloud of darkness loomed above the shield, wanting so badly to penetrate and conquer. It never again attacked the shield and finally passed eons later to conquer the rest of the universe. Odin held the energy shield in place while the rest of the defenders left and joined the rest of the souls in their slumber. The elders were satisfied that their powers of ascension had been used to the greatest of their abilities and could sleep once again with that power no longer needed. Each of their powers were left in the energy shield, and their souls found their eternal slumber. Odin could hold the shield himself, indefinitely, as long as Jade was safe in its containment.

He could sleep knowing that all evil had passed over. He could exist in peace, believing that everything was safe once again. Utopia: that was the Sovereigns' great vision. The bubble of souls contained in a small energy field would be all that was left in a scoured and desolate universe. Nothing would harm them; nothing would hunt them. Odin was the key to all of this, and Jade was his heart. Of all the powers that he held inside, none of them could outmatch his love for her, a love that had saved him in the end.

The universe was dead. Stars, planets, debris, everything, disappeared in the wake of the Ragnarok. The future held nothing. No wars, no conflict, no threats foreseen. All was at rest. For the entirety of eternity.

EPILOGUE

"No," Odin muttered, after ages of silence. "It cannot end this way."

"Earth," the other voices in the bubble called to him. "Take us to Earth."

Earth; the origin of the powers. Once, the gods called that planet their home. Now, Earth was all but a legend.

"Abandon Utopia?" Odin thought. "Would Earth accept us for committing such a sin?"

"Send an emissary," Lara answered. "Aten and his family. They can make way for all of us as we maintain Utopia."

"All of us occupying the promised land? Is such a thing possible?" Magnus voiced his doubts.

"If the Ragnarok hasn't destroyed it already ..." Decimus thought aloud.

"We can repopulate with our own souls. They need a home," Lara answered.

Odin had a deeper thought on his mind. "Maybe we should join them as mortals," he said, "and remember how to live off the power of the universe itself." The other powers widened their eyes at the thought. "To crawl, to cry, to beg, to make ourselves weak so we may better appreciate godly strength."

"We would have to descend gradually," Stratus reasoned, "becoming mortal over time would take ages."

"Ascending from mortality would be all the more difficult," the father reasoned. "All the more worth achieving."

All eyes were once again on the key to the Sovereigns great vision. Together, they made their new vision known. "Take us to Earth."

Without pause, Odin directed Utopia across the dark void of empty space to their new home. Earth, it seemed, was waiting for them.